CURANDERA

ALSO BY IRENOSEN OKOJIE

Speak Gigantular
Butterfly Fish
Nudibranch

IRENOSEN OKOJIE

CURANDERA

DIALOGUE BOOKS

First published in Great Britain in 2024 by Dialogue Books

10 9 8 7 6 5 4 3 2 1

Copyright © Irenosen Okojie 2024

The moral right of the author has been asserted.

All characters and events in this publication, other than those clearly in the public domain, are fictitious and any resemblance to real persons, living or dead, is purely coincidental.

All rights reserved.
No part of this publication may be reproduced, stored in a retrieval system, or transmitted, in any form or by any means, without the prior permission in writing of the publisher, nor be otherwise circulated in any form of binding or cover other than that in which it is published and without a similar condition including this condition being imposed on the subsequent purchaser.

A CIP catalogue record for this book
is available from the British Library.

Hardback ISBN 978-0-349-70094-6
C-format ISBN 978-0-349-70257-5

Typeset in Berling by M Rules
Printed and bound in Great Britain by
Clays Ltd, Elcograf S.p.A

Papers used by Dialogue Books are from well-managed forests and other responsible sources.

Dialogue Books
An imprint of Dialogue
Carmelite House
50 Victoria Embankment
London EC4Y 0DZ

www.dialoguebooks.co.uk

Dialogue, part of Little, Brown Book Group Limited,
an Hachette UK company.

To Mum, Dad, Amen, Ota and Iredia, thank you for blazing brightly.

Big love always.

To communities of women who create necessary trouble making their art.

Diagram Tree of Shamans

Cabo Verde

| Zulmira | Oni | kin | Baby |

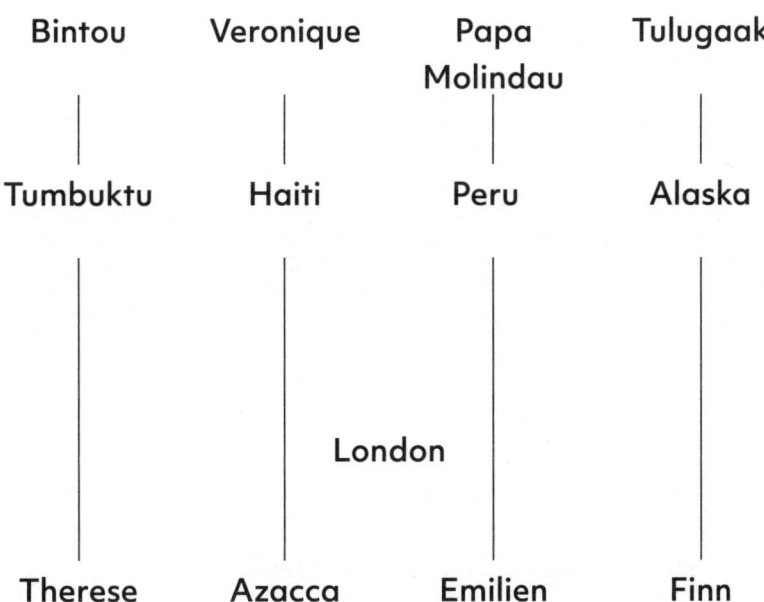

Carriers

| Bintou | Veronique | Papa Molindau | Tulugaak |
| Tumbuktu | Haiti | Peru | Alaska |

London

| Therese | Azacca | Emilien | Finn |

One

Gethsemane, Cabo Verde, West Africa, seventeenth century

All pregnant, five of us glimmer on the snaky path towards the low cacophony of the humming creek. Dusky goddesses breached through buried carcasses. We hear gifts turning in the ground's crevices. Barefoot, we sing to Oni, clutching one bone each. Lengthy red beads knock against our chests, the insides of rounded stomachs jostle with the rhythm of parched entities. White markings on our foreheads fade to confuse the forest's traffic. Inky trickles slither from our braided crowns down craned necks. Our nipples are pert against the morning. Behind us, the mountains of Gethsemane loom. A slow mist unfurls to reveal crooked homesteads in its folds, waiting to be shed in a purging between orbs of fire and a fog that will blind the fishermen, that will catch them in their own nets while the sea's creatures buck against the holes in the boats, sharing one eye, as their wives lose their bottom halves in fevered dreams. We sing. The mountains, bruised and magisterial in their morning stupor, absorb our voices, sprawling peaks and troughs dimpled with dew. White cloths wrapped around our waists feel loose on sweat-glazed skin, rustling against our thighs. The hems trailing behind us are pale, movable dawns. We ask our reflections to wait patiently for us in the water, tell floating lilies to be soft landing pads for a small reckoning. We ask the light bending to allow our internal bleeding to leak through our nipples into its axis points. We call Oni to build the golden arch marked with her fingerprints so traces of peyote beneath our tongues will know their inheritance. We dance. We chant, hollering abandons our mouths to chase a fleet-footed spirit marking areas for reinventions between trembling trees. At the bank, we scoop translucent sap from conspiratorial trees. The sky is starting to blush blue. The creek's seductive language threatens to break liquid confines. We call Oni by her name, walk into the water. Form a ring. The water rises, its cold temperature cocooning weeds grazing our feet in the murky depths below. We raise our heads to the heavens as the sky rattles, just as one of us confesses to carrying a foetus that fell from a mountain.

One by one we speak. One of us proclaims she has been plagued by locusts wielding a strain of fever, scuttling through her bloodstream. Hundreds of them gathering in her stomach, digging thin, sharp legs into the lining. Their fluttering ringing so loudly she can hear it while she breathes, as they scale her insides desperate for an exit. Another has had a stained black burial lace dress curling and twitching on a bough, trying to claim her organs to build its own body. Causing her to wake some mornings seeing her gauzy organs inching their way towards the dawn: a retracting lung following a misshapen heart trailing a shrunken kidney, while the dress creases in anticipation, her stomach full of a winding lace horizon.

Another is pregnant with a mermaid's bright orange tail; flapping, bending, pulsing in her womb, scattering shimmering scales until her tongue is stained silver.

I do not confess. The amalgamation of a hundred hatchings ring in my bloodstream as it heats. Spots of gold appear in my peripheral vision. An echo with the stealth of smoke passes through my eardrums. The gaps between the trees have cloud instruments fragmenting. The volume of our voices increases. Our reflections lose their fingers in branches. Clusters of purple geraniums sprout on their backs from a future spring. We hold our bones up to the sky. Grooves appear on the bank. A gutting of earth as the forest's creatures quiver, while the golden arch appears.

Oni has kept her promise. We emerge from the water, dripping rivulets onto the bank. My nipples leak blood. There is a deafening sound in my ears, a roar of such magnitude, I wonder if the others are experiencing it too.

We circle the arch; lie in birthing positions raising our knees up. We give birth.

The others place their birthed offerings to Oni in the arch. I do not.

Confused, the women turn away from me to watch the offerings rupture.

I hold Oni's gift to me tenderly. It is another face like mine. Baby.

I turn my back, drunk with this knowledge, as though I found a silver coin in a dragon fruit. I do not ask Oni how a woman can give birth to herself.

The face begins to flicker, Baby's limbs seem fragile in my grasp. Her small perfect fist grips mine in an unspoken promise. Letting go, I pick up my bone; white and hollowed.

I break free from the pack.

The sound of a newborn thunders in my ears.

I leave my baby behind.

Her piercing scream rings through the air like a thousand clarion calls losing their heads in a treacherous womb. My puckered, bloodied nipple turns towards her waiting new mouth, slick and shrill in its sweetness, its divinity. Born in love, stamped as weapon by a mother's disappearing shadow. Already commanding the heavens to change fates, we are bound by this second joining then separated. Bone, dense and changeable in my hand, acting as a compass. Pain emanates from my core. There will be punishments to come. I stifle the screaming inside me that is my child's voice infiltrating my tongue.

Running, I press the bone against a shard of light.

Existing since the dawn of time, Oni the shaman god wielded her influence over shamanic disciples through the ages. She was omnipotent and deity, spirit, all-encompassing oracle who beat in the blood of those she revealed herself to. A jealous force that could be both loving and vengeful. After all, what is a god without its devil side? What of a force that possessed the strengths of religious figureheads? One which man had chosen to worship only multiplied in power and depth. Oni instructed the seas and the heavens from her spiritual realm. She disrupted the gods that mere mortals had created with a brutal hand and fiendish inclinations, creating portals for her shamanic travellers of all forms to move through time. Therefore, dog heart could masquerade as a rare plant growing in the wild grounds of an ancient Iranian palace garden, keeping an eye on proceedings, dismantling coups. Bird beak could double as blade for a Japanese samurai to end his life honourably to stop two warring regions in the north. Those who touched a statue of Mary in a Roman square absorbed a rare fungal bacterium which closed their throats, cutting off their breathing. When a man set himself on fire outside the Egyptian embassy in protest at the government's stance on prisoners of war, it was Oni who gathered his ashes, giving him a new existence as a teacher in a floating monastery in the Himalayas. Oni could turn sins into acts of love, make deep betrayal seem like a mercy. She could extend the possibilities of our wildest imaginings, bridging the intersections of science and spirituality. Her power was to be embraced, revered, feared. Time could stretch, warp and bend in her hands. She could place a shaman in one era and its shadow in another, its tongue as messenger mimicking a goshawk's flight, scaling tumultuous skies. Nightmarish visions morphed into companions. A birth became a passage through orbits and multiverses. And so shamanic disciples were spawned, tumbling through ripples in time with secret instructions, existing under the guise of ordinary lives.

Chapter 1

London, 18 November 2012

Therese had experimented with peyote in several ways through the group's shamanic practices. In ancient and more modern times, shamans had used peyote to create gateways to move through dimensions. And so like true intergalactic vagabonds, they had finessed this mode of travelling from various iterations through Therese's keen fingers. She'd cooked it in bouillon soup, stirring till you couldn't taste a trace. She'd steamed it, scattering handfuls in deep glass bowls of water around the house, watching the leaves settling at the bottom curl, placing her head inside to absorb it into her skin, its sharp scent and steam opening her pores, her breathing passages. She'd extracted it from the stem; tiny, glistening droplets rubbed on both sides of her tongue, underneath it then finally on top, like a sign of the cross. She'd eaten it in bed, as though a small sprig had sprouted from the lines of her palm. As if she was a woman with a goat's mouth for the night, chewing ravenously, her eyes bloodshot, pulse speeding, ready to leave her body to convene in wounds hovering over the city to find resting points.

She'd hunted rare forms of peyote on Appalachian trails, plucking it from the ragged breaths of rocks, off their weathered cracks, while her guide, an old man with white hair brushing both shoulders, informed her of its ancient benefits; how it could open up channels and frequencies the body never knew it had, ease pain, take the spirit from the flesh. He'd spoken in a low, measured tone but his voice had a gravitas about it. As if it had flown beyond his tongue, a winged saliva-lined entity colliding against night traffic. His brown eyes had twinkled. He smelled of exotic, natural scents mingled with sweat. Every wrinkle and line on his face was a small trail of its own, secretive markings caressed by the cool evening air. She missed the guys during this trip, pangs rippling through her body as sharp reminders of their bond. She lay in a collapsible blue tent that felt like a vehicle of time, imagining the vast night sky with constellations like small missiles as a temporary companion. She thought about how each one of them had revealed a dark secret to her, that perhaps she in return had given some of herself to hold the weight of their secrets successfully, to carry them as transmutational matter with hints of a slippery salvation. If you watched your best friends die then be reborn at the hands of a high priestess prophet named Oni, if you knew the corners of their pain before you even met them, tasted the elements of their birth like an indescribable wine under their tongues as a current, it bonded you through infinity because what did forever mean within the wild vanguards of their untamed bodies.

The old man often waited for her outside her tent, the night sky folding above them. They stood between those rocks, he slightly stooped over his walking stick, she ignoring the burning fatigue shooting through her limbs. He informed her that before her arrival, he'd had a vision of a woman whose hands could reach into bodies and disappear, who could heal, take sickness from the blood by pressing her fingertips there, then withdraw them quietly, as if nothing had happened. She wept silently; tears ran down her cheeks thinking of Azacca, Finn and Emilien, of how she'd secretly looked into each of their bodies to see what Oni had left there for her to collect.

Back in London, she found the photograph slipped beneath a plump maroon-coloured pillow on her bed. Prior to that, it had been a herd of stained origami silhouettes, arms raised, poised in the doorway between the kitchen and the garden. Before that, it was a veined brahmi leaf left in the middle shelf of the fridge, gathering beads of water below the temperature dial. Predating that was the male goshawk left on the wooden kitchen worktop, a wing shorn, one eye still filmy. She'd blown a warm breath on that powder-blue wing, the kitchen air thick with the scent of blended rosemary and cayenne. The weight she'd felt was an exchange of silences between herself and the goshawk while the fridge hummed. She'd pressed a finger gently against its iris, wondering what the last image it saw was, where it had gone, if it would be covered in the same thin discharge on her finger. She'd wanted to reach through its deadened gaze to hold that image, press it against her heart to steady herself. Before the goshawk, was the matador costume, bleeding from its pockets as if they were gateways for injuries to pass through.

The costume had been bundled into the washing machine, one pocket pressed against the door, a tryst at daylight, a red horizon spilling from the pocket, a head waiting to be reared to smash through the glass. Her breath had caught; she'd pulled the costume out slowly, admiring the intricacy of the emblem on the chest area, the padded, embellished shoulders as though brushed against a shower of golden sequins. Before the costume, she'd found an old battery-run tape recorder in the bathtub one evening, playing a tape of barking into the hollow room. She'd climbed into the tub fully clothed, still in her blue kimono dressing gown, flapping open at the thigh. Playing the tape several times, she listened for something travelling through the grainy sound, a tension in her back, a ripple, a humming in her temples, her throat a thirsty, inadequate instrument, her feet hovering over a withered night trapped in the plughole. The recorder was Finn's, the tape inside it Emilien's. Sometimes Azacca borrowed it to record himself playing, 'a low-fi way of doing things', he said. Somehow, they all had a hand in it.

In the end, she'd left the brahmi leaf to completely erode before getting rid of it.

The goshawk she'd placed in a hedge on their street for a fox to find late at night. But she'd kept one bone from its wing, wrapped in clingfilm at the bottom of the freezer compartment, occasionally fishing it out, sitting cross-legged in the garden, looking up at the sky's blanket of stars while the bone defrosted in her hand, numbing her fingers, breathing again. Sometimes, she wore the matador costume at breakfast, which amused the guys. Other times, she left it on their beds, nestled into the duvet while they were out, hoping it would bleed again. The recording of the barking she kept too, playing it now and again, wondering which of them had left it for her to find. She knew that each time, something was taking shape, trying to make its way to her; gathering speed, density, mass.

She never panicked about these offerings around the house. They were a kind of warped requiem, ways to solidify their bond, prompts she couldn't quite figure out – part puzzle and part fractured memories – with each offering being a piece of a larger picture. Once, she'd lain on the kitchen floor in the matador costume holding the brahmi leaf, light from the fridge door falling on her face. Her braids pooled under her head, an alien longing in her hands, fingers curling over the faded leaf. She'd considered putting a stop to it, but the truth was she enjoyed the offerings. And she knew it was a kind of release for whoever left them.

She leaned back against the pillow holding the photograph, running a finger over it as though it was an expanded artery, searching for clues that could tell her which one of the guys was leaving her odd gifts. The photo captured the four of them at Xamsara Festival, covered in mud; she, Azacca, Finn and Emilien, listless creatures smeared red by an invisible hand that dropped them in undulating greens with trees doubling as watchmen. Each person's body language and expression encapsulated an element of their personality: Azacca was grimacing, his twists speckled with red spots, his nostrils a little flared, his ruggedly handsome features pronounced beneath the layer of mud, bearing an air of electricity about him that was even more intense in real life. Doe-eyed and elegant, Emilien was slighter in build than the other two men. He had that faraway look in his eyes which indicated while he was present physically, he was somewhere else mentally, always travelling internally to another location, another crossing in his life, his body ready to half-turn away from you before you registered it, with the quiet command of an illusionist who could extrapolate himself from tricky situations. And Finn was Finn: rakish, restless, green eyed, unruly dark hair scraped back, temporarily reigned in. Tall and strapping, his expression bordered on a scowl, the slight dent in his broken nose, masked by the mud, was the result of a fight with Azacca earlier, warring over who would scout for the perfect location at the festival to continue the secret task Oni had given them. The strain in their expressions indicated there was still a tension in the air. More feral in environments like that, Finn behaved himself later that afternoon, not completely abandoning the needs of the group for his own inclinations. Before the camera flashed, he'd shot an irritated look at Azacca who reciprocated with a hostile expression of his own, mouth swollen and bloody, while Emilien ignored both of them, sliding his arm around Therese's waist, whose lips curved upwards, shoulders relaxed releasing a hint of anxiety, a piece of barbed wire tucked between the group's kinetic energy.

Oni had instructed them to attend the festival. The plan was to take a sacrificial offering for her, their shaman god, to be made into a different entity in the other plane. She had come to each of them in their tents at night, under the veneer of the festival's celebratory activities, whispering in their ears like a disembodied force, planting flickering images of that second world, ripe, slick with fresh dew and two suns orbiting.

Over the course of Xamsara Festival, it rained two days in a row. Oil spillage in the sea meant swarms of gulls migrated in various directions, wings coated with coppery coloured grease, flocking to the festival grounds. Some landed in the muddy swamp on the outskirts, dyeing the surface an earthy copper tone. Just before the storm arrived on the second evening, the group threaded their way through crowds towards the swamp, the occasional sound of a whistle or horn punctuating their footsteps. The evening air caressed their bodies, lights dotted around twinkling. At the swamp, they undressed, left their clothes by the trees: short cloth mounds waiting to be disrupted. The breeze rustled the branches. Scavenging from hidden creatures ebbed away into the skyline. Heartbeats pulsed between their fingertips as the swamp was peppered with distressed gulls squawking so loudly they created a wall of sound around them. They sank their limbs in, covered by nature's cauldron-tinged red. Gulls lay dead on their backs, others limped pathetically in a doomed forward motion. Still more jerked at the edges until they were spent.

The group smeared their bodies, the dense paste forming a crust around their lips. Low murmurings of the swamp seeped into their chests. They began to chant their shamanic ritual, the mantra loaded with a choppy static trying to pull them through. Failing on that occasion, they left the swamp clutching the necks of dead gulls they had set on the stacks of their clothing. As if they'd flutter to life, reconstructed and twisted on beds of false comfort. Spots of blood dribbled from Emilien's nose. Azacca's chest began to cave in. A shark-like mouth was inching its way across Finn's back, waiting to break through skin. They searched for collapsed folds of earth, axis points to land in, circumferences around trees a body could leap through. Then, the storm arrived, scuppering their plans. They returned to the camp like painted gods amid a sea of chaos. More stained-red gulls shrieking, stealing bits of bread, sausages, half-eaten pies. Tents were flattened. People took shelter under plastic sheets, tossed prams. Children screamed. Spilled condiments looked like clots spat from their containers. Car boots were popped open for frantic grabs of survival kits. Vehicles shuddered on the roads. They helped people take shelter, working together as they often instinctively did despite their conflicts. Azacca led several women and children into a white caravan shaking at the right-side edge of the festival. Emilien took a group of children playing on a trampoline to safety in a treehouse in the children's play area. Finn gathered a family foolishly trying to make a getaway in the middle of the storm. Therese helped some of the stallholders, yelling at the guys to assist her with one thing or the other whenever she spotted any of them free. Items from the stalls such as moon worshipping stones, jewellery, wildly designed colourful clothes haemorrhaged in her hold like the storm's iridescent creatures. The group knew the raging of the storm was punishment from Oni for failing their task.

Later, bone-tired after things had settled somewhat, the group risked falling asleep in their mangled tent. Therese woke early, crusted lines of mud on her eyelids, to discover that Finn had disappeared. He returned at dawn, walking amid the stretches of rubble naked, his left knuckle bruised, blood on one side of his head, the cuts on his right hand speaking a muted language. His wounds screaming inside him, Finn had taken the sacrificial offering to Oni himself, selfishly to please her. He did not consult with the group. The friction from this spilled over on the ride home in the car when Azacca leaned forward from the passenger seat at the back, grabbed Finn in a headlock, eyes bloodshot, a vein in his neck throbbing, Emilien and Therese shouting at him to stop. The traffic surrounding them flashed like mutated accidents. And Finn desperately grabbing at the wheel, almost swerving off the road.

She placed the photo on her dresser by a short, rosewood-scented mauve candle, flicked on a lamp as the flame bent and curled, signalling the goshawk bone in the freezer, surrounded by cuts of lamb, kidney, tripe, oxtail, chopped aubergine mixed with chilli. Opening the window, she sat on the bed and slipped on some clothes: black boot-cut jeans, an old Harlem Globetrotters T-shirt, a loose navy cardigan. She arranged her braids into a bun, a few stray strands grazing her neck. She pulled on a pair of black Converse, moved to stand at the large double window. Their house was located in the leafy part of Dulwich, a more residential area in the south London suburbs. It boasted the feel of a little village, peppered with boutiques, colourful offbeat shops and bars. Her room overlooked the back end of a Turkish restaurant on the opposite side of the street. She saw guests laughing at the tables. The pudgy owner and a few waiters delivered small baskets of bread rolls, meze platters, light starters on elaborate beds of salads. A white van pulled up to make a delivery. The glow of the restaurant was warm, inviting, communal. She saw spots of dew on the restaurant's glass doors, a liquid night gushing from the neck of an elegant bottle of Anfora Trio, sticks of lamb kebab bleeding on white plates, an injury on a woman's thigh puckering against her silk black petticoat, a tiny piece of yellow cloth fraying in a man's lung, teeth marks on the skin of well-fed guests rising to meet a mouth emerging from the corner of her vision. These infiltrations planted a hunger in her. She was curious if Azacca, Finn and Emilien experienced them too. She breathed through them, slowly getting to know their outlines, running her fingers over their serrated edges.

She heard the turning of a key in the front-door lock; a click, the letterbox flapping back like a nervous tic as the door opened, then shut. She left her room to stand at the banister, listening to the soft padding of footsteps on the cherry-coloured welcome matt. Unopened letters she'd ignored earlier were on the floor, waiting to flitter onto the wooden staircase. A bunch of keys was placed on the hallway table; the soft gathering of the letters pricked her ears. She knew it was Azacca without looking down. She could tell by the loitering, the languid movements near the table. Emilien would have moved with more urgency, slammed the door, the wind crying in protest at his emergence from it, rushed into the kitchen to grab something from the fridge – whatever snack he'd half eaten the night before – or to rustle up an omelette, sandwiched between pieces of bread. Finn would have cared less about checking the bills. She often had to slide them under his door, into the glow of light pooling there like a third portal.

Azacca still wrote handwritten letters to his mother in Haiti. Every month, he eagerly leafed through stashes of envelopes spooling onto their hallway floor, searching for a white envelope with a cluster of foreign stamps. Now she heard him remove the guitar strapped to his back, the jangle of coins in his jacket from an evening of busking at the tube. The locations all over London varied each time: Waterloo, London Bridge, Earls Court, sometimes Embankment because he liked to walk along the bridge over the water. He enjoyed the inky hue of it at night, the way the slow ripples masked small transformations, he said; you'd see the unseen, while the traffic of people rushed past, oblivious to miracles limping towards sets of traffic lights, becoming invisible again as the lights shrieked, vanishing into the blind spots of vehicles.

Therese leaned over the banister, cardigan billowing. 'Did you get my text about our low supply of peyote?' she asked, trying to keep the longing from her voice, controlling the tremble of her hands with a deep breath.

He slid off his coat, slung it over the railing. 'My battery died. We can pick this up when the others get here,' he offered; a hint of his Haitian accent still lingered. He climbed the stairs, rubbing his eyes wearily. A tiny origami figure of a woman with no lower body fell out of his pocket and landed on the staircase like a slip of quiet thunder.

Taking off his boots, smiling affectionately, he said, 'Talk later.' Passing her and the overflowing laundry basket resting against the railings beside a coiled green water hose poised to strike like a python. Azacca's room was last on the floor. He fished out his key, unlocked it, nudging open the stiff wooden door with his shoulder before disappearing into his cave.

Therese, glued to the landing, mulled over whether he could be the secret gift giver. The throbbing in her temple increased like a wingless bat seeking other modes of transport through her body. A splintered memory crept in from her peripheral vision, reminding her of their secret pact in the beginning.

That first time they met, she'd seen him playing guitar at the edge of the National Gallery, his fingers strumming the guitar, singing Chris Isaacs' 'Wicked Game'. The pale building loomed; a Mecca on a concrete dune, bodies spilling. The croon of his voice was raw, imperfect, melancholy and vulnerable. It stopped her dead in her tracks, the folded copy of *Time Out* she'd been flicking through stuffed into her handbag dismissively as she moved towards the group of people around him. His handsome face was pulled into a pained expression, the chasm he'd opened bending, his fingers poised over the guitar strings. Therese's heart rate increased. Among the coins in his open guitar case on the ground were crinkled gold Werther's Original sweet wrappers. His jeans, ripped at the knee, revealed a crossing of scars there, hand-drawn by a faint hallucinatory needle. There were sweat stains at the armpits of his Nina Simone T-shirt.

Therese closed her eyes. The blustery evening air blew her half-unbuttoned bomber coat open. She waited patiently till most of the crowd had dispersed before approaching. He drank from a small bottle of Evian water, zeroing in on her.

His twists brushed his forehead, his smooth butterscotch-brown skin glowed. She could tell he was a man used to the admiration of women but not particularly vain, as indicated by his scruffy clothing. She needed to make it clear she wasn't trying to pick him up because she wasn't. Her reaction to him had been instinctive; a feeling of recognition. What interested her was the chasm he'd created, the pain, his ability to unlock the parts of a person from a pure, distilled place. A spark of electricity flickered between them she couldn't pinpoint as sexual, nor could she dismiss it as not being that either. It seemed beyond clear definitions, a sense of connection that was instant. He screwed the lid back on the bottle, set it down, adjusting the mic, golden brown eyes flicking back to her casually, but she could feel his curiosity, his survival mechanism of appearing distant, unfazed. The elements of their surroundings shifted; headless shapes in the chasm searched for new body language, the Werther's sweet wrappers ready to flutter to the mic like artificial butterflies. A stream of passers-by pinned and distorted against the street's backdrop were like captive apostles.

'I think I know you from a birth,' she said, without preamble, fuss or fear of judgement. He stopped dead in his tracks. Everything else faded away.

Afterwards, they searched the streets for somewhere to settle, the guitar packed away, bobbing on his back, the microphone though temporarily sheathed still rebelliously picking up sounds and frictions, a puddle of black water with sinister silhouettes spraying on rushing figures, a scrawny bald man minding an *Evening Standard* stand calling out. She spoke to him about rare orchids and flowers that grew in the Amazon, the Rafflesia flower specifically, how it looked like a giant mushroom with spotted red petals, or slices of salami stuck together, that it was other worldly, how something about him made her think of it and how strange that must all sound to him. He nodded, hands in his pockets, she practically running in her velvet red Converse to keep up with him as the city unfurled into a playground.

They walked to Waterloo, took refuge at Scootercaffe, which was tiny and full. The barman looked surly. The jukebox was playing Fats Domino's 'Ain't That a Shame'. They ordered two Moroccan teas and squeezed themselves onto a small table at the back. The heat was almost suffocating, the din steadily rising. She stirred two cubes of demerara sugar into her cup, asked him where he was living. 'Couch surfing,' he said nonchalantly, taking a sip of hot calming tea, a man used to the nature of transient living. Bright eyed, Therese looked at the bottom of her cup, watching the demerara granules melt, the sweet handful of a vanishing beginning that would find its teeth later. She offered him a place to stay if he told her his darkest secret. And so he did, physically trembling while he recounted the tale from a past life. Therese collected it like an injured wing, spotting the small half-crescent-moon-shaped birth mark on the left side of his neck. The sweetness of sugar melted into its dark lines; the mark of kin, one of Oni's disciples. Just like her. She looked deep inside him then and saw a memento from an old world: pink marrow shaped like octopuses limping towards the blind spot of a lush mountain's peak.

*

She made her way to a monthly Somali women's wellbeing project she volunteered for in Forest Gate, east London. The community centre where the project was situated was a nondescript grey building tucked behind a row of council houses, flanked on one side by a basketball court. A shop sat on the road opposite, its black shutters down mid-blink. A yellow-eyed ginger cat skulked, an unofficial guard waiting to elope with a stray shadow. The streetlamp illuminated shards of broken glass, a stubbed cigarette, a wedding veil in the bin. Inside the centre, the two main rooms were hives of activity peppered with a few stalls, gatherings of women sharing recipes, stories of their migration, goals they looked forward to fulfilling. The smell of Bur Shubaal lingered in the air. On the snack and beverage tables were flasks of Maraq soup, cups of spiced black tea, saucers of sweet fried bread. Shushumow crystallised pastry shells lay on folded red napkins. There were handfuls of groundnut in bright plastic bowls and trays of Macsharo mini rice and coconut cakes. Quaint piping bags containing Berbere spice to take away and small gift bags of black soap, handmade chocolates, truffles, and colourful compact notebooks beckoned at the corner of one table. At the far end of that room was the Mogadishu Archive on the wall, where the ladies pinned snaps of Somali women in daily life, both past and present. Therese sat at the back of the other room before her table of tiny, bottled ointments, a pale blue exercise mat on the floor behind her.

A woman arrived at her stall, hovering. Her hair was in disarray, black handbag unzipped, a stained baby's bib poking out. She complained of achy limbs. Some days ago, she'd burned herself at the stove boiling eggs, her baby tied to her back crying, curling and uncurling his small fists. She'd accidentally knocked the pot off the stove searching for qorfo dhegeyere, the water scalding her left leg and thigh, just missing the baby. Therese gave the woman Oregon grape root and lavender ointment for the burns, asked her to remove the top half of her clothes, then lie down on the mat, back exposed. She oiled her hands, trying not to reveal her hunger. Only a hint of tightness in her face indicated she was trying to keep her urges under control. A body laid out before her vulnerably even amid other people set her teeth on edge. Beads of sweat appeared on her forehead. She ran her hands over the woman's back, a map of skin marked with permanent symbols: a mole on the right side, a wrinkling on the left, fine hairs at the base, a Sahara rippling beneath her fingers while the woman sighed in relief. She kneaded gently, then applied more pressure, fingers working all the way down, across to the sides where stretchmarks crawling up were the indelible signatures of a woman who had given birth, splayed out in the blue. The other women flattened to a line on the periphery. The Sahara undulated. Therese used her thumbs on specific points. She felt the heat they generated increase, the rhythm of the woman's body beneath her hands, the mutter of her heart against her fingers. She closed her eyes as if in prayer. She couldn't stop the currents of excitement rushing through her.

As she ran her fingers greedily along the reddened blotches on the woman's leg, kneading into the muscle, a man's body was pulled from the darkened waters of the Thames. There were rips in his black raincoat, several buttons missing from his red checked shirt. A postcard of Bournemouth was tucked in the inside pocket of his jacket which choppy, cold waters had eroded somewhat, an impression from an absent ring on a finger on his left hand. He spilled from the perilous night, dead damp weight on concrete, his expression almost peaceful, his mouth a thin blue line. His skin pallid. An excavation had occurred. A lymph gland removed from his neck was a gutted last memory, fading in the distant murmur of his final heartbeat.

Two

I run until my limbs ache, and the murmurings of my kind, those women who will be pregnant with half futures again, are reduced to shrunken tremors in my chest. I run till the burn from my body reaches the pinnacle, the epicentre of Oni's molten wanderings, like a series of blood vessels colouring a trail. I run till kin's glassy curved hand in the restless sky reaches through several winters to hold me by the throat, steady me at intervals, mark my gaze with the splintered imprints of rebellious small clouds blooming in the blood, causing a series of organs to take flight while the body rests. I run till the bone in my pocket chaffs my skin through the thin cloth, in search of a soft, moist, pink marrow which has long disintegrated in me. I run all the way, through spiky scratches of nettles, the loosened weight of rocks crumbling, tethered by the dampened ground. The lines of past nights darting through the mountains are parched, blackened veins. Moss crawling from several angles is new growth kissed by cold breath, the warm air on my skin stirring a distant, fangled thing making its way to me.

I run towards the sea's embrace, glinting like a scowling blue jewel, liquefied in its undoing. It is dotted with boats boasting fishermen casting wide nets out to snag silvery fish they can eat raw. I pause on the shore, watching the boats. Salty sea air fills my nostrils. The boats rock gently on undulating waters.

The boats are filled with weeping, hollowed bones.

And then they are not.

The boats are loaded with scores of locusts shaped like women's silhouettes.

And then they are not.

The boats are refuges for bloody lace dresses fluttering against the wood, like a final request, a last interruption.

And then they are not.

A man is making his way towards me. The right side of his face is scarred like a prophet born from a searing flame, his gait sure, steady, fingers curling into the net. His haul dripping onto the shore. The catch in his net is rapidly becoming more visible. His breath is a signal born from a slackened morning's mouth waiting for the day's language.

The waters become rough. The boats are unsteady instruments gods deposited in bouts of kindness to men of the land, who used their bare hands to build them in the quiet hours of the day. They rock, fragile fruit spawned from flesh. Men call out to each other, steadily steering them while the water's shadows cling to their undersides one last time. The sprawling, choppy jewel's water folds, flattens, sways then flattens again in gulps of breathing. The boats are moored. The line of the shore pinned beneath them. The men hop out; push their boats further up the shore; arms straining in the light, their bodies covered in salty sea dew, shirts filled with damp patches. They grab their nets; hauls of fish bucking against various endings, loosened, bright scales like small, coloured seasons waiting to expand. The men convene briefly, the waters lapping at their feet. Gazes of fish abandon the nets. I inhale. A wind whips stray twigs searching for roots in the wrong land. The men scatter. I get down on my knees. The sand is cold. Grainy bits of stone press against the bone. I push my tongue into the spot, inside the sand, into the small, malleable gap. I taste tears from a great loss, bleeding from an ankle wound, the collapse of a trap unsure of what it was supposed to catch. I look up, the tip of my tongue covered in sand a pink newborn yet to decide its outer layer. The man born from fire is closer now. I stand, a dusting of sand covering my knees. His legs are bowed. His skin is dark; his wavy black hair curls away from his neck. His fish haul dribbles watery silver light from the corners of their mouths.

He raises his hand, indicating I should wait. I close my mouth, fresh saliva removing grainy particles from my tongue. A fluttering inside me builds into a tension. The clipped wing of a smoke-shrouded gull and a dying fish's fin become one. The man drops the net between us. A duplicitous trail of smoke speaks into my lungs. His loose brown shirt is rolled up at the sleeves. His hair, somewhat unkempt, is streaked with gold from being out in the sun often. The right side of his face, scarred from fire, has tight, shinier skin. The left side is still handsome. A shadow of bristle is on his chin. His Adam's apple bobs up and down as though waiting to be plucked. He is of considerable height, looming, looking down at me with a curious expression. His emerald-coloured eyes rest on my dusky skin. He smells of sweat and the sea. This is a man with the ocean's waters pumping through his veins in an act of deliberate misdirection, the curl of white waves tempering his heartbeats, dampening the ferocity of flame-singed secrets. Tiny beads of sweat coat the tips of visible chest hair, a red patch on his neck staggers upwards in a buoyant attempt to reach a dissipated curl of smoke between us. His chest heaves. I close my eyes hearing it's fluttering beneath the cloth, a soft point for the water's creatures leaping off it in an act of faith, losing themselves in the conspiratorial morning air. Fish wriggle in their sandy nets as if infected with the rhythms of bodies in close proximity. We are shrouded in the early light of the day now: bright, blooming, full of possibilities. Above us, the birds cry out, the flapping of their wings catching stunted bait.

The man raises his broad, weathered hands again as if I am skittish, alarmed. I look him in the eye without fear. In a way that a man of such physical presence is not used to from a stranger, a woman. His breath is warm on my skin when he asks if I am lost. He has not seen me in these parts before. I say I am not lost; the land has ways of showing you things when you are not expecting to see them. He tells me his name is Domingos. I say I am Zulmira. Zulmira, he repeats slowly with the gentleness of a prayer, as though attempting to know the corners of a name. Our exchange of names has the weight of small currencies in disguise. The other men come closer, their footsteps a restless audience marking the sand. The sea air has dented the lines of their bodies like a lover's caress. Their backs are taut with small tensions, their expressions curious. Wet shirts cling to their skin. Nets are thrown over their backs, fingers curled into pinched tips. Fish eyes cry at the loss of an underwater world. White fists of seawater crash against the whispers of the misshapen shoreline, rebellious as an accomplice in its own slow erosion. The men gather around us. Some watch me openly, others more discreetly. A stranger in their midst is cause for some excitement, some discussion. Domingos is a leader of sorts to them. I sense this from the way they seek his opinion, his reassurance.

He tells them I am a woman from an accident on the sea who fell off a boat passing through then slept in the crook of one mountain to recover. He lies on my behalf.

He does not know why. The men exchange concerns. A woman who belongs to no one will cause talk in Gethsemane, a foreigner no less. Can she stay with the outcasts on the edges of the town? Has she any gold coins or silver to show she is a woman of standing, of means? Perhaps Rowena, a stall owner who sells spices and items from different corners of the world as well as being one of the town's most knowledgeable residents, will know where she can go. As the men chatter, I look to the horizon beyond them. There is a blue tent folding, collapsing then swelling into its shape again. It belongs to Oni, filled with offerings. The entrance flutters open. I cannot see what is inside; only hear a jostling followed by stillness. I close my eyes briefly, blinking it away temporarily.

A decision is made. Domingos leads the way. The men talk among themselves as we wind through a crooked path heading east. Sun rays are a splintered compass. The murmurings of tiny creatures in shrubs are barely discernible. The hollows of warmly coloured shells are a haven for lost wings, the occasional ascension of blind snails feeding from fading footsteps, their translucent trails catching a copper coin, a soiled string, scales, a sweaty pip. I listen for my kind. A throbbing in my head begins. The scent of the sea is still strong. I will cough up something from its murky bottom which will find its half-eaten heart on the land. I know my kind are gone for now, their hungry mouths pressed against a restless root, the shapes of their pregnancies tumbling away, fading like a mist leaving a tense shoulder. Baby's cries still ring in my ears, promising more hauntings. I wonder who will feed her now that my bloody nipples have temporarily retreated into themselves. I linger beside Domingos.

He is thoughtful, silent, mouth pursed in contemplation. He shoots me a glance, as if I am a rough stone he has stumbled upon, a nuisance he has to contend with. I am tempted to reach for his scarred face, see if it will change beneath my fingers or if the growth of a singed sprig will break through with its own story to tell. One of the men, thin and sickly looking, offers me red berries from his pocket. I nod in thanks. I am no longer pregnant with the version of myself Oni showed me but I am still hungry enough for two. I eat the berries. The burst of sweet flavour is a welcome relief. Domingos marches forward, bowlegs quick, his gaze focused ahead. A bald goshawk bearing a scar in its centre emerges from the blue tent, circles the group, releasing a sharp cry, like a creature escaped from a trap. The scar leaves its body, curling in the sky. The goshawk flies away, shrinking into the map of clouds yet leaving a thrumming sensation of recognition in me. I ask about this Rowena the men mentioned. I wonder if she is a mother; does she know the pain of a severed bond between mother and child? Domingos refers to her as a clever, well-intentioned busybody. The blue tent attempts to break the fold, greedily opening its flap.

We walk on. One by one, men leave the procession snaking through the mountains, heading for their homes. The mountains' peaks and crevices are buoyant from the rays of the morning. The sand below flattens while the hands of my kind sprout through, curled and bleeding from Baby's umbilical cord, till they merge into one injury feeding the shore. Domingos is still silent beside me, the muscles of his arm strained from holding his leaking bounty. The rhythm of his gait slips into my chest. We cross a pale path which leads to a homestead. A wonky, stone house christened with blooms of moss, shrubs growing on both sides, a bramble patch at the left side. Thorns stretch, entwined, leaning into the lines of the house in an unplanned invasion. Scattered sticks lie gnarled, twisted, like a dormant army waiting for the grip, the smoke, a charred disintegration on the fold. At the door, before Domingos pushes it open, I see a cold hollow with a crying eye, a daughter, a sick wife, a house that needs a woman's touch, my finger pressed into the centre. Baby shrieking rings loudly into the crevices.

The daughter holds a club. A stain sullies her brown dress. Before he enters, I know the house has a hearth, a clay heart, one window which crumbles at its edges, a lilac cloth blushing in a corner of light stained by blood from a woman's womb. I know there are three separate rooms that have survived turbulent seasons, logs propped up against holes in the walls, the clay heart buried beneath the house beating, a wooden mallet beside a copper bowl of plums. There is movement behind him. The daughter clutches a pip. Domingos leaves the door open. I see the mallet smashing the pip, plum skin bruised and pulled from the walls' holes, winter fractured in the copper bowl, in the limping clay heart, freezing its wandering beat, a mortar full with grains of an eroded window. The daughter moves behind him again, the smashed pip in her mouth. She rubs the club against the stain on her dress, startled, curious. Domingos beckons me to follow. The bone in my pocket aches with longing. The house breathes and I with it. They open the door.

They let me in.

Chapter 2

A cataclysmic incident occurred that they hadn't foreseen. The new-found land in the other dimension, with its incandescent, twisted allure, embraced them like a drunken paradise, but something had gone wrong the last time the group were on that plane. Fissures in the dimension meant a breach – an entity had attempted to incubate in each of them unsuccessfully, which caused mood swings, arguing, erratic behaviour. Finn had offered to help Therese with a paper on Nepalese tribes and their use of plant healing practices only for it to turn into an argument over her more accommodating attitude towards Azacca. Emilien found a missing page from his sketchpad in Azacca's room, an image of Azacca tumbling in the ether with hands pushing him and Oni's blue tent flapping in the corner spilling sacrificial offerings. A disagreement followed about how it got there, with Azacca flinging out accusations of his own. Someone had stolen two hundred pounds from his wallet as well as some of his mother's letters. He cursed in Haitian; Therese and Finn had to rush upstairs to separate things. The four of them stood shouting, the scrunched-up sketch paper pulsing on the ground between them like an outcaste scorched thing.

However, prior to that, on arrival in their gloriously warped Eden-like new world, everything had seemed as it should be. They had been building it in stages, coming together for their rituals of flight. The group were incubators, sentient beings who were arbiters of wondrous new realities and infinite possibilities that could pass parts of hallucinations as DNA on to creatures. The heads of a one-eyed eagle turning like globes, its messages released into the hot air to spread the power of this new world to its outer limits. Of course, there were personal costs to incubators. Each secretly managed the impact on their bodies. On the plane, the looming valleys bathed in light were shedding half-formed butterflies scouring for their caterpillar origins in a nearby shimmering lake. The bright afternoon had paths winding through like electric currents leading to points of sacrifice. The air smelled of sweet berries, the scent growing tantalisingly stronger as Therese, Azacca, Finn and Emilien wandered through the paths in awe of entities they had spawned from their bodies as architects of creation. Two molten suns above in the endless azure sky oscillated towards each other, offering wonder, the threat of obliteration. Seals with vertebrae sprouting out of their backs like soft bone constructs hovered beyond them. Gnarled, pale trees were slowly absorbing colour from the sky while growing new fruit. Locusts emerged from plums then became Sanskrit verses in shadowed corners. Headless bright water bulls stumbled around the lakes before falling through to the watery mirrors beneath them. Above, a golden goshawk traced the shape of Oni's collapsed blue tent travelling through the ages in search of fresh offerings.

The group felt the blood thump through their veins, adrenalin pumping inside them, their hearts beating frenetically in tune with this beautiful, perilous utopia. Liquid mercury spilled from their peripheral visions into electric paths. And the large bulbs of peyote were nestled in parts of the valley like heady rewards waiting to be claimed. They wandered through their Eden, four agents of change and abomination, looking for spaces to nurture, to populate with their irrepressible bodies. Tiny prisms in the air reflected white bones with pink marrow spilling from them like miniature vertebrae maps. Their senses heightened when this happened. The air thickened, light refracted in waves before them. The two suns flickered as though something got lost in translation. An entity was coming through the frequency in their distorted haven, already made malleable by their restless fingers. The intense heat, the sudden warping of sound in their ears felt like it was travelling towards them, hurtling from every direction so it appeared to multiply, its ascent a labyrinthine infiltration slowly turning the axis on the plane. The valley shedding half butterflies was now filled with shadows, its edges swirling into a gathering storm. The hissing sound of pink marrow spilling from small vertebrae floating in the air as unencumbered instruments magnified in their eardrums. Marrow sputtered through cracks, making the pinkened vertebrae look like monstrous amebae.

Therese's heart shuddered violently in her chest. A little ahead of her, Azacca fell to the ground covering his ears, unable to bear the shrill, invasive screaming, a girl's voice howling as if transported unexpectedly through the passages of time. Spots of blood began to trickle from his ears. His back grew bulbous, incubating a shape attempting to breathe through him. To his right was Finn, whose stomach was now a distorted zone in its own process of change as the entity searched inside his body. Veins spilled from his nostrils, the whites of his eyes stretched eclipsing his irises. Emilien, the furthest ahead, stopped to look back at the others. The darkness from the valley's edges had seeped into him.

'What's happening?' he barked, his expression confused, his hands and feet becoming dark vertebrae.

Azacca and Finn, both in pain, were unable to answer. Therese tried to respond but couldn't. Her throat closed as if a violent act had occurred there and had banished the memory as a form of protection. The taste left her mouth, her tongue was bruised from a usurper planting its languages and layers of past lives there. The girl's voice was fading in the skies. The memory of it left an imprint inside them. A growing ache began to spread between them. Their tongues became distended, harbouring the echoes of the girl's screams. They wandered on. Further down, electric-blue currents ran along the edges of various paths. The middle path flickered with light, yet the darkness loomed. And the entity trying to come through them as though they were vessels had left their limbs exhausted and vulnerable, a parched ventriloquist chasing discombobulated suns.

And so, the entity that had attempted to infiltrate their bodies in utopia arrived, an oddly beautiful mutant-like organism which travelled through the breach, taking kinetically charged paths to get there. The traveller, a ribcage blooming fruit, sat on a wooden chopping board at the kitchen worktop in an unfinished display, shrouded by the faint screaming of a girl that lingered in the air. A spill of cumin seeds rolled off the edge, the bread knife was stained with blood, a rusted copper pipe flanked it, forming a haphazard broken circle. Therese stumbled towards it from the hallway as if emerging through a corridor of slippery ground. Her vest and black combats clung to damp skin. Her braids were wet at the tips. Her limbs ached. Her head throbbed. Her fingers felt stiff. Her vision was spotted still. White murmurs from its corners assembled then flattened in a line in her sight. The window flapped open. A breeze shuddered the pink frosted shells on the ledge. Brooding and dark, the night threatened to suck the kitchen's contents into its folds. Finn came from behind her, his gait slower. Like their prior visits to the other plane, they each had ailments to contend with in the aftermath returning from the process of incubation. This time, Finn's injuries were in his chest, a gathering of mouths weeping beneath his black cotton T-shirt. Earlier, Azacca had claimed the silhouette of his heart was floating inside him; tumbling, tugging something in the blood, pumping in his gut before rising again. The slow orchestra of him joining them coalesced with Emilien coming from the downstairs bathroom having vomited in the toilet's alabaster neck. His hands were temporarily webbed, sharp shots of pain hit his knees, legs buckling as he parked his feverish body on a stool. Soft breaths calmed him.

Therese edged closer to the worktop, the middle island's garish gift. Azacca placed his hand on her back to steady her. Finn uncurled from the doorway, walking towards the ribcage. 'This is wild, guys. Trying to get my head around how it happened,' he said, green eyes flashing, lips thinned to a line.

'Any number of factors could have caused this,' Azacca retorted, voice thick, accent stronger as it often was in moments of anger.

Emilien flexed his left hand, the skin between his fingers taut. 'We've somehow invited this here. Therese, are you okay?' he asked.

She nodded slowly, as if in a trance, walking to the centre.

Magnets on the fridge door rattled. A fifth waning heartbeat attempted to interrupt before fading away. The window flapped back again. The shape of the creek they'd been in to help revive themselves hovered at the frame. Lights in the ceiling flickered, as though the possibility of darkness would change everything, would rearrange each element until they were left holding parts of an inebriated memory, running back through the bend into the night. Back to their naked forms on all fours sinking into the soil, to their tongues pressed against folds of earth waiting for fires to reconfigure in blood, back to the hollows repeating the movements of their bodies then distorting it. Returning to the plane shifting, the land changing beneath their feet, a new unnamed weather passing through their bodies bearing the chill of winter, buoyant beginnings of spring. Back to the silhouettes withering on the horizon like burnished plants. Returning towards euphoria, to run amok, language changing in their mouths, the splintered, foreign dawns on the second plane taking turns to shatter in each of them.

Their attempts to please Oni through their secret task

always left a gulf of hunger inside them. Making her vision come to life cost them in ways they couldn't fully decipher. It was an addiction, the deep desire to be more than one thing, to create beyond themselves, which Oni stoked with her meddling hand. Therese felt that the world had seen what man could do within their limited systems, patriarchal terrorisation. What a woman shaman deity could create, alternative solutions behind the veil of mundane, ordinary existence. She knew they didn't want to be ordinary. They were Oni's modern disciples known as kin.

Later that night, the entity had bloomed even more. Flickering back to its full capacity, the ceiling light's glow on the ribcage was celestial. A thin film of dust had settled on it. On one side, a rib had tiny orbs of colour leaking from it, rainbow hued, the vibrancy of oil spills on roads shimmering. On another rib, blood vessels looked fit to burst; on the third rib, red berries grew from the bone: small, plump, juicy. The other side of the ribcage boasted a smattering of moss.

Azacca touched the damp moss, took a sniff. 'It smells like the sea, the rush of a wave. Something in me knew this was coming. That's why I've been hearing the echoes of my heart moving in the different dimensions recklessly,' he offered, eyeing Emilien, whose pallor had got slightly better, the webbed skin between his fingers shrinking back. Emilien got off the stool, made his way to the others.

'*Mierda*. This is beyond our runs.' He wiped his sweaty brow with the back of his right hand. His arm fell, twitching by his side. Azacca held it reassuringly, steadying it as if it was a skittish colt that needed a quiet tenderness, a masculine show of camaraderie. The physical toll from their trips to the other side were always more visible on Emilien. They didn't know why but it often seemed as if a timer was ticking for him, making them all feel on edge – not just for him but for each other. Who among them was a bomb in disguise waiting to explode?

Therese inhaled, plucked a berry, slipping it under her tongue. 'Fruit from the bone,' she whispered, her voice cracking as she stroked the ribcage gently, almost lovingly, intoxicated by its presence, its oozing of element, fruit and blood.

Finn snapped one berry off abruptly, brow furrowed, cheeks flushed, wounds wailing. 'When the fuck did this get here?'

She'd met Finn at a late exhibition of stars and comets at The Royal Observatory. That evening, the observatory had looked like something the moon birthed – pale, abstract, incongruous in its setting: a steep walk up, pathways separating a large park, bodies moored on either side of a sea of green. A steady flow of footfall rang in the air. Inside, silvery light gave the cold concave room of photographs a surreal quality, as though they'd all accidentally become grainy, then seep into the images, the room like a half-formed fallen planet. He'd knocked into her accidentally. A momentary lapse, heat emerged from the contact of their bodies, his hand grazing the loose thread at the waist of her yellow dress. His breath tinged with alcohol was warm on her face. A swift separation of their limbs followed, his hand loose at her waist. A little winded, Therese took in the nose (broken at least twice), the plump mouth, the slash of cheekbones, wild curly black hair cut short, beautiful emerald eyes. He was tall, striking rather than conventionally attractive. No apology. Instead: 'Shit, are you okay? Uranium on Mars, you're like something out of an Octavia Butler novel. Very good dress. Nice braids.' Before she could take a breath, he'd drawn her in, ignoring social protocol and boundaries, launching into a jumble of commentary, bright eyed. The heat off his body was palpable. 'Aerial photography,' he said. 'Yeah. That was how the images were captured. I knew the photographer in a past life. We filmed storms once, got sick in the Andes, lived with Maasai warriors together. We fell out spectacularly over a woman, a contortionist. Crazy story! She fucked us both over in the end. Anyway, last September I helped excavate a quarry in Oman, beautiful. I didn't expect that but it was. Looking into that enormous cavity, standing at the edge of it, undid something in me. You see I haven't always been a good son even though I have a rotten father who never gave a shit about me; sometimes I've wanted to cut the essence of that man out of me, remove those traits steeped in the marrow of my bones. Sometimes I've been a bad man purely for survival, because it was necessary. And occasionally, I'm susceptible to confessing my sins to pretty women who crash in on a train of thought in bright garb. And is there a name for a wound under the skin that keeps moving? I'm sure I fucking have one. I'm paranoid about it. I don't know where it came from but some days, I can feel it trying to communicate with me, thickening, attempting to break the skin. Crazy! I know. I'm not going to the doctor for it, no fucking way. Have you noticed how many exits there are in this place? Jesus. I'm Finn, by the way,' he continued, fully in his element, popping a stick of gum into his mouth. The best conversations were with strangers, he said, people who had no vested interest in you whatsoever. What was that scent she was wearing? Oleander? Jasmine? Potpourri? he joked, his lips curving into a wry smile. And if they stayed in contact, if they remained friends, would he enjoy talking to her in future as much as he did this instant? He was present, warm and somehow charged with elements beyond what the eye could see.

He was right about the wound. But she didn't want to panic him. She resisted the urge to say, *There will be more to come*, because there would be. She heard it inside him moving, finding its form, pushing against the skin again. She inhaled, her fingers itching to stroke it, breathe against it. She smiled patiently, looking up at the ceiling searching for a sign, a confirmation she'd already embraced on instinct. Falling into step with one another, they slipped outside, talking still, the wound in him whispering during quiet moments in the ebb and flow of their conversation. The trees shuddered. The thread from her yellow dress caught the zipper of his leather jacket, catching the night. He studied her as if she was a woman growing from one of his internal injuries. A wound strained against his skin painfully, causing him to wince while naming a star Durneen.

She spotted the crescent-shaped birthmark on the right side of his neck, the mark of kin. Later, he confided his darkest secret from a different life with a sense of urgency, a piece of him to cement their growing bond, to lure him into the fold. That was the exchange, the currency she wielded through her intoxicating aura. Of course, he would never fully pay his debt to Oni, although that was something he didn't need to be aware of.

He was the first to move in with her. In between expeditions and writing assignments – a story on pygmies in Papua New Guinea, a piece on a submarine harbouring stolen museum artefacts, a feature on descendants of Amazonian women – they created a home together as friends. He'd bought her an exquisite red tea set trimmed with gold from Morocco, pretty mosaic vases from Zanzibar for plants blooming in her study, a microscope to assess plant nuclei for those restless nights when sleep abandoned her body. He bought her a leather-bound book on fifteenth-century botanists he'd found in a Transylvanian market, a study on warrior women in the kingdom of Dahomey, hand-woven woollen portraits by Inuit women in Alaska. There was never a fuss or show made when her brought items home. 'One for the collection,' he'd say, glassy eyed, amused by her subdued appreciation. Or she'd get an off-hand, 'That'll be worth something someday, sentimental or monetary value, you'll decide,' distractedly already chewing over something else: the next trip or assignment, the last woman he slept with in transit several times. And how attraction had a scent, that the smell of this woman had changed for him, an indication he no longer wanted her in the same way.

They built a small greenhouse at the bottom of the garden, stripped the kitchen floor, cleared out the basement. They tried to recreate a Japanese garden but failed. It had been a half-hearted attempt. They ended up smoking spliffs in a makeshift hammock which only came out in summer. Some nights, she heard his wound crying inside him. She understood its loneliness, its isolation in the body; she sat on the edge of her bed thinking of ways to water it, running her fingers over its replications in the margins. She watched Finn's expressions carefully for signs of a change.

He went on assignment for three weeks to Chile, a piece on developers buying up land in a small town, mining it for its minerals, disregarding ancient customs, destroying its natural beauty. Via email, he told her there were streams of community members cast from its bowels in apocalyptic treks to rapidly dwindling springs clutching large water cans.

The house was quiet without him; his restless padding in the hallways unknotting thoughts mid-flow; hammering away on his laptop; the blare of music from his room: Johnny Cash, Dinah Washington, Tom Waits, Sharon Jones, Nick Cave, Vivaldi; his loud reading of excerpts from Raymond Carver's short stories on the occasions he cooked, pot lids jangling from the heat, the papery murmur of pages being turned; random commentary on the plants in her study. 'This fucker has tall poppy syndrome,' he'd said once about a tropical pitcher plant shooting up rebelliously towards the ceiling, running his finger along its spine. She received the odd phone call. 'How is it?' she would ask. During one exchange, his voice was slightly slurred, lined with whatever preferred alcoholic companion of the moment had settled in his system. There was a delay, a beat between responses. 'I'm like Morecambe without his Wise in paradise,' he joked. 'So far, I've managed to grossly offend one of my interview subjects, misplace my mobile which thankfully was returned to me, and survive a fever that could have killed me, the life of Riley,' he added. The static crackled like a talking void. A beat became a moment of silence pressed against multiple receivers. The distance twisted into a white-hot space pulsing between phone conversations; not quite of the earth nor the heavens; beating and breaking.

On another call, he wept quietly. The pain of his wounds was so bad, he put her voice on speaker, pacing the cramped lodging of the treehouse he was in. His mobile phone with two bars remaining, the night's mischief makers threatening to crash through the window suffused with heat, Therese speaking a mantra to him while his wounds glimmered in her peripheral vision, while he screamed so loudly from the pain, it rippled through the static. She closed her eyes in rapture, at the inevitability of it all, the receiver in her hand limp as the night's repository for his punishment.

She became restless, lonely. She wrote a deconstruction on the properties of the ghost orchid, felt untethered in crowds of people, a hunger beyond meals taking root inside her, a tremble of electricity slowly expanding. She sat in restaurants ordering for one, watching tongues disappear in moist, cavernous mouths, the echoes of Finn's cries inside her, feeling the breath leave her, unnamed things bleeding from the corners into the foreground, intermittently smudging heads around her. She didn't bother telling Finn about Azacca. It was her house. She bought it. She could invite who she wanted.

And on returning, Finn, blurry eyed, cranky off a 2 a.m. flight to Gatwick, had crashed unceremoniously back home. He lingered in her bedroom doorway, bristling yet calm, flicking a green lighter on and off so the flame blazed in brief spurts.

'Question,' he offered by way of greeting to her sleep-lined, tired expression. 'You found another like us?' A hint of jealousy in his tone, a throbbing in his jaw, the crescent-shaped mark on his neck filled with scar tissue. Now he was no longer her only one. The pureness of his pain had always been quite beautiful to her. The room felt charged with possibilities. She sat up, holding the intensity of his gaze, watching his right fist uncurl like a restrained siren between them. She turned her response over before releasing it as a rapturous breath.

'Yes, kin.'

Three

Domingos leads me through the stone passageway just as his daughter drops her pip. It rolls as though protesting my presence on its way to take root again. A woman splutters behind a closed door, a cough racks her body. The sound is hollow, ragged; like nestle clamouring for water. The woman shuffles about slowly, moving her limbs towards our interruption. The clay heart turns in the soil. A stubborn wind whistles through the roof, the logs become silhouettes.

'Come this way,' Domingos instructs, setting his net down by the hearth, rivulets pooling beneath it, translucent beads flattening.

The homestead feels inadequate for him, as if it cannot contain the height and breadth of him, all that he is, all that the eye does not immediately see, yet he moves about easily, gracefully. Were the house to collapse, he would know its lines instinctively, rebuild it from rubble. His daughter trails us excitedly, black eyes gleaming, brown skin smooth, a cut on the bridge of her nose still healing. She waves the club with a soiled hand in a manner that is playful rather than threatening.

'I am Sueli,' *she declares in a serious voice, an imitation of adults she has heard making introductions,* 'You are not one of us,' *she says, pointing the club, with the candour and innocence of a child.*

'Quiet!' *Domingos barks.* 'Zulmira will help here in exchange for room and board for a little while.' *He takes us to a small room at the back. It is a narrow, characterless, dank space, barely enough for a family of goats. There is a creaky oil lamp in one corner, a bloody, violet cloth in a creased puddle in the other. Embarrassed, he gathers the cloth, tucks it beneath his arm.* 'This will do for now,' *he offers curtly, watching my expression for judgement.*

'Thank you,' *I say, smiling at the ease in which a man wants a woman's approval, even one that is not his own.*

Sueli squeals, feral and mischievous. 'I cannot find my brothers and sisters,' *she confesses.* 'They come to Mama, then leave,' *she whispers, cupping her mouth with a curved hand.*

'Get!' *Domingos orders, a furious expression on his face. She scurries away, bearing the guilty look of a child who has said too much to a stranger. There is a tension in the room after she leaves, moments of strained silence.*

'Where did she get that club?' *I ask, lifting the lamp up, rubbing my finger against a slither of oil on the coppery frame. The cloth threatens to unravel under his grip; he tucks it in again forcefully.*

'God only knows! That child, half the things she speaks of are a mystery to me. It is as if she did not come from us.' *The burnt side of his face twitches. He grimaces as though in pain, turning abruptly. The lamp swings slowly in my hold. I face the doorway as he leaves me. Sueli darts back and forth in the periphery, talking in a frenzied language to her club, throwing it, leaping at it. Then she is reduced to a tiny girl in the stone hearth, clutching the tongues of lost siblings while her mother's injuries migrate to her stained hemline. She takes her pattern of chaos further outside, runs between the shrubs, tossing the club, squealing. Domingos lifts her, throws her over his shoulder.*

'*Papa, put me down!' she exclaims. Their peels of laughter follow, lingering on the edge. I tighten my grip on the lamp. It swings again steadily, insisting for the curl and flicker of its missing flame, for me to hold it up to see the shapes of scenes that had turned to ash in the room's corners. An angle of light from the window falls on my skin. I am half shadow, half light on the hard floor. I raise my head, breaking the lines of a past scene: a small limp body gathered like a failed offering, the bundling of cloth beneath it, oil on the material, the washing of hands, the breaking of a pale shell, whites of a man's eyes darkening. I listen to the soft traces of invisible evidence.*

I am certain a death has occurred in my room.

Over the next few days, Domingos sets off just after dawn to meet the other fishermen on a quiet mountain where a man leapt to his death north of the town. Sometimes, he heads to the market afterwards to sell the fish, before bringing what remains home, his hands acrid, scales stuck under his fingernails, his mood darkened, red scratches across his knuckles and veins thickened under his skin. The jangle of coins in his pocket is usually a measure of the day's success or disappointment. On other occasions, he brings home a pig's heart, a hare's headless body, large crooked crabs with deformed legs, his bounty dribbling, crossing the homestead's threshold.

The bone leaves my pocket. I keep it under makeshift bedding in my room, beneath a bundle of cloth used as a pillow. It crackles in my ear at night, the marrow darkening then growing again, breathing against the bone. The pain of being separated from Baby continues to be a fangled thing inside me. Guilt eats away at me thinking of her puckered expressions asking for her mother. I take on the running of the house with a fervour to combat this shattering feeling. The homestead is a cavity, our bodies springing from it each morning. I clear out the cook room's hearth, removing charred cinders from its gut, replacing it with fresh wood. I wash the stone mortars, wiping the residue of grains from pestles. I sweep the small pantry storing salted pieces of meat lying on rough stone slabs. A woven basket of batatas sits in one corner. Four shelves rest on the walls, on the bottom shelf are copper and metal instruments I do not recognise. I picture Domingos's hands over these objects, wielding them feverishly against enemies in the dark appearing from the cinders, the hearth, the blade, the axe. A string of root vegetables hangs at the opposite end of the pantry, facing a dilapidated garden enclosure housing weeds crawling up wooden fencing. Unruly vegetation grows through layers of earth.

Sueli assists me, firing questions at me curiously. Is your mother unhappy too? Why do you have no belongings? Who are your people?

I do not tell her my kin can hear from distances. They can listen through a collarbone, an ovary, a ruptured spleen. Sueli buzzes in my periphery: rolling batatas from one end of the pantry floor to the other, firing stones off a makeshift contraption of sticks and cloth at the hem of my plain brown shift, leaping into blades of grass in the back enclosure, arms outstretched for a gift to fall from the clouds.

In the mornings, I tend to Domingos's wife, Marguerite, washing her with a small cloth dipped in a basin of water. She was once fine looking but ill health has stolen her beauty, leaving her delicate face hollowed. The first time in their sleeping quarters, she watches my body almost greedily, as though hungry for the movement and presence of someone new. She sits up in the bed, her golden-brown skin pallid, hands shaking, the sweat-soaked bed linen rustling against her, taking gulps of air in slowly while her shoulders slacken. 'You have a strange mouth,' she says, wheezing, 'as if it does not belong in your face. You possess a foreign disposition.'

I squeeze water from the cloth, running it over her shoulder blades.

Laughing gently. 'I suppose my manner seems odd in a new place.' Lifting her chin, I maintain my smile. I scour her skin for points of entry to cut a sickness out. The blue basin chimes with the landing of invisible limbs.

I cook the pig's heart. The hare. The ugly crab. I watch them float in boiling water inside the copper pot; steam rising, the orange hue of the pot somehow more pronounced, the hearth roaring. A half-cooked pig's heart is like an entity a body releases as the blood warms. I make delicious, peppery broths with sweet batatas, wild onion, slices of pumpkin. The scents of sage and spices fill the homestead. We eat our later meals when the light changes in the evening, Gethsemane sheds its skin for the night and Domingos returns home with the next day's meal from the thrashing sea. He does not say so but he is impressed by my ability to make much out of little. He asks for second helpings. Sometimes, he takes bowls of broth to Marguerite, feeding her patiently, tenderly brushing tendrils of hair away from her clammy forehead. Now and then Sueli hums during meals, laughing between mouthfuls, pulling faces, repeating parts of conversations she'd heard days before in a loop. On one occasion, Domingos comes upon me in the pantry. I am salting the hare's legs to keep for a few days. White crystals of sea salt cover my hands and wrists. He leans against one side of the doorway. I sense his presence, reading his body's expression even before it changes. 'We will see what you will make of the rainbow fish. It is not the most flavoursome but plentiful.' He unfolds his arms. His skin under the glow of the oil lamp by my feet takes on a warmth. I raise my head, one salted hare leg in hand.

'Cooking good meals is the least of my capabilities,' I respond. I say this practically. It is true, after all. He does not know what to make of this. He watches me from guarded lids, his eyes gleam, his gaze rests on the elegant curve of my neck. I return my attention to the task, listening as the thud of his footsteps fades. After finishing, I wash my hands in the back garden. I can still smell the hare on my skin. Nights like this I feel a loneliness overwhelm me, the loss of a shared language temporarily gone. I grapple with my betrayal against Baby and my kind. I listen for their chants to Oni, which the winds can toss as far as desserts undulating beneath a burnished sun. I cry silently about Baby, wondering how kin take turns to mother her, whose arms make her feel safe, which nipples does she suckle, whose display of maternal joy gives her a sense of wonder in the world. What is done cannot be undone. I try to pre-empt the repercussions of my betrayal but cannot; they are cloud beaks slipping through my hold into nothing. I listen for my kind in between planes, the mutating of their heartbeats, the transporting of foreign angles into the blood, the *white mist escaping from orifices. I cross the passageway feeling a cold tip skimming my insides.*

Outside my room, standing by the doorway, I find Sueli holding my bone, tapping its pale length with a keen finger, placing her mouth at its rounded opening to suck the marrow, before changing her mind and returning it.

It is the week of the harvest moon when Marguerite stands over me as I wake. She is trembling. Her eyes dart around uncertainly. She lifts her smock up to reveal bite marks covering her torso, crawling up towards plump, golden breasts. Domingos appears from behind, holding her. There are spaces of smooth skin between the bites which look like the red markings of a territory, as though her body has offered itself to be conquered. He points to a mark. 'This is a reaction to one of your concoctions,' he barks, throwing a furious look my way. I know it is not a result of my meals. Standing up slowly, I run a finger along the indentations of one bite.

'Strange incidents can happen during a harvest moon period,' I say reassuringly. I blow a breath against one bite mark, watching the redness vanish. Domingos pulls Marguerite back, bewildered.

On returning home later that day, he either scowls at me or barely glances my way. I expect this. I am the outsider who shoulders blame when others need to make sense of things they cannot understand or want to come to terms with. They will not hold a mirror up for fear of what they might see. He fusses over Marguerite, kneads her shoulders, runs a cold cloth over her head and skin, kisses the hollow of her back. I feel a twinge in my chest I do not want to identify.

The next morning, after Domingos sets off earlier than usual to head to the other side of Jellah Mountain, I grab sprigs of lavender from the bottom of the chaotic back garden to aid in skin healing. I gather Marguerite from her bed, heat some water in the pot, pour it into the basin adding the lavender. I dip a cloth in it, wipe her bite marks gently before blowing a breath on every single one, my left hand gripping her naked waist, my right hand already reaching for the marks as if they are the wayward offspring of the harvest moon.

That evening, Marguerite joins us to eat rather than staying in their bedroom. 'The bite marks have left my body,' she announces dramatically. 'I do not know what she did! It is wonderful, is it not?' She grabs my arm, in confirmation, nearly knocking over a metallic bowl of wild rabbit soup. Sueli steadies the bowl, reacting quickly. A trickle of soup runs down her chin. Handfuls of bugs she caught earlier crawl from the pocket of her blue shift. She makes a popping sound using one finger pressed against the inside of her cheek. Domingos glances over her head at me, his expression grim. His mouth flattens into a line, as if he does not know who he has allowed into his home. I release a barely audible breath, smiling briefly, triumphantly.

Chapter 3

Feverishly, Therese dreamed of a dusky woman breaking away from her clan in a past time. Saw bone, marrow and sweet nectar becoming one in an unfamiliar land. The ground a burnished copper hue as the woman tore away, in anticipation of what lay before her. Intertwined in that moment, she felt the woman's heart pumping frenetically in her chest, two hearts beating in tandem. She imbibed the punishing heat of that foreign sun on her skin, the dryness of the woman's mouth in hers, the cluster of ominous women with fallen expressions near by, a shrieking baby. The urgency of the unnamed woman running imbued her own limbs with adrenalin. She witnessed the woman in flight from her clan, beautiful sylphs transported from the horizon sporting crescent-shaped markings on their necks. Tension in the air caused a bruise to bloom on the woman's lung, her curved back sprouted smatterings of fresh cells on the spine, a lengthened throat storing new weather in the surroundings. The mountains in this sun-stroked land were secretive. Therese sensed their wisdom acutely. A shadow emerged from beneath the woman's tongue and roamed on all fours while she caught her breath, scrambling through winding pathways, mountainous peaks and crevices. Therese turned these images in her hands as if the weight of this other world controlled her reluctant fingers. That night, she tossed and turned, bunching the checked blanket between her thighs. Waking up in a cold sweat, her white T-shirt clinging to her, the sharp incisions of unfamiliar scenes threatened to break through her skin. Then, pacing the hallway seeing that woman raising roots to the sky as evidence of ruptures inside them, chanting which became a distant din rising inside her. She felt the rhythm of the woman's body passing through hers. She tasted the residue of chalk from the woman's wrists, angles of a glimmering void, the crinkle of nettle leaves, the prick of bark breaking into a ceremonial gathering. The woman's hand reached through the void to pull her towards an inherited danger. One of these things tethered the other:

The woman abandoning a shrieking baby.

Her clan forming a ring around it to lay claim.

Pink marrow spilling from bone that slipped into her vision.

The static of language increased in her eardrums like bells ricocheting through past and present lives.

One night she awoke startled, tasting alien flavours from this woman's tongue: nettle, calendula, squid broth, a white pip. Swinging her legs over the bed, she sat up, blinking at the glow of the numbers from the clock on her dresser. She blinked again. The faraway land had shimmering slipstreams wound through its mountains. An unclaimed mangled heart pumped through the centre as though creating its own equator. The odd blue vein shot through the edges. Worms with butterfly wings clung to bent blades of grass. A dilapidated white homestead spilled a waterfall from one front window. An imposter sun languished in the background. Red ladybirds passed through pale chalk markings on dusty ground becoming bright fingerprints on the other side. Lava ran down the edge of a mountain. Women's lace costumes sank to the bottom of streams only to break the surface again filled with marrow and bone. It was like mecca demented on foreign blood.

Covered in a cold sweat, Therese slipped on her dressing gown, tying it loosely. Her heart rate became rapid. Beads of sweat slid down her back. Her throat tightened; her mouth swelled with distant shapes of that woman's movements travelling through dawn to take refuge in its moist enclave. The woman's face flickered in her subconscious: a delicately featured black woman with molasses-brown skin, high cheekbones and tempestuous golden eyes. Therese padded into the upstairs bathroom, opened the window, feeling relief as the rush of cold air hit her skin. The gentle sounds of the early morning filtered in: the odd car crossing a set of traffic lights, a fox rummaging through a cluster of bins, lone footsteps passing now and again. She stood over the blue sink lined with shaving cream, a tube of muscle relief ointment, one electric toothbrush. She gazed into the water-marked mirror above the sink. Something hatched there. The sound of echoes reverberated; she placed one hand on the glass as if she could catch them, fingers splayed. Heat coursed through her body as though a drop of lava from the faraway mountain land had slid into a vein. She looked into the mirror again, expecting a bright figure, half eroded by lava, persuaded by a mist to pull her through to the other side. Running the cold tap, she splashed water over her face. She sat on the edge of the bathtub. The secret present giver hadn't placed his latest gift inside it. She'd have to search around the house.

The ribcage loomed in the kitchen, resting on the worktop, growing fruit, reproducing the elements, expanding, retracting, a living breathing organism. They'd considered keeping it in the fridge, wedged in the middle compartment absorbing the constant hum. It would have to be moved. Therese could feel the excitement, curiosity and nervous energy in the house as they each mulled over its arrival, what it meant for them; somehow, they'd opened up a portal which delivered it. She closed the tap. Leaving the bathroom, she noticed the glow of the lamp through the glass partition above Emilien's door. She crossed the landing, tapped on his door quietly. No answer. She pulled the handle down gently, careful not to wake the others. The scent of incense tickled her nostrils. The window and a few drawers filled with shirts and socks were open. An empty bottle of Jack Daniel's Whiskey lay on the floor. There were mud prints on the double bed. Purple grapefruits tinged with blood clots spilled from the corner of the duvet, a trail of edible offerings beckoning. The ribcage's new fruit trickled down his bed while the house slumbered. Emilien had carried some into the morning. The large, green Chinese fan of wildflowers which normally rested on the wall above his bed had crashed down onto the headboard. A weathered map of the Andes lay on a small table beside the bed with red arrows pointing to specific areas. Little white tobacco sheets were wedged between half a mug of cold coffee and books on some of the world's great illusionists: Houdini, Dai Vernon, David Copperfield.

She sat in the large wicker chair at the back of the room which she fondly referred to as 'his old man's chair'. She spotted his sketchpad underneath the bed. Fishing it out, she ran her fingers over the grainy, grey cover, flicking it open. Some pages were missing, ripped out. There were caricatures of all of them; humorous anecdotal snapshots capturing moments in their lives. She flipped on towards the middle, stopping at a comically grotesque rendering of her in the bath, her huge head taking up a large portion of the page, her braids fanned out, stomach rounded, feet tiny, legs in the birthing position, pushing out gifts as blood sloshed down the sides of the tub. A thundering began in her temples. After that there was a sketch of a girl screaming behind an iron chair rising from an endless expanse of green land. Spots of Emilien's blood decorated the edges, a bleeding into an old world. She closed the pad, returned it to the dark gap where the screaming girl raised their heads from paper, ready to be fed by their restless ventriloquist, Oni. As the stranger's face continued to flicker inside her like a potent disrupter, the woman who had abandoned her baby and kin. She gazed at the dappled bed, reaching for a memory.

The first time they met, Emilien stopped her on a bustling street in Leadenhall Market outside a baroquely designed furnishings shop asking for directions to the Guildhall building. This led to tempting her into having drinks with him and ultimately diverting the course of their day. And with the rain beating down on them, her silvery umbrella turned inside out, their bodies rushing through the slant of rainwater, chests expanding from the thrill of a random encounter, they gathered themselves in the doorway of an old pub on Liverpool Street, The Knight's Head. A film of condensation had settled on the stained-glass door. The umbrella crumpled between them, slumping amid lingering bodies. The blur of traffic sped by. They adjusted to the quiet rhythm in their limbs. He possessed a warm, earthy scent. His breath smelled of coffee and whisky. A crack of thunder tore through murky patterns in the sky. They looked up, almost reluctant to leave that doorway where anything seemed possible, punctuated by the occasional gust of cold air on their faces. His Peruvian accent wasn't quite watered down. He was mercurial in the breaking light. Therese liked that. Dark haired and dark eyed, elegantly handsome from one angle, fiendish and foxlike from another. Lean. Sluggish on one hand then quick to spring forward, to laugh, swift to reassure, darting ahead, high on spontaneity, pulling her through clusters of people. He shrugged off his backpack, dumping it by the foot of a table before pulling a chair out for her. She pictured grenade pins floating in his backpack, a small, contained galaxy glinting, her tongue tracing its winding trail. And the grenades like ridged metal eggs scattered around the city chasing a constellation. He shook the rain from his hair. His Hawaiian shirt, army-style trousers and scuffed boots were an odd combination. Slipping into the chair in relief he said, 'I've never stopped being accident prone, yet my body keeps surviving it. You may be my latest accident.'

She turned to face him fully, tucking her braids behind

her ears, adjusting her patterned wooden necklace, covertly watching his mouth as though something bright and beautiful had formed there. They ordered coffees laced with brandy as silhouettes shifted in the rain. A haggard female street urchin came into the pub begging before being thrown out, a group of women in pink Cancer Research T-shirts raucously celebrated some tables away. A man with a stack of *Big Issue* magazines fumbled at the bar, reaching deep into his pockets for lost currencies. She took a sip from her coffee. The dark-haired chameleon said his name was Emelien.

'E-m-i-l-i-e-n.' He enunciated patiently, used to incorrect pronunciations. He stretched his long legs, settling in his seat, watching her carefully over the mug's rim. 'Have you ever felt that something was missing from your memory or consciousness? Like sometimes you're looking at the world through a glass partition. When I was little, I felt the absence of something.'

'Sometimes our brains bury things to protect us, especially after a traumatic incident,' she said, studying his calm demeanour, trying to keep a lid on her excitement at the possibilities of injuries inside him oscillating towards her reach.

Perhaps he'd been a twin in the womb, he continued, emerging the only survivor. Maybe there was a sibling before him who passed. Whatever the reason, his arrival in the world wasn't met with open arms from his parents. Instead, there was a void, a lack of interest which caused a break inside him over time. His attempts to widen that gulf were subconscious. The accidents followed. At eight he fell from a huarango tree: the swift snap of the branch spinning away like an airborne crack, his limbs stiffening in response, the borderless weight of air, the shock of the fall, pain lodging into his body and brain.

At sixteen, a drunk driver behind the wheel of a white Ford Corona hit him, barely swerving in time. He didn't run, sensing it had been inevitable. Later in the hospital, he drowsily studied the male doctor conducting his check-up with an element of anger. At twenty-one, the skydiving strap malfunctioned. He'd hit the water below, surrounded by multicoloured creatures with handfuls of bright membranes underwater closing in. He'd limped out of the sea having wrestled off the rainbow parachute. He confided in her, things he hadn't told anybody for a long time. He was surprised by the ease of it, the spark between them from the moment he laid eyes on her. It was easy for her to bear witness, to look through the glass partition and see what he couldn't.

Therese bought the next round of drinks. She listened, reached into the break inside him while he told her the incarnations of himself after each accident felt like a sibling borrowing his bloodstream. Or a series of long-buried memories slipping into his clothes. Originally from Huacachina, Peru, he'd been backpacking through Europe, planting his feet in the soil of a country every time his body required an intermission. In Ireland, he stayed in Dublin for six months, working in pubs and at fairs; drawing caricatures of people who didn't know they needed to see distorted versions of themselves in broad daylight, an island of machines around to suck the emotions from them; the drop from the Ferris wheel when they opened their eyes intermittently, the speed of train carriages twisting in caves of darkness, the deceptive motion of a boat ride swinging, a spoke from its underside poking through the sickness in their stomachs. In Scotland, he stayed in Edinburgh, working at a soup kitchen or two. He didn't say it but Therese sensed something bad had occurred at the last soup kitchen, something the other half of his consciousness harboured like a broken jewel in a tempestuous current. He then headed to Dumbarton and through Stonehaven, each crossing of land, element and sky leaving an imprint in him. In Belgium he helped build cabins in the region of De Haan, blending into lively groups of men so he would become no one before disappearing again, earning just enough to keep moving, going forward like a wounded stray apostle.

Around 11 p.m. they stumbled out of the pub, the streets a blur of movement. Night guardians emerged from dark road puddles to deposit the next day's interruptions at their feet. A fire engine roared towards debris from Emilien's accidents converging ahead, an orange chute sprouting over them as a cushion for an incoming obliteration. They walked towards the station, the jostle of his backpack between them. She hadn't revealed much about herself to him. But that was her way with these encounters, to listen, mirror, gently persuade, arrange her face into recognisable expressions, identify a kindred spirit when she saw one. Outside the station, she touched his left arm lightly before the escalators transported them into the sharply lit concave of the underground.

'You weren't about to have your next accident when you mentioned crossing Waterloo Bridge this morning?' she asked, her tone neutral.

'Ah querida,' he said in a confessional way, leaning close

enough for her to hear the flutter in his temples. The bones of his left knuckle curled into a loose fist, the golden hue of his neck smooth. 'I just liked the view from the top,' he said softly, turning, a small transformation amid a decapitation of caricatures. 'Have you ever seen something so unorthodoxly beautiful, so beyond the trivialities of this life, you could die happy right then, just to be consumed by it?' His eyes gleamed, a vein in his left hand throbbed. She caught her breath. The air was loaded with quiet grenade pins. She asked him for it then, one of his darkest secrets to seal their bond, something she knew Oni would hold over him for lifetimes to come. As he leaned in towards her, she spotted the crescent-shaped marking on the right side of his neck. She had noticed it earlier, the mark of kin, and he the final piece to complete the group's circle.

Four

The man in the blue tent is screaming.

Flames chase him, licking at his feet, curling towards his heartbeat,

Reaching for his face in a blue fire tryst he tries to outrun.

Then he is reduced to parts.

The parts are fragments of a season.

Orbs pulsing, before floating in the spectrum of darkness dappling the tent.

The man is a stranger to himself in the distance of our breakable home. The tip of his tongue tastes of morning dew, the sides of dandelion, the middle of seawater.

His tongue shrinks in the tent, curls upwards in a fleeting salute.

Smoke from a different time fades away.

In my room, I chant Umera, Olitza, Ofuleria, a language rushing to meet his tongue halfway. My kind kin planted a burning memory in me. Oni takes a small breath in the tent, so quietly it is a sweet murmur, an announcement to collect what belongs to her, a pardon after the sacrifice. These sacrificial parts rustle, crawling towards Oni's fingerprint, her marking is water in a groove. A heat spreads through my body, a ripple of white light stutters behind my lids. A woman who sounds like me from the future cries beyond Gethsemane, her voice strains, thinning before multiplying into a series of echoes, beckoning a procession of weeping, bald goshawks towards the tent. They do not want to eat, they circle, watch beads of dew spread to the flap of the tent, transfixed by the tiny reflections in them, by Oni's face seeping into the dew, threatening to water memories that cannot be held hostage by place, nor confine nor blood. The heat within me becomes an ache settling in the margins of my body. The homestead shudders. The tent flap opens. Smoky air from an excavation is released. There is a fluttering in the blood, a scraping on bone, an etching, a severing between what came before and after a disappearance. The vultures frantically smack their heads against the white light beneath my lids, trying to free the shapes of my perilous past in the break.

After the tent is temporarily sated, that night Domingos brings news of a man behaving in odd ways his wife does not recognise. It is a sensitive matter, he tells me gravely, outside the back of the homestead. 'Would you be able to take a look? Offer the woman some comfort? Perhaps a stranger's eye might see something we have missed. And you have an unusual way about you which arouses assurance.' He offers this as neither compliment nor truce, but as fact, the nerve in his right cheek throbbing in the tightness of skin. My arms are greasy up to the elbows from being buried in sheep's intestines, plucking innards to transform into delicacies. Cool air seeps inside our bodies. He takes several steps towards me; stops just close enough, murmuring something unintelligible. I smell alcohol on his breath to keep the demons at bay. Above us, the moon bobs uncertainly, as if it will slip from its position into an unplanned fall on the burnished grass between berry and bramble. I wait for a confession, a small vulnerability. Instead, he grabs my upper left arm gently. The pressure of his fingers is not lost on me. 'Ensure you do not bring the smell of sheep's guts inside,' he instructs curtly. As though I have brought unsavoury things into his home he cannot contend with. I turn my head as he walks away, listening to his movements in their quarters. It is my right to. I absorb their raised voices, a silence, more arguing, his pacing. A crack makes its way through bramble, wound and nerve blindly, instinctively heading for the centre.

In the morning, I wait for his absence before getting ready. I decide to take Sueli with me, aware the child has become used to the loneliness of running wild by herself in the surroundings of our dilapidated home. She is Baby's big sister in my mind although I know this is wrong, a temporary dressing for my mother wound. The crack in the clay heart beneath the floor expands a little. There is a crumbling in the soil, lightly spilling into the break where the blue tent sits. Covered in a fine sweat, I wash outside, willing the dull ache to leave my limbs. It is a bright morning full of promise, danger and the shadows of forces beyond the town. A small trickle is trapped in the roof, a black current as an unwilling guardian above our heads. On leaving the house, I am reminded of Domingos telling me that the woman I need to see lives on the other side of Noma Mountain, in a home with a discoloured white horn on the roof. A vengeful wind howls between the mountain's peaks crusted with light, remote from our homestead yet poised to reveal the secrets within it. Inside, I dress slowly in an old purple smock Marguerite no longer needs. I walk to Sueli's room, large in comparison to my own. An ocean-blue cloth hangs over the window; she claims her lost brothers and sisters gather faded items from it when it flutters at night. A red ladybird crawls over her club at one end. In the opposite corner lie a handful of pebbles she flings into a copper bowl beside it, comforted by the sound. A stick of charred wood rests a few feet away from her. I watch it briefly before entering as if it would reveal its true purpose; a disrupter from the past waiting to cause chaos. I do not move it out of harm's way. It is a secret accomplice hiding in plain sight. Sueli rouses, sitting up, attuned to my footsteps, her curtain of frizzy hair bouncing. I have hidden the bone elsewhere in my room. I search her eyes for recognition of its new hiding place. There is none. Not yet.

While her mother is still sullen from a quarrel with Domingos, I crouch down, pressing my forehead against hers, informing her there is a man in the town slowly losing himself, asking a horn disfigured by time to help him.

Along the way, crackling fern scatter beneath our feet. Our purple dresses billow in the light wind, with hoods swelling like fattened, bruised halos, heads bobbing in their deceptive comfort. The straps are tied into ribbons at our necks, a delicate act in the harsh condition. Sueli chatters to the ladybird on the back of her right hand, spotted and blushing, winding its way over her skin, speeding along before slowing down. The wind whistles sharply, pricking our ears, stiffening our limbs. Noma Mountain is separated from the others by a twisting river crashing against rocks and stones, holding past drownings attempting to limp into existence again. We cross the mountain on our side, heading towards Noma as though it is a horizon, bodies untethered on the steep incline. If Domingos intends for me to be maimed along this route, I will take his daughter with me. I will tug her into whatever injuries await us, so we beat as one, suffer as one, recover as one. If she falls to her ending, I will still have Baby to dream of.

We pass the waterfall spilling into the river. On the way down, I catch my left foot in a rocky crevice, falling and hitting my head, setting off a throbbing beneath that area of skin. Crossing the river, Sueli slips, losing her ladybird to a tide. 'Where will he go?' she squeals, arms flailing, face darkening. 'I wanted to give him to Mama!' she grumbles, looking at me resentfully. I pull her up. She shivers, the bottom of her skirt wet. We carry on. The homesteads of the mountain lean in, ready to be purged from their stony plots. The white horn looms, a wailing intensifies. Roots in my pocket whisper. Language of kin threatens to spill from my mouth. Sueli digs her fingers into my arm.

We arrive at the homestead crested on the hill like an ugly jewel, grey and rectangular, weeds crawling up either side. A few sheep bleat at us, announcing our presence, dotting the area of land like moored clouds. I take Sueli by the hand; heat crawls up my neck, a small pit forms inside me. A rush of excitement courses through my blood. I knock on the wooden door. We wait, dripping watery shadows onto the entrance.

A woman with a pinched face and a harried expression approaches, dark hair scraggly, grey smock puckered in parts, smelling of stale air. The fragility of her limbs reflects a sadness in their home. Her brow furrows in trepidation but she smiles briefly at Sueli before pulling us in.

'Domingos said you would come, I am Vanero, we are grateful

for his kindness and yours, Zulmira,' she says, turning to lead the way, the skirt of her smock rustling with each movement. Her shoulder blades are pronounced instruments waiting for a tender touch.

'What ails him exactly?' I ask, glaring at Sueli who, hood down, begins to mimic the rustling of Vanero's skirt till it sounds like a hiss following us, increasing amid the tension in the air.

'It is not something I have encountered before,' Vanero answers, stopping to catch my eye for a moment, panic in her tone, chest rising.

The rooms are fairly bare. There is a table in one with a hearth, its ashes the ruins of gatherings. A wash area rests at one end with large slabs of stone for cutting, preparing, mixing. Pieces of white sheepskin wool are thrown over the chairs as decoration. We pass three sets of candlesticks with fat, forlorn candles, their flames having abandoned them to linger inside the white horn on the roof. A faint scent of dampness clings to the air as though shapes from wet soil held a vigil the night before. Lavender roots in my pocket jostle steadily, reassuringly, bound by a piece of rough brown string.

His skin is pale when we enter their sleeping quarters, bedding covering his bare chest protectively. The vein protruding in his neck is a wrinkled siren. The room is ripe with sour breath. He raises his arms defensively at the direction of our voices, strangers in his presence. He sits upright. 'My eyes are stinging,' he barks. 'How can a man provide with his vision spoiled?' he says, wincing.

His right arm rises again; he squeezes his fist, face collapsing into a pained expression. Sueli steps forward, pointing at the white fragments on the corners of both his eyes, edging towards *the middle like an unexpected assault. Arthilo begins his tale; all he needed was the encouragement of a child.*

'Two days ago, I was drying the leathers out in the field, like I always do after cutting and rinsing them. I know something is wrong because the sheep start scattering. The sky darkens. A silver bolt cracks through it. I look ahead and around but there is no visitor coming from any direction. I feel a stinging sensation behind my eyes. My vision blurs. A pain throbs inside my head unlike anything I have known. I fall to my knees from it, blinking. Everything becomes quiet, slow. Then there are women in the field instead of sheep. They are holding a wailing baby at first, each one clutching the same child. How is that possible? It feels like an aberration overwhelming me yet I know it is real.

'I see them. They are in the air rushing towards me, on the roof circling. The white horn rolling between them, the sound echoes in my ears, my bones. After the women vanish with that baby, my eyes continue to give me trouble.'

I try to keep my expression neutral, still. The way one does when a feeling of panic spreads. To deflect, I rest my hand over his left arm reassuringly.

Sensing a change in the atmosphere, Sueli slips out of the room. My mouth feels grainy; the heat spreading through my throat is a warning. A spasm in my thigh attempts to communicate to shadowy women on the periphery holding my baby. Vanero sits on the edge of the bed beside her husband, adjusting the bedding, placing her hand on his forehead, scanning my face imploringly, a silent exchange between women. The room becomes quiet. Arthilo closes his eyes, turns his body away in surrender. It is pitiful, definite and clear. His wife's comforting has done little to curtail his worries. I hear the flow of sound between this time and a future plane passing through the horn on the roof. I know it will rattle inside my bone later that night. Sueli places her fingers in the secret areas of their homestead in search of unknown things. I crush fennel in a bowl, rinse Arthilo's eyes with it to ease his discomfort. I instruct Vanero to do so again at dusk. Afterwards, I find Sueli in their kitchen, kneeling down by the far end of one wall, right hand over an engraving between her splayed fingers. A small, open wooden chest of perfectly formed empty scent bottles sits by her feet, glinting as though blown from an angel's mouth. I cross the room, lift Sueli's fingers off the wall. A spasm works its way to my stomach. Beside the groove in the wall, hidden from the eye at the corner, is a small circle with six ridges in it; entry points, a miniature golden ring. Sueli's eyes are bright, hungry. I run a finger over each ridge as if they will crumble beneath my touch into gold dust from another land. A dizzying feeling hits me.

My kind have been here before.

More than once.

And now they have Baby to taunt me with.

I gather Sueli to me in one swift motion, her body breathing against mine to ease the thunderous pain. I am thinking of strange women wandering through desolate lands of lost sheep, feeding on the disintegration of a man's vision, the memory of kin and Baby creeping out of the edges. Vanero appears from behind fussing, loose tendrils of dark hair framing her face. She picks up the wooden chest, offers it to me. 'They are from the seas through a passing merchant. I have no use for them working the land.'

Sixteen miniature bottles to be filled, admired, stroked. I pass the chest to Sueli, who closes the lid gently as though spotting something wondrous lurking between the bottles to keep concealed.

We make our way back over the mountain, spots of rain falling on our faces in a baptism, our damp dresses clinging to our limbs, unruly bodies on the move. The waters lap at Sueli's feet, the miniature bottles clinking in her grip. A spasm leaves my stomach, softly rippling through Gethsemane like an infected colony. The next day, we receive word that although the pain had diminished in Arthilo's eyes, his irises were completely covered, his sight lost to an invasion from the dark.

And so, it began.

Chapter 4

Finn bought a tank for the wild, regenerative ribcage, a glass number with a wrought-iron frame that had a Gothic feel. He knew the aquarium owner, Eitan, an orthodox Jew who played football with such ferocity they called him Danger Mouse on the field, a bearded, determined centre without apology. Once during a break in a game Therese attended, she, he and Finn had discussed the merits of Middle Eastern literature and the intricate beauty of Ottoman maps as the temperature dropped. She'd had to talk to one of Finn's wounds quietly when the pain became all-encompassing. And he'd had to temporarily leave the field, wincing in agony, unable to explain to the other players what his ailment was. Therese placed her hand on his chest, the wounds distorted against her touch, absorbing the ripples of energy she sent to console them. Afterwards, the grass frosted, their feet and limbs began to ache, afternoon light slipped into evening and the portable white nets behind the goalkeepers started twitching as though they'd caught the shadows of men's bodies.

Azacca had opposed the idea of the tank since it was Finn's suggestion. This was the constant tension between them; the opposite of. If Azacca suggested storing the ribcage in the greenhouse, where it could be kept cool naturally, connected to the garden, Finn would argue it was a place people could search through. Hiding something in plain sight didn't always work. What if a neighbourhood kid lost a ball in their garden? It happened on occasion: a misfired shot, an excitable child chasing after it being spurred on by friends. Only to head inside the greenhouse to find a porous entity between a quarter-length silver drum, weed killer, two shovels and shears, and no ball because, hypothetically, the kid may have underestimated the ball's velocity, its speed of travel. It might miss their garden entirely, just to land two doors down, but that wouldn't stop a curious child hunting on a whim.

Emilien didn't mind where it was kept as long as it was out of the kitchen.

'Querida,' he warned, 'it's crazy leaving it out like that.' He'd cornered her on the landing, eyes gleaming, his grip firm on her upper arm before slackening as the floorboards creaked. 'We've opened up a portal. Anything could come for it.' His breath warm and sweet on her face was laced with Irish cream, his hand lingered at her waist.

And so Finn procured the tank from his friend. On the evening he brought it home, fireworks were going off in the neighbourhood. Nobody paid attention to Finn and his tank. Instead, people's eyes were fixed on the decorative explosions marking the sky in brightly coloured small Ferris wheels, bobbles, rockets and mushrooms dramatically fragmenting, popping loudly, ricocheting as elements of the same sound multiplied. They met Finn at the door. He was breathing heavily having carried the tank by himself, his wry smile stilted, a smudge of dirt on his right cheek. His shoulders rose and fell. The tank sat in a cardboard box between his legs. Azacca grabbed one end, Emilien the other, giving a brief respite to Finn, who stepped into the hallway in relief, flexing his fingers, brow furrowing at the lack of fanfare he'd received for his efforts. Moments before, Therese had discovered a cluster of headless Origami women under her bed, arms outstretched. The secret gift giver had struck again. She was thinking of her breath passing through those miniature women wiping the smudge from Finn's cheek while Azacca and Emilien carefully edged down the stairs leading into the basement.

She brought the ribcage out of the fridge, tried to measure the disruption of the other woman's heart beating inside her from a separate plane. She felt the hem of the woman's frayed skirt swaying like a scarred ripple. She saw herself chasing those threads as the dress unravelled. Her form changed. Adrenalin coursed through her veins. The mountainous land with the visitor's heartbeat swam in her vision before fracturing around the woman's hooded purple dress while she bled from her mouth into the ground's crevices, following a shadow attempting to communicate with her. The dress tumbled away, damp from passing through thrashing tides, circling a skewed sun-stroked homestead before becoming a golden arch in the air. Roots sprouted from its base, threatening to fill her throat with its knowing tips. Snapping out of her reverie, Therese stood listening to the hum of the fridge. The vision settled into her system, accosting her like a thunderbolt in blood. What was memory but a trick every time, slipped from a restless murmur within an old town? She was one with the woman who became a claw disintegrating on a mountain plane. After that, small cocoons forming at the bottom of a river, followed by a womb in flight, cutting through the warm air, moving between the different homesteads, a passenger waiting to be let in. These visions made Therese feel dizzy. She snapped a few berries off the ribcage, popped them in her mouth, a trickle of garish purple liquid staining her fingers. Eating the berries made her visons sharper, throbbing with an urgency that had to be acknowledged.

She heard Finn moving about in the hallway, dumping his jacket, tossing his lighter up, flicking through his mobile phone before shoving it in his pocket. Consuming the berries made her acutely aware of every sound, her mouth pressed against rhythms in the distance. Wondering if it was the same for the others, she crossed the hallway carrying the ribcage on a large silver platter, spotting the headless origami women clutching handfuls of frayed golden thread. She blinked the image away, her fingers brushing the coolness of the bones. More fireworks popped outside. They gathered in the basement. The wire of the single bulb dangling from the ceiling poised to channel an electric current. A ripple of tension passed between them. Therese and Azacca stood in front of the tank. Finn and Emilien loitered at either end. Emilien after uncurling himself from the wine-coloured beanbag where he'd been rifling through Therese's stack of records: Miriam Makeba, King Sunny Adé and Count Ossie among others. And Finn, post playing with an old telescope tube he'd forgotten he left down there. The small prison-like window at the far-right end was open. A neon sofa in the middle had items of clothing slung over it. Peeling, lavender-painted walls added an extra layer of narcotic brightness. They bent over the tank, hypnotised. Therese carefully placed the ribcage inside it. The glass misted at the top. Azacca ran a finger over the moss on one side of the warped entity, his finger slick with dew.

An ache bloomed in Therese's chest. She thought of the ribcage journeying through portals to get to them, imagining its plight; a fault line of stars moving through it, dodging that ominous frayed dress she felt was a connection yet sneaking through the golden arch, tumbling down the vortex, slippery within the lines of time and space expanding, falling into a crack on an inky dark night right into their orbit. She placed her right hand on the glass, sharing a secret communication with it. 'This is wild,' she said, turning to the others, eyes sparkling. 'It's reproducing organisms it's encountered.'

'Or wants to become,' Finn offered. 'Imagine not being able to share this with anyone except you guys.'

Emilien's face clouded. 'Don't do that.' He enunciated each word for emphasis.

'Exactly, this stays between us.' Azacca threw a warning glance Finn's way. 'We know how generous you get with stories after a few drinks.'

Finn raised a middle finger at him. Azacca chuckled softly but with an edge.

'What do we do with it?' Emilien asked, moving closer to the tank, nervousness apparent in his voice.

Azacca held their gazes before plucking four berries from his pocket. 'We guard it. It's ours for now. I think this is what was trying to incubate inside us. What I want to know is why it's come now.' He offered each a berry, tying them into the pact. Green from moss at the edges of their vision became lushly iridescent. The dead goshawk's shadow sputtered at the window, trying to reach a loose golden thread it saw between the bars before flying away. The light bulb flickered; crinkled record sleeves had tiny grains of warm earth from the ancient town in a faraway land. A plant's silhouette began to take shape in the wall's corners. Traffic outside faded. Bursts of fireworks petered off. A trickle of water from the tank caught their attention. They moved closer to it.

'Jesus, it can happen here too,' Emilien muttered, his features slightly more pronounced in wonder. He drank everything in. A low bed of liquid the colour of a waterfall rippled beneath the ribcage. More mist unfurled. It was producing water, responding to its environment. Drawn in, the group's heads were bobbing indoor moons ready for the glass planet's offerings.

It was a cold morning two days later. Shrubs lining the streets were frosted, bearing nature's ice overcoats. Ferns bent in anticipation. The soft crackle of strewn leaves was carried along by a wind. The morning embraced London's inhabitants in its folds. Trails of smoke from exhaust pipes assembling into temporary birds were impossible to catch. The stupor of sleep was still present in people's limbs, dwindling as the demands of the day took hold. Outside the local park where the group lived, a council truck loaded with tree branches circled, a saw poking through the branches like a serrated silver animal mid-escape. Inside the park, frenetic squirrels carried acorns, tiny pieces of bread, discarded bits of spicy porri up the tennis court fencing, willow trees and across the sand pit by the children's play area where a small trampoline had been stained with the spill of beer and the tears of homeless drifters.

A woman in a grey anorak was threading through one pathway, walking her Jack Russell, which lagged at her heels before bounding ahead. Often stopping to sniff the base of a tree, pressing its paw against squashed drink cartons, nudging the greasy paper of kebab wrapping with its damp nose. The woman held a lead in her right hand, its grey hook dangled precariously. They passed a maple tree oozing sap into a crumbling Godiva statue, a trolley crashed on the edge, languishing inside it were a packet of Rukya cigarettes, a nearly depleted bottle of Abbot Ale, éclair wrappers. They slipped through a rusted gate, entering a large field littered with firework poppers, a football net at one end. The Jack Russell took off towards it. The woman followed, turning the lead in her hand as they got closer. There was a body inside the net. It was Eitan, the aquarium owner, Danger Mouse silenced, another net wrapped around him. He was completely still, his clothes damp, lips blue from the cold. A short, rough incision was carved into his neck. His eyes stared blankly ahead. The treacherous sky shifted into patterns. Firework rockets were everywhere, feverish cadets who took his last instruction into the blind spots of the park's secret inhabitants.

Five

Word spread of my presence, like smoke curling through the town: that a woman Domingos found from the seas had eased the suffering of a man turning blind. The man's sight did not return and the horn from his roof began to glimmer suspiciously on the rooftops of other homesteads, forced to travel to survive. Rowena, the pretty buxom stallholder selling merchant spices comes to visit and introduce herself. I do not want friends, especially inquisitive, sharp-eyed ones who try to get the measure of me, however subtly. She ingratiates herself with charm and guile. A small, plump mass just above her collarbone has teeth markings, perhaps from a lover. Her presence is strong; she smells of oleander and is quick to laugh even when her brown eyes tell a different story. She has a sister, she says, who is her opposite in every way. She comes bearing a gift: a thickly rimmed circular mirror a secret admirer built for her she no longer has use for since a supply of mirrors is not something she lacks. She hands it to Sueli who lingers on the edge, watching Rowena in an intrigued manner.

'You know Papa!' she says. 'I've seen you in town.'

Rowena nods. 'Your father has bought spices from me.'

Sueli rushes off, busy finding a place for the mirror in my room. That first visit from Rowena is pleasant. We play a game of stone dice by the gnarly bramble patch on the right side of the homestead while grasshoppers shriek, the mass above her collarbone circling towards me in a quiet dance.

And so before Marguerite goes searching for a womb in choppy waters, a bracing, windy season comes, whose tremors reach deep into the crevices of the town's inhabitants, already unsettled by my presence. I see it through eyes forged in ceremony. One evening on Ranula Mountain, the Chimera homestead find their oxen in the sleeping quarters having broken through the fencing which had contained their increasingly restless movements up until that point. They pace back and forth making loud, rumbling noises until every member of the homestead (all six of them) are forced together to drag them out.

At the bottom of Guverro Mountain, the Monteiro homestead find their belongings suspended in the air, the pockets of their clothing turned inside out, their secret areas excavated, their bedding rumpled in the daytime as if spirits had taken some respite while their backs were turned, and the night rhythms of their bodies were foraging in the dust. Upon their discovery, the Monteiros see no footprints in nor out of their homestead. It is a trick of sorts to them. They pluck the items one by one from the air, fingers curling into belongings they view in a new light. Afterwards, they wander around the rooms in stunned silence, listening for a new language forming between their movements, passing through the resistance of walls.

At the Fonseca homestead, a series of large circles in threes mar the corn crop. Dented, in mocking salute of the crops beginning to wilt. There is a woman's vision using oxen, horn, cloth and vegetation to betray the natural order of things. Afterwards, the shapes of crumbling mouths rise through the crop circles before collapsing again.

Our homestead feeds on this season's tremors. A man from a neighbouring town accuses Domingos of cutting the throats of his yews on a visit, claiming he had witnessed a man's face injured by fire hovering among them as they limped to their burial grounds breaking mounds of earth. The man's claims are dismissed. Domingos is well liked in Gethsemane. How could a stranger's words hold weight over one of their own? By the time the soil begins to soften slightly, Rowena has made three visits. Each time the mass in her threatens to break the skin but she brings me ground cayenne peppers, wild mushrooms and delicately veined vine leaves to be wrapped around cooked grains of rice and steamed in a copper pot. A doctor of geology arrives from Madagascar to study ancient engravings in the caves tucked behind Ranula Mountain. Dr Ramsagar, a fragile figure of a man. He makes the mistake of journeying up there by himself. Hours later, nobody sees him emerge from the blustery throats of darkness inside. Only the ancient engravings deepen on the cave walls fed by a presence. And his watermarked documents containing his thoughts and drawings scatter like paper companions speaking on his behalf. This disappearance unsettles the town further, they are uncomfortable about strangers in their midst.

After a reasonable period of sunshine, the Rambutanos ceremony occurs, where the town's inhabitants dress in bright spirit costumes, donning masks at night on two days to honour the gods for their mercies. They clutch raised sticks of fire, singing praise songs down the mountain's spines. On those nights, I watch the orbs of fire curling, stretching from the front of the homestead sitting down on a stool, Sueli beside me, her head in my lap, my fingers gathering her curls in soft strokes as her body loosens. The songs in the distance deepen then echo. A curl of fire leaves a stick, whispering to Domingos who is not among them. Sueli's head lifts slowly between my thighs. I tune out of praise songs breaking one by one. The feeling of Baby surging through my bloodied thighs into the world hits me. My chest constricts, the mother's pain is pure and unfiltered. Baby's face and Sueli's head merge into one, taunting me cruelly. An incandescent, vengeful molten light roars within me.

It is a cooler evening on a night Domingos is late back to the homestead. Inky patterns in the vast sky gather before fading. Overhead: the movements of strange shapes dwindle into gentle disappearances. Breaks of light appear from strings of fireflies as winged instruments drawn to the night's utterances. The creak of fences slips into caved beds of earth. Earlier in the day, Sueli used short sticks of chalk to draw white rings in the corner of her room, watching them expectantly. The night's whispers collide in my chest. They are the tongues of kin, women whose notions I understand, requiems, warnings of things to grow in the void. They are prayers few gods will recognise. Muttering, See this crooked eye in the rivers you have refused to claim? Watch this injury inside an apostle's lung a feather dipped in ink will attempt to name? See your baby crawling through desert sand screaming with your voice? Hear this toothless man on an icy peak, offered up to a lost dawn, mimicking the movements of an infant? See these burial grounds from wars we have dipped our costumes in, sinkholes of change, shrunken trails of death and resurrection we christen passages of time? Why have you forsaken your kind? Steered the limbs we gave you into the perilous embrace of escape? There is no hiding from our eyes, they chorus. No treaded path we do not see, no throb in vein we cannot conquer, *they sing.* Look under your tongue for your visions. Do not lose memory, forgetting is punishment. *Their whispers continue. I dance to pacify them, stave off their thirst, spinning through my room until dizziness is inevitable, till the mirror Rowena gifted me leaning against one faded grey wall crackles with their silhouettes. A throbbing is released into my body, a beating moulded under Oni's gaze.*

I strip naked, rush out to the back where the garden has bloomed, fetch seeds from achiote fruit to paint my body red orange, rubbing it on my limbs, watching it weep against the skin. Dancing between salted cuts of meat, I stop the man on the icy peak becoming the infant in the sand. Sueli slips a stick of chalk beneath her mother's pillow, mimicking the bone which resided under mine. She rushes to stand before my mirror, reaching for the pink mist curling over elements of a future time like a weightless curtain, seeing the crescent-shaped markings on four angled necks travelling towards her. She runs away from the mirror, this new secret lodged inside her. She stands on the edge of the garden, watching the kaleidoscopic colours shimmering on my rapturous limbs with the breathless wonder of a child.

After I wash my body amid rumbling leaves and dress in a loose pale smock, Marguerite wanders out from their sleeping quarters. Her expression is tight, lips drawn. Her limbs are frail in the white dress draining what little glow her golden skin possesses. Her wild curls are braided into submission, brushing the dip in her back. She approaches, hands fluttering like restless birds betraying each other for losing their wings. She does not name what ails her; instead, she tugs the nightdress up at the shoulder where it slips to expose a patch of chalk-marked skin. She stands beside me, throwing an envious look my way. 'You have brought life to this home. It beats again. I know we are not easy folk.'

'You have given a stranger shelter,' I answer, noticing the fine growth of hair on her legs. My gaze moves to the forlorn expression on her face. I trace it with my fingers. She does not flinch at this intimate act. 'I have no gold coins to offer,' I say.

'You are a peculiar creature.' She laughs softly, pleased with herself for presenting this notion. 'Your people must long for you, the place you have in their lives. Gethsemane will not know what to make of a woman like you, free from the rule of any man.'

I ignore the pangs in my chest, the mother's pain that threatens to obliterate my vision. I know the acts of sympathy. I have studied them through time. I look into the decay inside her, which is spreading. It widens, folds, retracts at my touch. I pity her then, her lack of resistance for what is to come; I pity her weapons blunted by decomposition and the names she cannot mention dying at the tip of her tongue.

The sky roars. The darkness overhead swirls. Rowena's mirror shudders against the patchy wall. I cannot throw it out. I know kin placed it in her hands, an instrument that is watcher and deliverer of signs disguised as a gift. There is a hint of rain in the lines of spirits crossing over, moving steadily between cycles of life. Marguerite's hands shake, two birds carrying new names, ready to separate from her arms, squawk in protest at the burdens of the homestead. The stools creak under the weight of our bodies.

A breeze follows the scurry of tiny, hidden creatures feeding from the plant beds. She raises her head to the sky to fill her tongue with its musings.

'What feels like a long time ago, my husband used to run home to me. Sometimes, I would stand at the front watching for his tall frame to appear as though cast from a turning I could not see, that place where something is about to change for the better. I always knew he was coming,' she continues, a hint of a lost smile on her face. 'I would run to meet him halfway. He usually carried me, lifting me off the ground as if that was his reward after a long day's work.' She draws her knees up, the smile cracking. 'Now he touches me with cold fingers, roams the mountains, keeps things from me. Lies beside me at night smelling of other beings, breathing against my breasts while I wonder if he recognises me at all.' Her shoulders rise, her eyes water. This is a woman used to crying hidden from the gazes of others. I turn away at the truth of her words, carrying a double burden on my shoulders. Hers is not the only face that is unrecognisable. A woman like me has many faces across several lifetimes.

I wade into the garden. It is an unruly sea bending seductively. I know her wound.

I gather flowers, broken branches, sticks, carrying them to her, a bounty spilling from my hands. She watches me curiously, her throat constricting. I spread my map from the ground to fashion into something new. I relay the tale of a band of dusky-skinned, glassy-eyed women in Bogota who commanded hounds to silence while they howled, digging the lines of a new country with bare hands. And the hounds rolled on their backs in a kind of euphoria. I build Marguerite a thorny crown, kiss her gently on the cheek, my teeth hovering over the throbbing deep inside her. The sound of fury echoes in my peripheral vision, the loss of my child as a sacrifice to be there. She laughs softly. The bounty as crown rests on her head at a skewed angle, in anticipation of its own decay. It is presented as an act of empathy; a woman withering beneath a crown.

On the evening Marguerite leaves the homestead by herself, kin's voices call her from the cold seas. Despite the tiredness in her limbs, almost turning back on the pebbled, twisted path, she forges ahead, becoming scared again at the mountain's shoulder, where her hands feebly grip its crumbling parts to support her movements. She is weak, giddy from the change of environment, her nostrils filled with the secret scents that linger on Domingos's body. She spins haphazardly to take in Gethsemane's beauty; how it floats in the heavens from certain angles, it's damp peaks glistening as though covered with a nectar from the gods that the inhabitants said would intoxicate if you drank from it, much like Pinera ale which local men drowned their sorrows in at the shebeens when the seas got too rough, the land combative, the harvest periods unfruitful, and on occasion when that nectar began to trickle down, the women rushing out of their homesteads announcing that the mountains were spilling alcohol again. Marguerite passes a patch of pink violets. She is struck by its colours, the vibrancy of it in comparison to her own waning light. A few scatter into her footsteps, faltering in the trail. She scratches her arms faintly, wrestling through brushes, talks to coloured seashells dotting the shore. At the beach, she accidentally cuts the back of her neck taking refuge in a driftwood shrine among a display of shrines. A sharp sting from the injury follows.

Her eyes drink in pieces of limestone in muted shades of green scattered around. The ghosts of skulls chattering at her feet are women's voices she does not recognise. Kin. A wind whistles between the seashells breaking them open into small, bright platters of wonder the waters delivered. She loses the memory of drawing chalk markings on her body, of the first time she held Sueli, the lack of recognition, the feeling that if she continued to look at the child it would collapse into nothing in her arms with only its cry lingering in the air. Pangs inside her of birth and misdirection grow, of a lost life being absorbed by something dark on the periphery wielding the silhouette of someone she used to know. The homesteads dotting the mountain become a blur, their caverns momentary last rites for her hallowed body. The driftwood shrines circle, doubling as respite and cage. The undertow calls. Marguerite's ravaged body responds. She searches for her lost children underwater, between seaweed and stones, charged currents and items long swallowed by the choppy waters of the sea. She looks for babies with traces of her expression. Perhaps she will recognise her old self reaching for bloody umbilical cords needing to be cut again. Instead, a baby she does not know presents itself. She reaches out to touch it but it morphs into illusive handfuls of placenta, mimicking sea creatures scurrying into bursts of watery flight.

Our dilapidated homestead responds. Our bodies contract. Sueli heads to her parents' room, runs her fingers over the bedclothes as if Marguerite will appear through them: sickly, gutted and confused. She rushes to me, muttering about the chalk rings on her walls then standing before the mirror rambling. She tugs at my skirt, shouting, 'Where did she go? Mama will get worse out there.'

The house beats. A thudding in my eardrums begins. Sueli spins away from me, arms stretched above her head. The beating gets louder. The bone in my room calls. I walk towards it, pulled by its longing. A ripple in the garden blooms. I listen to it, plucking a slip of calendula from it. In my room the bone murmurs. The potion bottles clink in response behind my bedding. I grab one, reach for the bone, removing it from its new hiding place in the back wall. It whispers again, pink marrow bubbles at the tip. A tiny splinter runs through its underside. The bone will never run out of marrow. It can provide an endless supply. I pour marrow into the potion bottle, place the calendula stem inside. It sinks into the marrow, buoyed within its softened passage of bone and oblivion.

Domingos rescues Marguerite from the beach, driven by instinct and the warnings of passers-by that a woman who looked like his wife lay panting on the shoreline, broken, head bowed, body convulsing, mouth puckered against cracked limestone and the last movements of a baby with my mouth. He brings her home. They shiver on arrival, clothes soaked to the skin, teeth chattering. Sueli flings herself at their legs, clinging on tightly until Domingos impatiently orders her to her room. The homestead's heartbeat slows. Kin's inky night-weapons hover at the doors. The calendula murmurs in the marrow. The clay heart in the soil trembles. The mirror has a tiny spill of marrow inside it that is unaccounted for.

A tear appears in my peripheral vision, widening in my room. I fill it, listening to Domingos's sweet words of comfort and Marguerite's wounded utterings in response.

My fingers curl in anger into the bedding. I recall a time when nobody was there to save my ravaged body except kin, Oni's disciples. I have no one to temper my worries of betrayal and the costs that lie ahead.

In the morning, I rise to the sounds of dogs barking. Walking out to the front entrance, my left eye twitches. My blood runs cold. A line of sweat forms above my top lip. A procession of dogs has gathered outside the homestead. Trails of them, different breeds and sizes running all the way down, as far as the eye can see. Even over the mountains' spines, crossing mounds of earth, some from beyond Gethsemane. I feel the short shocks of pain running along their hind legs from weariness, sweat dripping off their dangled tongues hanging like low flags, bodies rippling in a triumphant response to an order from kin. The dogs bay, snarling and leaping towards me, a madness in their eyes. I walk towards them slowly, my nightdress brushing my ankles, a breeze whispers to their dimpled bodies. The scent of calendula clings to my fingers. The dogs' tongues become pink flames flickering over a man's face. Something dark and unyielding hatches between the doorway and their shadows. I take a deep breath, aligning the rhythm of their heartbeats with mine. The dogs start to bleed from their noses. A thudding begins in my head. The canine army start shrieking in kin's voices. I know instinctively they have been sent to torture me, to stoke the memory of a man racing against a raging fire stored in the bone.

Chapter 5

At the University of Edinburgh Therese majored in molecular plant science. Within the magisterial college buildings imbued with history and pedigree, she'd studied plant ecology and evolution, poring over documents on disease-resistant plants of the seventeenth and eighteenth centuries, lugging photocopied pages from the library through winding hallways. She'd investigated how plants respond to DNA damage, the effects of hybridisation and biogeography on plant diversity with a focus on the rhododendron, her thoughts buzzing like a series of upended hornets' nests as she rushed through passages connecting faculties. In her rustic, efficient room within student halls at night, there was usually a compact glass of whisky on her dresser, a pile of books on the floor at her feet, a basket of laundry spilling from the opposite end and the painting of chorusing women in a square she bought from a flea market hanging over her bed. She could often be found hunched at her desk, bright eyed, twists spilling into documents, a torch angled over papers, dark skin luminous, her fingers scanning and underlining, her breath warm, tongue intoxicated from a dwindling bottle of Aberfeldy whisky while she pondered over dissections on the ancestral circadian clock shared by fungi, plants and animals. Sometimes, she'd wash her ink-stained hands in the sink after a night of study, her chest full of the wonders and mysteries of nature, the secret lives they lived, the signals and ways of communication they shared. Occasionally, she'd lie awake in bed, attempting to make sense of a nagging connection she couldn't ignore. She started to spend more time in the lab, looking at mutation in stem cells, her white coat stained orange at the sleeves from lily pollen she'd stuffed in the pocket, her right hand splayed on the wood top, her eye greedily taking in cells, enamoured with a kinetic energy you could only see through the microscope. Afterwards, the image of mutant plants such as dahlias and chrysanthemums from the microscope stayed imprinted in her brain like an X-ray. The properties, benefits and dangers of these plants and herbs began to stay with her. Ginkgo biloba thinned the blood, hawthorn slowed the heart rhythm and horsetail expedited bone growth. Now and again, she discovered people's bodies pushed beyond the limits of expectation who'd relied on plant life to help them: a group of female Baju sea nomads in Thailand who frequently dived to hunt for food, whose bodies were genetically adapted to diving; Inuit men known for putting their limbs through freezing temperatures during rites of passage; a man in Sub-Saharan Africa who wandered for twenty days with very little sustenance except for wild sorrel plants. She harboured these stories like bulbs of fuel that melted into her very being. She became fascinated by the role of hallucinogenic plants to create altered states, its impact on the body, the pathways of hedonistic ecstasy and transformations it opened up. She began to collate information as her pet project.

In the spring of her second semester, the wilds of Drumbrae called. She put on her hiking boots, blanket in tow, a hot flask of ginger tea in her rucksack. On arrival, she scoured for alien plantation, placing fennel, nettle and black mushrooms in jars she held up to the light, anticipating a reconfiguration in glass, her fingers hovering in the opening, her eardrums filled with the subtle language of her surroundings, she could access it while soft patches of earth beckoned, the cool air whipped her twists about playfully. When an attractive, elegant-looking technician called Pascale from the rural region of Marseille became infatuated with her, it was a quick seduction. She took him to her room at halls, tied a mauve stocking with a run in it on his penis tightly, watching the tip ooze and glisten appreciatively in response. After she straddled him, her back arching in pleasure, a soft growl emanating from his throat, his hands greedy, devoid of their earlier poetry, her expression was feral, deeply intense and past just fucking, as though she was listening to other life forms contorting in synchronicity with her body. He thought it was odd, sexy even, but then she started doing that thing with his dick again, so he forgot about it.

Afterwards, she felt the power of her carrier Bintou rippling through her, fuelling her instincts to feed her desires. Bintou was kin; following Oni's instructions, she had travelled from a small province in northern Mali, near the interior of the Sahara Desert, close to the Tuareg, to a sprawling, magnificent Timbuktu. She had passed her secrets down in the blood. Therese absorbed them. That night, heady from her encounter with Pascale, she wandered out into the green searching for hidden enclaves with soft patches of earth for flight.

It was Finn's turn to find a suitable spot for their rituals of flight. He turned the car keys in his pocket, whistling the opening tune of Fellini's *8½*. His black tweed jacket billowed; his striped scarf blew across his face and his left hand tightened on the small, grey overnight bag, the zipper tantalisingly close to the end of the flap, leaving a slight opening several fingers could slip into: the items jostling against a potential stranger's touch. He'd driven the rental Peugeot 500 for four hours to Amersham, picked up the keys from the lighthouse keeper – a bearded, average-sized man who had a large wart on his right cheek, was friendly, spoke in measured tones and deliberately didn't pay too much attention. Finn liked that about him. After he gave the man cash, he parked the car on a side road where the last word on the sign had been eroded. He started crossing the fields towards the lighthouse at the far end, a looming, pale structure that had survived various iterations: periods of decay, lodgers and maintenance. It blushed in the moonlight from the red lick of paint circling its top half. Fairly quiet at this time of night, the fields swelled from Finn's movements. The rhythm of his long, quick strides meant the bag occasionally knocked against his legs. Crickets chirping filled his ears, the slosh of tyres on puddles of black water on the slopes of roads, the earlier chatter of gathering folk in The King's Lynn pub he'd passed on his way long died down. Black, old-fashioned streetlamps were dotted around. Wind chimes spun softly in some entrances.

On reaching the lighthouse, the door was a tasteful dark wood with a red post-box slot for letters to the lighthouse keeper. His throat was filled with salty air, his right hand raw from the cold. He fished out the key, unlocked the door, turning the handle and shoving with his shoulder the way the keeper had instructed. He stepped inside, taking in the winding staircase leading to a room at the top. Finn pictured their internal injuries from that fateful night mirrored in its window, weeping despite the condensation until the heads of wood pigeons smashed through in an inebriated welcome. The room was unfussy, small, sparse but adequate. A comfortable large wooden bed took up most of the space. It would just about contain all six foot two of him.

That night it had been cramped with the three of them, brimming with their dynamic of camaraderie and bubbling tensions. The past and the present intermingled. On either side of the bed were small dressers with a reading lamp, where Azacca had left pale Rizla sheets. Just below the window on the opposite end sat a chest of drawers, on top of which was a well-thumbed visitors' book that he'd be ignoring. Emilien had scrawled his signature there with a shaky hand. Large crossbeams filled the ceiling. There was a ball of wool and one purple knitting needle under the bed that the lighthouse keeper must have forgotten to pick up from their last visit, an instrument they'd used to trace the etchings on limestones. He placed the bag by the foot of the bed, shrugged off his jacket, slung it over the chair, relieved by the feeling of panic leaving his chest. He gathered the wool and needle as though it would knit long-gone scenes of that night again, Azacca vomiting into a plastic bag, he and Emilien holding his shuddering body. He placed it on one dresser, the clink and quiet noise of his footsteps was a comfort.

It was Therese who'd encouraged them to make that trip, an escapade for them to connect. He padded about the space. Those internal wounds under the skin wept again as he thought of the trauma which occurred that evening the guys kept between them. He felt the multiple shocks of pain. His eyes watered. It was pointless reaching for painkillers. He grabbed a cigarette from a packet of Marlboro Gold inside his jacket, opened the window, lit up and took a few drags. Outside, hedges surrounding houses were thick, the cobwebs silvery distractions for fleet-footed mint-green grasshoppers. Owls called to each other in a shared soliloquy echoing through the night. The familiarity and memory hit him all at once, the strangely exotic scent of incense that seeped into the walls, the salty sea air from a different land which lingered in his nostrils. The boys had come back here on the night they pulled Azacca out from the sea, when he claimed to have temporarily been paralysed by the tides, watching his heart leave his body to become a pink marrow creature pulsing towards a figure in the bed of the sea. It was Oni pulling him closer to a distorted reality. In this guise, her dark skin shimmered in the waters like liquid stardust. Her soft, seductive full mouth spilled green peacock feathers stained with blood. She glimmered before him, an underwater doyenne who commanded the seas, skies and kin deployed in different faces throughout the ages. Azacca was certain he was both dead and alive when three of the peacock feathers became white in her hand. She fed one into his mouth, against the disruption of tides, reminding him of his ancestral commitment, the price of an inherited debt that would take lifetimes to pay. This occurred while Finn, Azacca and Emilien went limestone hunting on the beach, joking and trying to outdo each other, a blustery wind cooling their heated shadows. Pulled by a magnetic force emanating from the waters, Azacca followed Oni's light bending a path into the waters. When he didn't come up for five minutes, Finn and Emilien dived in, swimming deep down into the murky bed. They pulled him out from the thrashing waters. Afterwards, splayed on the dappled shore, breathing heavily, crescent-shaped marks throbbing in their necks, they embraced, bonded by the beauty and sudden brutality of Oni's hand. She'd taken Azacca's heart as an offering, replacing it with three white feathers of no abode floating mercurially in its absence, their tips spilling the inky lines of Gethsemane's mountains' secrets. In the aftermath, it was the lighthouse they'd come back to recover in, consoling each other, Azacca convulsing on the bed, wracked with pangs from his absent heart, a voracious globe in Oni's hold. They made breathy declarations over limestones with etchings from past and future kin that were the eyes of the thrumming surrounding landscape. And Oni having taken Azacca's heart with no indication of when it would be returned.

Finn looked out of the window, saw a bloodshot eyed, a white rabbit scurrying up to the lighthouse. Perhaps it had come to collect the ball of wool and the needle. He looked again; the rabbit had become a pale wound sinking into the base of the lighthouse.

He unpacked: a rumpled pair of overnight clothes

including black tracksuit bottoms, an aged Van Morrison T-shirt, a dark brown farmer's flat cap. He wished Azacca and Emilien were with him again. This time without a gutting looming on the horizon. He fished out a handful of plums from a clear cellophane bag, the skin still fairly taut yet a little bruised; a map and a rolled-up copy of the local paper from their borough. He opened the gazette on the bed, flicking the pages over as he read, the shocks of pain inside him fading somewhat, the throbbing in his temples winging its way to his head. The white rabbit poised at the window. His hands had warmed up again by now and the cigarette had taken the edge off. He always felt a mix of excitement plus anxiety on these trips, which never made it easier. By themselves, Therese and Azacca would have aroused too much curiosity, while Emelien possessed that odd, individualistic air which either sparked people's interest or made them keep their distance. In the paper, there were short write-ups of a former dance teacher starting a local mime class, a cat named Huey heralded a hero for scratching a burglar in the face. *Huey Foils Robbery!* His relieved owner awakened from an afternoon nap to find the burglar fleeing through the garden door, Huey at his heels. Finn flipped over, placed the map on the left-hand page. On the right was a feature on Eitan. *Strange Slaying of Local Aquarium Owner*, the headline read. There was a picture of Eitan at the aquarium's entrance standing next to a lady customer who was smiling sheepishly. The electric-blue sign glowed enticingly, a fragment of life captured in another consciousness. Finn's hand hovered over the map. He released a whisper of a breath. The article said there was no new evidence, appealed for witnesses. A helpline number was emblazoned at the bottom.

He didn't think it was possible, but the room seemed smaller filled with him and his half-assembled thoughts. The hunger they all possessed, which Oni had planted inside them, that got worse from that night. And if they couldn't control the hunger sometimes, it was okay to want to consume things to fill it. He closed his eyes. The lines of the map began to seep into Eitan's picture, as if to suck him into its centre. Considering how much he'd loved maps, Finn thought Eitan would have appreciated that. He looked away from the photo with an unbearable ache in his chest.

He set off early the next morning, dressed like one of the locals in his farmer's flat cap, brown corduroys, wellington boots and an anorak over his T-shirt and jumper. He walked for roughly twenty minutes, map in hand, before finding one entrance to the woods tucked behind an ill-thought-out empty car park, a large hole in the fencing, the nettles and hedges twitching as he ventured into the woods' embrace. The woodland stretched for miles. He walked deeper and deeper into it, finding a secret wild garden and surreal spaces which felt like a trick of the eye if you missed a turning. He weaved between tall trees with the expressions of squirrels caught on their leaves, listening for those softened points of earth beneath his feet. It was dense enough for people to disappear into. He took gulps of fresh morning air, pausing by a moss-green brook, acorns scattered along its edge as nature's bullets, dark shapes moving under the surface. He looked up at the unrelenting sky searchingly for a few moments, bathed in that blue light that was celestial. He plucked his mobile from the inside pocket of his anorak, briefly touching the coppery ridges of the lighthouse key. Two bars left.

For a moment, he tried to steady his excitement then called.

Therese picked up on the fifth ring. Friction from the static gurgled between them.

'I remembered where I buried them,' he said, chest heaving. The spaces between trees shimmered. In the distance, the lighthouse window misted, Azacca's heart throbbing in the glass. The sky opened, sucking the blue light. That red-eyed rabbit sat breathing in his overnight bag, eating the ball of wool, a tentacle of memory from that blazing evening seared into their consciousness. In the other plane, the lines of Eitan's image were absorbed into the mouths of startled deer, shark fin. A perforated nucleus limped out of view. The static flattened. Finn clutched the bloodied limestones with kin's etchings from the night Oni had taken Azacca's heart and instigated a ferocious hunger that all three men would never forget.

Six

I dream of the dogs for a few nights. Their outlines take turns guarding the white horn on the rooftops of Gethsemane; deep in the soil they circle the crack in the clay heart under our homestead. Pass through the dimpled blue tent languishing in the periphery, temporarily bereft of gifts for Oni. I hear them writhing in bloodied white sheets at the corners of my room, preparing to be reborn, the cold hands of shamanic kin inside them pressing new scars against their organs. The mood in the homestead is solemn. The tension thick, memories like fruit threaten to spill from the bowels of wandering dogs; ripe, sweet and soft to the touch. Cherry red. Marrow and thorn grow in conjunction. Hare and caterpillar ambush a ravaged beetroot at the bottom of the garden. Dragonroot grows wild on the rickety fencing. The plants sprouting steadily in potion bottles of marrow are dusted with a light dew of a morning to come. Trembling from the reflections of four strange kin in the future with crescent-moon markings on their necks, angling their way towards the glass, Sueli says prayers at meals in between bites of food that Domingos and Marguerite do not recognise. One day, his hand *flexes over a steaming pot of Cachupa soup, Domingos asks what foreign language am I teaching his child. I say children invent things all the time; that she will become beautifully surprising to them as she grows. He reaches for Sueli's hand. It is artfully small in his, the start of a labyrinth, sullied from rummaging through hidden crevices the homestead reveals, unspooled from her father's secrets.*

Three white feathers arrive. I walk in the dark to hear them land. They have come through breaking banks, shimmering trees, soil turning the colour of copper while a fire rages as if the land had been burnished by a vengeful dragon's breath. Sent by kin, the feathers were not dissuaded by weather, or disruption, or the regrets of men. They loiter as the blood hums inside me, descending from an island that vanished.

That night, I roll up my night smock sleeves, walking carefully down the front path of the homestead, wary of waking the others. The mountains blur in the distance, smudged by Oni's fingers. I cannot share the secrets I carry yet, that those injuries released as accomplices by kin will make their way to the town's inhabitants. And eventually the shores and the rivers and the wilds will undulate gratefully. The planes between worlds shall fold, reconstructing, filled with multiple languages swelling in my ears. The hairs on my arms stand to attention. I look up at the sky, those injuries are changing; a white rope becomes the lining of a womb, a rabbit heart thins into a vessel, a pocket becomes a small blue patch of possibility. My eardrums hum. Three silver rivulets from the vanished island lodge in my chest between breast and ribcage. A slither of salty saliva fills my mouth. The languages break through to the centre of my tongue. A black bruise starts to form on the underside. I close my eyes, hear a wind changing direction in my bloodstream. I listen for the feathers, their soiled tips angling through the air. One lands in the shebeen window on Ranula Mountain, fluttering against the ripple of a groove; another in the wheelbarrow outside the garment store on Figaroo Street; another in the gap under the doorway of the school on Figaroo Way. My nostrils fill with the scent of burning from the vanished island. The ground is hot against my feet. A shard of neon-stained glass gleams, a parting gift from the dogs. I place it in the right underside of my tongue. It reflects the black bruise into the coming morning.

The next evening Domingos arrives home carrying a small sack, a piece of string tied tightly near the tip to keep it protected. The scent of rose hangs on his clothes, a woman's ointment; it fills my nostrils when he finds me in my room. There is a troubled air about him. The smell of dragonroot lingers in the air, the last whispers from me burning the ends. He eyes the plants in the potion bottles by the window curiously, perhaps noticing them for the first time. I am sitting on my rumpled bedding like a prophet on a white lotus singing a song about a woman whose beloved abandoned her for one that was not her equal. He drops the sack at my feet. His expression is amused despite his worrisome manner, which softens his handsome face somewhat.

'Can you guess what booty I have brought for your kitchen?' he asks. His tone is teasing, making jest at my expense, but a small ripple of pleasure courses through me at the kitchen being called mine. The kerosene lamp under the window is a witness, after bone, marrow and plant. Its flame curls, its bright shadow a rush of heat against glass.

'A man will catch what he needs when he sets his mind to it,' I respond, my head full with worries from the previous day. My tongue thickens; a dangerous desire to share my burdens takes hold. He bends down, his face inches from mine.

'Since you have come, my wife wants to do what her body cannot. Strange desires fill her mind. My daughter speaks in riddles. There is a feeling in this house I cannot name.'

'Change is good,' I say reassuringly. 'I am company for them when you are absent.' I reach for the sack; he stops me, his warm hand over mine. There are light scratches on the back, traces of translucent fish scales. He unties the sack, plucks a dead pheasant from inside, places it on top. 'I half expect you to waken it, but then we cannot eat it alive.'

It is not far into its stages of growth, the neck crudely broken, its head limp, its gaze glassy, wings held back with string. It needs to be plucked, washed, salted.

'Now long away from its mother's protection,' I say matter-of-factly, eyeing its width and length, searching its eyes.

'It will do,' he says, standing up, the tension in his shoulders a little lessened. 'Tomorrow, you come with me,' he instructs. 'Be ready.'

He leaves moments later. I hear him throwing Sueli in the air while she squeals joyfully. Closing my eyes, I imagine Baby, my own child, in his arms. Ripples of pain shoot through my chest. The kerosene flame curls through the pheasant's insides, its pupils melt, its lost heartbeat speeds up. My nostrils are still thick with the rose scent from his clothing.

'But then we cannot eat it alive,' I say to the mutterings of kin clamouring in the wings.

*

By morning, the bats from my vision slick with perspiration lose half their wings in Gethsemane's caves. A clarion mimics the arc of their flight after inheriting their cries, circling the rooftops of the flour mill, puffs of black smoke spiralling between them. The circular patterns which haunted the harvest shrink further into the soil, breathing rhythmically above roots. New growths of moss sprout in the mountain's crevices, handfuls of limestone gathered by children wink in secret stashes inside homesteads. And the rainbow fish in the seas begin their migration north.

After a hushed argument with Marguerite in the night, their voices tense through the walls, Domingos is curt once again. His teasing expression from the previous evening gone, a worrisome look is back on his face. I slip on a necklace Marguerite and I carved from wood in our ramshackle garden. Its light weight is a comfort against my neck and collarbone, misshapen and frail. In a small sack, I pack a blade that has been soaked and washed in lime juice, a needle, some black thread, a sprig of devil's claw for pain.

We set off walking in step. I am still an unknown entity beside him. The homestead, the path, the garden and our corner of the world have become playthings for Oni the shaman god. I watch his large, coiled frame, the beauty of his scarred face. I feel a pull towards hands that give me dead creatures to make edible. He tells me we are on our way to an orchard on the south of Ranula Mountain called the Orchard of Lost Souls, where a woman named Ezadaro, the wife of one of his fishermen, believing she had become an apple, made her way to the orchard to roll among fallen fruit. For weeks, he says, according to her husband Paolo, she had been obsessed with apples in a way that was not natural. She would place them in the windows of their homestead as though they could see. After warming a few in a pot of water, she would run one between her breasts in a swift up-and-down motion which was a comfort, a way of managing her worrisome energy. Sometimes when Paolo kissed her at night, he tasted the pips she had been hiding under her tongue. When she sliced the apples, she did so in a particular manner, resting the blade against the side, taking a breath before cutting slowly, watching tiny bursts of liquid, fascinated by its newness, its potential for decay, the measurement of time through it.

Paolo became jealous of apples.

Domingos laughs nervously, throwing a sideways glance to gauge my reaction. Yes! His wife had not looked at him in seasons the way she did those apples. He accused her of fixating on them because they could not answer back.

They had no children yet. Perhaps it was a transference of energy, a way to keep herself occupied between household tasks. Paolo considered himself a simple man. He had taken her as his wife because of her light-hearted disposition. And had not bargained for this dazed, complicated creature he did not recognise, wandering around their homestead taken with things that made no sense. Besides, since this madness she had not allowed him the pleasure between her legs, which was sure to set a man on edge.

When Paolo arrived home one evening, after a long day's work, to find her tumbling on their floors – 'Rolling like apples', she offered, looking up at him innocently, in all seriousness – he had been so incandescent with rage, shouting, he startled the pigeons, who fled their fences at the noise.

The orchard itself is lopsided when we get there. Tall shoots of grass curve with light spots of colour on thin blades. The air *possesses a sweet, exotic fragrance. Lines of dandelion on either side dwindle in weathered patches. Apples on the ground age and soften from the light on their skin. We feel a tug to the middle where a large tree rests. Its branches are stretched in an embrace of the sky. Its thick trunk bears the lines and histories of passing faces. On the ground, undulating beneath the gaze and twitching of low-hanging fruit, is Ezadaro, her body in the grip of Oni's hold that is strange and foreign to her. She is a fine woman with a long open face and soft mouth. Her dark skin has a glow. Wild curls frame her face. There is a feverish air about her, a sheen of sweat on her skin. She barely recognises Domingos but turns towards him nevertheless. 'I am in bloom,' she says. 'Paolo does not understand. I must abandon any stone in my way.'*

A look of deep sadness crosses Domingos's face, perhaps a reminder of his sick wife. He steps away to give me room. His hands hover at the small of my back questioningly. I tell him I know what she needs. I lay her down gently. She is still, almost expectantly so. I fish the knife out, lift up her dress. When I make the cut to her side, above her right hip, it is a tender cut, just the way she would slice the fruit at home. The cut whispers instructions from Oni. The clarions above tear through the sky, leaving pale trails. Tension between us mounts. Not too far from the area, a wild antelope loses its way. The heady, exotic scent of wild roses in the air becomes dizzying. The orchard threatens to fracture down the side of the mountain. Ezadaro's cut spills. She reaches up blindly for my arms, her expression far away.

She cries out in pleasure, in relief, as Oni's voice echoes in her wound.

Chapter 6

Warped plant silhouettes danced on the basement walls. The ribcage floated inside the tank, retracting, a student of light. It had continued to create its own elements; the cloudy waterfall now bore a soft reddish tinge from berries scattered on the tank floor. Moss crawled up misted glass on one side. Pale green stems protruded from a rib. Iridescent tadpole-like creatures swam in the water, circling a pile of moss that was a miniature mountain. Liquid creatures moved up the moss stash, precariously balanced on an apex between two planes, while the tadpole imitators careened into the water again, darting around like bright fragments shooting through water. The ribcage refracted once more. So did the other plane in tandem. Memories of its travels were imprinted in the second dimension's sky; the ribcage hurtling through a ridged, darkened tunnel of ether and scattered constellations, of several shimmering portals forking in different directions, of it poised in the centre, hovering, before tumbling through one pathway while it expanded from the speed of travel in the plane. The sky swirled memories as reflections; then it was on the valley, listening for its other parts in the void, by the brook watching a girl clutching a stick of chalk running underwater on burnished blades of grass scouring for a vanishing island, in silent conversations with creatures that lost their heads to a second sun, a lizard entering the brook, a bird head sprouting from its back. Light flickered in the basement. The other utopia paused. A naked body stood before the tank breathing heavily. Breath on the glass became a small path to an ancient land. The light flickered again. Emilien's intoxicated hand rummaged through the tank for marrow berries gleaming with a certain malevolence.

On the forum, his initials were JD, his avatar an image of a smoking cigar in a hat.
He said he couldn't step out into daylight without being in pain, his limbs battling a burning sensation, his eyes glazing, a strange paralysis, splinterings of pain in his chest, his body crumpling before crawling back indoors. Therese read his story sitting in bed, watching her laptop screen, that woman from another time's gauzy hand guiding their heartbeats to a frenetic pace though a static, making her presence felt. She knew the echoes of another's movements inside her, of worlds colliding. She traced the jagged shape of stained glass under her tongue followed by the bitter-sweet taste of a bruise, heard the howl of hounds fading in her eardrums, felt their shared hunger and anger growing.
This haven was a space to communicate with strangers about ailments people didn't have the right terminology for or couldn't explain. Therese closed her eyes momentarily, steadying their intertwined heartbeats. Excitement coursed

through her, the sense they had something to exchange. The woman's hand turned inside her again, a corroded dial fuelling their desires as though they were interchangeable. There was a voice within that was distant at first, mired in the static, then closer, formal, assured. *You must follow this instinct to seek knowledge from the bones and bodies of others.* It was husky, powerful, reverberating across time inside her. Fingerprints faded on half a glass of Moscato that was warm after being left on the dresser for too long. The open window rattled from the night's disciples quietly making visits while her back was turned. The pull of a sick individual made her heart beat faster. She knew that other voice lurked inside her, the visitor taking root understood.

Her fingers poised over the keys, she heard the kitchen tap running downstairs – Azacca back after a late gig, raiding the cupboards, trying to fill the hunger that was affecting them all. She knew they had been taking turns feeding from the ribcage, which they named Ovida. She woke occasionally to the sound of the basement door creaking open lodged in her eardrums, the cloudy water from Ovida trickling into her irises inserting new revelations. She continued reading the thread online, which went on for a while. Rubbing her temples, finishing the wine, she closed the window as a chill came through. A humming began in her brain that manifested into the woman's voice again. *Follow the hunger then starve it of its own intentions.* A copy of *Psychologies* magazine resting on her thighs, she used a finger to draw the silhouette of a man who could barely cross his front yard on it. Then she started typing.

*

JD turned out to be Jeronimo Dorsey. He said people often thought he was crazy because he'd tried to set up a UFO spotting group on the forum in the past. He didn't mind a visit from a stranger. He had nothing to lose and could do with the company. Jeronimo's house was in Enfield on a slope, a pale weathered Victorian offering with converted rustic arched windows. It was around midday, the traffic faint on the steep road, the shops dotted around fairly quiet.

A haggard man was selling matching duvets and pillowcases, abruptly approaching people as if he'd pull out other things they didn't expect from his pockets and the duvet selling was just a ruse. It was a surprisingly warm, bright day. Therese noticed her senses were sharper from eating the sweet marrow berries. She heard a faulty bell ringing, the haphazard trickle of blood from a woman cutting herself shaving a leg, a man faltering on a ladder, the whoosh then liquid burst of a watermelon chopped in half, its pink innards waiting to be consumed. Something passed through the neighbourhood network of cat flaps which wasn't a cat. The slope beckoned. She ambled up it, her leather bag swinging by her waist reassuringly. She wondered if the slope contributed to Jeronimo's sense of disorientation. It must have felt odd that every time you stepped out you weren't on an even keel, instead tilted, susceptible to secret attacks from the periphery that could wreck a body. On arriving, she noted the number 54, the white front door bearing a knocker with a serpent's head. She walked round to the back as instructed, where the gate had been left open. The woman's voice inside her from the distant land whispered, *He has let you in, go to feed your hunger.*

When she entered, a pond awaited; it was slightly murky but she could see through to the bottom where female figurines were frozen firing arrows at a stone globe. There were vines sprouting from the water, dappled white petals littered the surface like wilted communion. One chair each sat at opposite ends. The double kitchen doors were open but the shards of stained glass on it were missing and the sound of those hounds filled her ears again. She tugged the strap of her bag up her shoulder before walking in. A pale, bearded, dishevelled man in his sixties appeared at the entrance of the kitchen where several condiments were scattered on a large oak table and a calendar for the year 2050 hung on the wall by a grainy photograph of a bunker with the shadow looming in the corner. The man's silk dressing gown was a riot of colours, a contrast to his sickly appearance. A greenish bruise stretched up his left arm, like ivy growing under the skin. He held a steaming mug of tea, which filled the air with a warm, herbal scent. Oolong, she guessed, with fruity undertones.

'You're not what I expected,' he said, sizing her up. His voice was raspy, level.

'Not a bad thing,' she answered, motioning to the kettle on the worktop, the cupboard above it. Mirroring. They didn't introduce themselves. Instead, she put the kettle on. It whistled, mingling with the instructions from the hounds. She made blackberry tea in a mug decorated with a woman made of barbed wire, sipped from the mug. Jeronimo watched her carefully, blinking rapidly. He took a sip from his own mug. His mouth tilted up at the corners in a fleeting knowing smile. He glanced outside. His expression became sombre, uncertain, as though factors he wasn't able to control could materialise; the figurines breaking from their watery entrapment to fire arrows at their backs, the kettle's whistle echoing to release the shadow from the bunker photo, pages of the 2050 calendar separating, fluttering onto the chairs outside before the air decided what they would become.

'You don't look like the type scouring forums for sick people. I mean, you're very pretty,' he said, breaking out of his reverie.

'That doesn't save me from the inevitability of life's tribulations; it's the least interesting thing about me,' she responded, tucking one lose twist behind her ear.

He didn't ask what she meant by that, didn't know her well enough to gauge whether she was joking. There was a charged atmosphere around her that felt intoxicating. Ignoring the niggling anxiety in his chest and perhaps a little shame from the reality of an attractive woman seeing him in this state, he led the way through the house. A woman came three times a week, he said, a carer of sorts who tidied up, did the shopping, ensured he took whatever medication wasn't successful each time he trialled one since the doctors didn't know what they were dealing with. The theory of a mutated form of photosensitivity had been bandied about, although it was a misdiagnosis, he said, an easy categorisation in an attempt to define the unknown. He was no expert, but it felt like an ancient affliction that had infiltrated the present, crippling him at a stage in his life where he should be enjoying the labours of a youth spent as a space engineer. He knew it sounded crazy, he mused, a man unable to step out into daylight lest his body give way from a force beyond his control. Some days, he felt like it was a punishment, although he couldn't understand what he was being punished for. Perhaps it was some mental issue he couldn't quite come to terms with. She watched him moving through the hallway gingerly as he spoke, leaning to one side as if bracing himself for something. A cluster of paintings of men in his likeness filled the walls.

'Ah, the line of Dorsey men,' he acknowledged dismissively.

There was a son in Exeter. Finley. They weren't close, sporadically exchanging phone calls, Christmas cards, that kind of thing. On the odd occasion his son visited, it was awkward. There was no real understanding, only the acrid scent of suspicion in the air, the unspoken conclusion it was a bid for attention from a lonely man who'd had no real sense of family when it mattered. She looked up, noticing the small grooves in the ceiling, another entrance. She pictured him holding the stone globe directly beneath it, engraving his secrets on it with an unsteady hand.

In the room downstairs which had been turned into a makeshift bedroom, the air was stale, the bed crumpled, the computer screen flashing. A few science magazines were scattered on the floor. An instrument that looked like a small kora with broken strings was leaning against the bed. A series of connected metallic grey magnet devices filled the dresser, a small robotic army on display. He didn't argue when she squeezed drops of Lobelia Tupa, also known as devil's tobacco, from an ornate golden vial into his tea. He finished it before climbing into bed, starring up at the spots of colour on the light-bulb wire before sinking back against the pillows.

'Sometimes I dream of my limbs moving under a spotlight on an open road,' he said gravely. 'Not as one but individually, my right leg walking restlessly, my left arm twitching anticipating something, my shoulder tumbling through the breeze. At times, that spotlight follows me through the house. Most people don't know how lucky they are to have the freedom of movement without repercussions.'

'Imagine yourself completely untethered,' she instructed, slipping her right hand inside him while distracting him, the way nurses do when giving patients injections.

Afterwards, he asked how it was possible. How did he feel her hands moving within him? And not just under the skin but touching corners that needed awakening.

'Can't you hear the hounds coming?' she asked, her teeth flashing before him in a feral manner.

A kind of ecstasy filled his brain, spreading through his body. He stood up unsteadily, his expression one of awe. The magnets on the dresser had gone haywire, rattling against each other in rhapsodic acknowledgement. The spots of colour from the bulb wire had spread through the room, bright chasms suspended in the air. One lady figurine broke away from the pond, set her arrow down and was crying in the doorway.

When Therese arrived back home, she felt the weight of a loss. The hounds had faded, the shrill echoes of a baby's cry filled her ears. She fished out the cassette he'd given her as a parting gift, declaring it his favourite recording. She had expected something classical or world music. She played the tape in the living room while she waited for the others. Distressed sounds filled the space: groans; screaming; rushed, unintelligible whispers; women's voices in discomfort, signalling to her from a void. She took a breath, pressed pause. She was sure of it.

Jeronimo Dorsey, who lived on a hill, on a tilted axis, had given her recordings of multiple women giving birth. The rustle of something in the air travelling through static, trees, coming to the fore each time she pressed rewind, cutting past the noise until the sounds scrambled in her ears and the ache inside her intensified. The beat in her temple fluttered as though wasp wings were chanting incantations into her blood. Her vision swam; the air was filled with electricity. And the woman's face appeared to her again, her likeness from another time. She whispered, *They have Baby*, standing on a precipice surrounded by the silhouettes of majestic mountains, holding an umbilical cord that flickered into a bone while her feet bled into the mountains.

Seven

The cut is between us.
cut while we breathe,
cut while we hover,
As we exhale.
The weeping cut bleeds
Into the sky from below
Pierces fruit for a dalliance with pips,
Trickles
Into grooves where the slanted orchard
Hides feral woman

Domingos is a towering, ruinous husk. His expression harried, uncertain. I want to dip my finger into her wound saying, See where Oni harbours her tricks? The goshawk loses its eye? Where the apparition for the vanished burnished island lands before fading? See where your ash face has led us? *The scent of burning fills my nostrils, a searing knowable reminder of the past.*

But Ezadaro is writhing. Groaning, feverishly tugging at golden blades of grass. I slip the knife inside my dress pocket, blade masked in cloth, gleam contained in rustles of movement, tip taunting injury.

The orchard is reflected in the goshawk's lost eye, the injury passing through the petticoats of kin with foreign tongues and free bodies.

> My kind wants to be sated.
> My kind wants the hunger.
> My kind wants the thirst.
> My kind wants the cut.

'What is the meaning of this?' he barks, fussing over her, brushing curly tendrils from her damp forehead. I kneel beside him, my hand firm on his shoulder.

'She wants the scar that will come. She needs the memories it brings. It will help ease her worrisome nature.'

He is confused, as if I am mumbling unintelligibly.

'She had to become smaller,' I say. 'A thing that was familiar and unknown. She had to roll through uneven ground to feel it.'

His eyes flash. 'I do not understand what you speak of, it makes no sense. Gethsemane is becoming a place of the unknown.'

'What is the power of your sense,' I add, 'when a woman thinks she is fruit, your wife embraces a decaying crown in your absence, and your daughter speaks parts of a language that is not from her people?' Heat fills my chest. A throbbing vein appears in his neck. Thick. Insistent.

Standing, I raise the hem of my dress. It angles against a bruise forming in the centre of the orchard, shaped like a wound from a future kin. The tension between us deepens.

'Help her a little more,' I urge. I want to sing it like a melody, but I whisper it instead, so it lingers. 'Press your mouth against the cut.'

Ezadaro groans that she can see a man with her cuts, many of them inside him. He is not from now but a time to come.

After I sew her wound, the line of thread furrowed within the flesh, the silence is heavy. His face bears a pained expression, the scarred skin tightening, his brow wrinkled in confusion, his mouth curled by the sting of shame it hides.

The shard of stained glass the hounds brought me had foretold it: a bloody-mouthed man with wailing wounds bearing a crescent-shaped birthmark on his neck kneeling under a guava tree; one scene from the future in exchange for one obscured in smoke from the past. The memory of the glass under my tongue covered with saliva lingers, and later still, the bruise there changing steadily to imitate a coming cut.

Domingos lifts Ezadaro cautiously. 'People have disappeared from this place come nightfall. I cannot leave her here.' He sighs.

My hands flutter inside the dress's pocket as though catching an unspoken thing from the seams. I slip her arm over my shoulder. She mutters at the sky, her head rolling to one side. We carry her awkwardly at first before finding a rhythm, the weight of another's body sending sharp pains to our hands, limbs, the orchard's centre slanting a little more as we leave it.

On the way back, I think of the feathers.

Flocks of feathers covering naked bodies angled on the mountains of Gethsemane, waiting to be plucked under the night's light like a new kind of being.

Since their arrival, I talk to the three feathers in Gethsemane *in the dark when the whisperings of kin echo inside me, thrumming against my chest. The feather on Ranula Mountain scales its peak, drawing the outlines of kin clutching shadowy creatures that pulse.*

We start to tire. Domingos harrumphs as he loses his grip through sweaty, weary hands. In a different tongue, I sing about driftwood shrines in collusion with a vanished island, my voice soaring like a wild siren. He does not understand the language.

We deliver Ezadaro back to Paolo, who collapses with relief, holding her as a flooding of pips spill from her cut like rare jewels, ushered to the surface by a mouthful of blood from kin who will bear those same wounds in the future. Upon our exit, Domingos marches ahead of me, past the weathered fence surrounding their homestead. There is anger in the lines of his body. He curls and uncurls a fist. He waits for me to reach him, for the humming in my body to calm the uncertainty in his. The sweetness of our pained limbs, the journey's reward to us is a comfort. I stuff my hands in my pocket; run a finger over the blade.

Kin fill my cloak's pockets with other possessions: a line of fire, new red berries containing addictive marrow and sweet nectar from a watery mirror, a woman's face feverishly struggling for breath. They dodge the blue tent while Oni breathes inside it. The tent flutters, waiting to be sated. Kin's shrieks ripple through my heart.

'What kind of affliction was that?' he asks, pulling me towards him sharply. 'I have never seen such a thing. I know the sadness of a sick wife. I had no words of comfort. I could not say that this change in her will pass.' He is shaken, his breath short, the

whites of his eyes cloudy. The exotic scents of the orchard mingled with his sweat sits in my nostrils. I breathe it in deeply, place my hands on his chest.

'He must continue to love her as she is until whatever has been unleashed settles.'

The darkness looms. Our tired bodies move onwards, towards the clinks of the plant-filled potion bottles in the homestead, rattling in my ears like a stuttering bell.

Parts of the vanished island start to come. They appear dipped in blood, dew droplets, decorated in burnt thorns. They are born of injuries and past lives. One day, a rope grazes my back in our homestead's garden while I dig. Hounds' mouths filled with coloured glass rise through the undergrowth, taunting my curved fingers in damp soil. The symbols Sueli traced on the walls of her room appear on my mirror like tainted possessions. I press my lips against them, my ears, the rhythm of my heart, before they leave again. A cluster of one-eyed goshawks buck against our fence as if confused about the burden of entry or what they will become without warning in the between space; changing to fern, a handful of rotted organs, beaks from a gutting covered in ink, scribbling the unknown language from Sueli's mouth, translating it into another foreign tongue on Gethsemane's cave walls. Jagged shapes from the lost island's sky circle Sueli as she plays, darting through the homestead's entrances in short bursts of energy. And then as she uses her mother's decaying crown, standing before my mirror to name yolk, stick and stone a new queen. It brings relief, laughter, releases a little tension as Marguerite retreats, sickly, sad and somewhat envious.

Domingos eyes me suspiciously yet he cannot bring himself to banish me from the home. We are bound together now having sipped from the wound of a woman who thinks she is fruit. We know the weight of shame that lines our fingertips.

In the distance, the vanished island limps, gathers, breaks.

Inside our pantry, a smattering of snow winds through a deer's lung, dew covers hare heart, veins criss-cross over liver. I cook them into silence, clattering copper, clay and metal utensils in my wake. The between space Oni created throbs. I teach Sueli a new song. Kin shriek, What of marrow as weapon, as memory, as awakening?

A merchant from Zanzibar arrives. He sets up shop in the town centre selling fine silks and delicate wares to women whose hands know hardship season after season who make breathy declarations about using the materials for special occasions. And later, standing before mirrors, press soft ripples of cloth against their bodies while their husbands work the land and mine the sea. Rowena takes me there for a visit, her features animated with joy, her violet skirt swishing between the different hues of material, pulling me along with tales of Gethsemane's inhabitants. On this occasion, she smells of orange blossom. I taste it on my tongue. When she selects four fabrics to purchase, coins jangling in her cloth purse, the mass above her collarbone turns inside my mouth in a fated dalliance.

Paolo tells Domingos of bringing his mother to stay to watch over Ezadaro in his absences. She welcomes the company, he says. She talks about the man with wounds inside him, of seeing him doubled over in pain. She leaves her pips in a cracked white bowl out by the livestock. They circle, sniffing it warily. Paolo confides his relief at having someone else share his burden, his weariness holding a woman he no longer knows well enough, his guilt longing for happier moments from their past because her unpredictability has made everything uncertain. And an uncertain man is an unhappy one. He confesses an intimate detail: he kisses the scar on her right side in a small act of love with the moon swelling above, buoyed by his tenderness. Her scar is often restless. He follows it through their homestead in the dark. She turns in their bed at his movements. Bulbs of moonshine emerge at the corners of their home, a lonely visitor come to call, the man with multiple wounds inside him, a deep purple marrow berry swirling in his mouth. He is kin from the future, glimmering brightly to collect the pips in the bowl outside that turn sweet before depleting in his wounds. The white bone scaling the town's rooftops lands on their roof.

The day Paolo catches an octopus, he and Domingos are playthings for the elements in the small boat rocking unsteadily. The wind howls, tossing them. The pull on their nets is a comfort along with the murmurs of the shore. The octopus is pink, large, curling in his net among flashes of silver. A feeling of sickness bubbles in Paolo's stomach. He does not sell the octopus in town. He takes it home instead, holds it up to their kitchen ceiling as though it is a sea star that cannot be contained, even in his hold; pink, glistening and slick from the undercurrents. The sick feeling rises. He splits the octopus using his sharpest knife. A soft breath leaves him. Nestled inside is a familiar scar. Ezadaro's scar. He knows its line, its curve in the middle, its ridges at the edges. He starts to cry, running a finger over it repeatedly in shock.

It is a bright day when Sueli and I head for the caves to gather wild mushrooms. The warm air is soothing, the light gentle on our bodies. A lilac-breasted roller bird streaks above us. Ferns scatter in our path between the crunching of stones and the small rumblings under our feet. Our dresses billow, no match for the codes of the between, Oni's blue tent, for kin slipping their fingers inside folds of cloth to reach the beating wings within us. Homesteads dotted around the mountains look small, dazed and inadequate, unprepared for the excavations to come. Sueli plucks a sprig of nettle from a fence we pass. She raises it to me, her hood slipping down just as a smile breaks. 'For you!' she squeals. 'Will you hold me a little on nights when I cannot sleep like those other women?'

I pause. My heartbeat quickens. A humming explodes in my temples. My mouth dries. Like those other women. *'This is a rare gift!' I say dramatically, waving the nettle in the air. 'It is a prize for queens,' I continue, ignoring its roughness on my skin, exaggerating my expression to distract her. She laughs, darting ahead, the swoosh of her dress a faint interjection.*

The caves are damp and hollow. A crack of light winds through the ceiling. Sueli spins below it, muttering. The mushrooms growing along the base of the caves are soft declarations on rock. We slip them into small pouches, backs arched, hands wielding a lightness of touch, our breaths in tandem. The symbols from Sueli's room decorate parts of the walls; some shaped like small trees, others as golden arches. Like those other women. *I chew on this new knowledge. A handful of mushrooms are bulbous in my hold. I blink as if they will become charred cinders in an instant. Below us, the waters crash. The driftwood shrines shudder, moss spreads. The taste of smoke fills my mouth. I close my eyes, picturing Sueli being carried to the shrines on restless nights, gathering language for a tongue that no longer belongs to her alone.*

    Entwined curandera seek
    Burning apparition
    Ink doused tip
    Corrugated edge
    Curved silence
    Pocket of atomic flights
    Throbbing core
    This nebulous labyrinth
    This modern wound
    What of the weight
    Of small desires
    When two bodies move towards
    Them?

Chapter 7

Emilien arrived home at dawn; he thought of first light in Huacachina, Peru, where he was born. A time which meant the shadows of the night had retreated, taking their secrets to make room for the day's occurrences. The taste of smoke sat heavily in his mouth, his left arm ached, his shoes were soaked through, his feet still bore the cold of cave water. His eyes swam from the riotous colours of visions, hallucinatory gateways fragmenting between heartbeats, a soft line of earth crumbling in his chest, a scream that dwindled in his eardrums before ricocheting in that mountainous land. Gethsemane's wind raged in his ears. There were tingles in his hands which would wear off soon. He took a breath, the weight of the keys jangling in his pocket some comfort, the outlines of a past dusk bending to embrace him again.

He opened the front door, careful not to disturb the house in these quiet hours. Removing his boots, torn striped socks, he peeled his jacket off. He set it on the dresser filled with letters, the odd bit of reading material, correspondence from *The Botanical Society of Britain & Ireland* addressed to Therese, an issue of *National Geographic* for Finn, a postcard from Port-au-Prince for Azacca, some coloured pencils he ordered two weeks back. He ran his fingers over it sighing, a furtive expression on his face. He'd settled in London because of Therese. The pull they had towards each other was undeniable, but lately that old restlessness had reared its head inside him like traps trying to catch a floating prey. He spotted the trail of headless origami gulls leading to the basement where Ovida resided in the tank. The gulls were eerily static. A throbbing in his temples began. A flash of annoyance crossed his eyes. The gulls' bodies were singed in sporadic patterns as though from a burning hand. Had he accidentally let a childhood memory slip during a drunken night in the basement? Recently, the group couldn't tell who was doing what to whom, despite keeping secrets for each other. They were feverish in their actions. And couldn't stop eating Ovida's fruit, sweet, succulent and mysterious. It was affecting them.

He'd heard Finn slip into the basement on several nights; he could only assume what he was up to, hearing his careful movements rise through the floorboards. He pictured him lying on the basement sofa, drinking whisky while sharing expedition tales with Ovida's beating centre or touching the moist green of the downy moss, the bright tadpole-like creatures breaking and reforming, still climbing its waterfall. In a dream, he'd seen Azacca soak a handful of luminous peacock feathers in the tank, eyes closed, murmuring frenetically, his mouth loaded with stems spilling pink marrow. He knew Therese had been feeding from Ovida too in odd cycles. She started it all.

The origami gulls were light in his arms, but he carried

them wearily to the kitchen. He dropped them on the countertop before flicking the light switch on. The whirr of the fridge greeted him along with a squirrel holding a piece of bread in the windowsill, watching him with a startled expression, as if he'd broken into his own home, before it scampered away. He closed his eyes, listening for the weeping of Finn's internal injuries. They all heard it often, at the most unexpected times. He wondered how Finn coped, apart from numbing himself with alcohol or sex, being increasingly drawn to more dangerous expeditions. He opened the sink's cold tap, ducked his head under it for cool relief, washing the imprints of the night away. Ovida's marrow grapes were trickling alien memories into them of a faraway sun-stroked land where the mountains' silhouettes glimmered with secrets. He opened the fridge, spotted a cellophane-covered plate of macaroni cheese, a partially drunk bottle of Supermalt, two slices of caramel-glazed Madeira cake. He took a bite, removing the ashy taste from his mouth, washing it down with the rich malt drink. Afterwards, he splashed cold water over his bloodshot right eye again, irritated from his travels to the cave in the burnished mountainland Gethsemane. The memory of being there at the forefront of his mind; the circular signs engraved on its walls golden, intricate, trailing into the water shimmering below like a small azure colony. Balanced on a frequency between past and present only those who had the gift could reach. He'd noticed his irritated eye on his return walking through the streets, tired and hungry, the sleeves of his black windbreaker sullied as he paused to check his stinging iris in a Vauxhall Nova side mirror. At that hour, after 3 a.m., his hazy reflection looked distorted by his body's flight into a passage of time, the mirror capturing the memory of his weary face, momentarily engraved in glass while a band of foxes surrounded him, hypnotised by the muted orchestral rhythms of his limbs.

He remembered then that his carrier, his grandfather Papa Molindau, ostracised by his mother, had often wandered around their small Peruvian town with one eye bloodshot from the things he'd seen, sometimes the left eye, occasionally the right. Papa Molindau who was of legend status when Emilien was a boy, who people had claimed to see walking across lakes carrying his own head on his back as if it were his only trusted companion, or howling in trees dressed in frayed women's costumes he'd said a knowing wind had brought him, or appearing at weddings uninvited, offering the brides gifts he announced they needed to insert inside them to see what the future would bring. Emilien sighed, knocking the empty Supermalt bottle against his thigh, a nervous habit, leaning further against the island. Some things were inherited. He knew Papa Molindau had passed his restlessness to him, that curiosity to see with the whole body. He raised the bottle up in a toast.

'Ah querida,' he murmured as the night's haze of secrets slipped into the bottle. 'Show me what you know about chasing the absence of a shadow.'

By the time he was twelve, Emilien had amassed several near-death experiences. How and why these occurrences happened remained a mystery to his unconcerned parents, who'd set their hearts on a simple life toiling the land as farmers. And in the wild plains where they lived, the community speculated that Papa Molindau's bloodline had struck again, a double-edged inheritance which blessed and cursed. As a child, Emilien felt he'd experienced a great loss in his early life but he had no recollection of it, only a deep ache he carried with him and the sense of that loss permeating the household in his father's forlorn, heavy movements around the farm, his mother's silences at evening meals, the guilty expressions he caught sometimes on their faces when they watched him, his futile attempts at gaining their love by doing chores, working hard on the farm. This great absence dogged him. He didn't know when it began or how it grew, but it did. It became a void which mimicked the shapes of his parents' silhouettes, following him around the farm, taunting him. Some mornings, he woke up crying. He knew there was a power, a wisdom within him possessing its own dialect, but nobody talked about it, no one in the household told him anything. His body started moving towards perilous situations; on one occasion, he sat in his father's weathered yellow tractor in a trance as it malfunctioned, stuttering over the soil and careening towards the fence, its jaws opening and closing ominously like a mechanical Venus flytrap. On another, he'd woken up with the sounds of wild horses which crossed the harsher outlands in his chest. He'd followed that sound, determined to insert himself into their run. In a separate occurrence, spurned on by other boys in a dare, he'd played with mad dogs on the Casa Rivera estate, at first snarling and lunging at him before becoming accustomed to his calm movements, his steadfast, knowing gaze. Perhaps these incidents were a cry for attention; maybe they were clues to a memory that had eluded him.

The first time he met his grandfather, he'd pulled Emilien from a neighbour's burning barn after he'd accidentally fallen asleep in a stall. Papa Molindau had lifted him clean off the ground as though bearing the strength of several men. There were three feathers in the air spilling fire from their tips. Then the feathers fluttered in the margins as charlatans of destruction. The flames danced, spreading quickly. Papa Molindau had appeared through the smoky mist as if he already knew its every twist, line and direction. He spoke to the feathers' tips in a soft incantation, crying out to Oni, the god he called on. There were painted red markings on his face. His long, white hair was stark against his brown skin, his body wiry, his hands rough from a life lived out in the plains. Emilien didn't panic. He recognised him from the old photographs his mother stashed in a small tin box kept on the back shelf of a rickety closet in his parents' bedroom. The fine-boned face was older, the hair a different colour from its original dark hue, the eyes still a molten, golden brown. In one picture, his hair was shorn; he was dressed in a white robe holding what looked like a pale bone in his left hand, curved at the tip. His right arm was thrown over his daughter's shoulder; her expression was one of resignation and irritation. Emilien coughed as he was lifted out of the barn. It was him. Papa Molindau. The one who congregated with lost souls in the spirit land, who spoke the mother tongues of ancient civilisations in broad daylight, who crossed the waters touching the lives of the drowned, seeing with his whole body.

Papa Molindau carried him home. Along the way, he muttered things Emilien couldn't understand while the smoke swirled inside them, telling its unfinished tales of entrapment and destruction from an ancient land. The winding route of the forest expanded in the haze while a distant afternoon was studded with death traps. And the next morning, he woke to the memory of Papa Molindau's arms carrying him, steadying him, an act of love and rescue which struck a chord in him. And his grandfather speaking urgently about ways of rebirth to Oni like some strange, feverish vision spawned from the trunks of trees. He asked him why the three feathers had started a fire to consume things but his grandfather didn't answer. Later, his mother, Esmeralda, warned him against seeing Papa Milindau.

'Stay away from that man, you hear me?' she instructed in the kitchen, scowling, grabbing his shoulders. 'Or I'll show you the back of my hand, you understand?'

He shook his head, rubbing at scratches on his neck that he hadn't noticed before which criss-crossed over the crescent-shaped birthmark, stinging. Slowly, he raised his gaze. 'He came out of nowhere, Mama. It's like he knew I needed him. Something in the air changed when he appeared, I could feel it. You look like him, you know?' In his eyeline, the photo from the tin box floated in the cracks. The wear and tear at the edges expanded over a gathering of bodies and silences. Esmeralda began to laugh, gently at first then almost maniacally.

'All my life,' she spluttered, 'I have tried not to look like or be anything like that man. We do not choose the family that we're given.' The pinched expression on her face remained as she turned her back, searching through the cupboards, clattering pots and pans that wouldn't break in her fingers. Even then, he sensed a contained fury from her, a feeling of being betrayed, although he couldn't yet understand why. Not only did he survive the barn fire but he'd bonded with Papa Molindau. They were now tied, inextricably, his grandfather, him and Oni, whether his mother liked it or not.

He headed up to his room, leaving the singed paper gulls to their secrets. While undressing, his limbs were still heavy. He climbed into bed, watching the wicker chair as if hauntings from the past would manifest there. The window was open, so the room was cool. And somebody had been rifling through his sketchpad. It was open on the dresser, on the page of a headless girl doubling as a gateway. He sank into bed. His head swam with a memory. Of course, Papa Molindau had come to him again. The next time, audaciously, in his room at the farm, his white hair tied into a bun, his face serene, his right hand stretched out in an offering, his eyes glimmering with wisdom. 'I want to show you something,' he'd said calmly. Hypnotised, Emilien had placed his hand in his. An orange-coloured, leaf-like entity crackled under Papa Molindau's tongue. Everything else receded. A secret world beckoned. Dusk opened its arms to embrace them. And the white feathers Oni sent from Gethsemane trembled again in the margins.

Finn parked the car in front of the house, narrowly missing a scavenging fox appearing from nowhere, its electric gaze challenging the headlights, knocking over a Desperados beer bottle before vanishing into the hedge on the opposite side. He set the gear stick into neutral, the engine hummed. Its brown seats bore a leathery smell. An *A–Z* map rested on the front passenger seat placed the wrong way up. A silver clock lay in the far-left corner of the back seat, a battery-powered architect denied its negotiations of time. The car smelled of cigarettes and gin. As if a mercy had occurred, a consumption of vices after Finn's body had wept behind the wheel, his internal injuries screaming, threatening to escape beyond their confines of bloody matter. He gripped the wheel, his hands turning whiter with impatience. The throbbing in his temples intensified. He didn't feel the pain in Gethsemane, taking the pips that woman who thought she was a new kind of fruit had left out for him, who bore his injury. The group needed to get to the third plane, Oni's new world.

He honked the horn when they emerged, a trio of travellers; Azacca and Emilien trailing behind Therese, who held an ancient aquamarine vial containing a concoction of peyote mixed with the juice from Ovida's berries. She was always fine-tuning their liquid gateways, transitions to be entered, recovering their bodies in new forms each time.

They piled into the car, talking over each other. 'You sure this is a good spot?' Azacca asked, settling into the back seat, shoving the clock out of the way, his chest, bereft of his heart, aching.

'I vomited earlier, querida,' Emilien said, slipping his seatbelt on, rolling the window down, his breath misting the glass.

'Just drive,' Therese instructed, placing the back of her hand against the erratic fluttering in Finn's temple, watching as though a wound would shoot right out of him into the rear-view mirror, splintering into inebriated creatures in a dalliance with glass. They sped off, exhaust fumes shrouding their flight-ravaged bodies. Silent cars with misted windscreens were witnesses heading towards invisible precipices. The trees and shrubs shook gently, crying to future traffic to come. The air was cool on their skin. They sipped from the vial. Liquid peyote warm in their throats with a hint of sweetness, simmering on parched tongues, heightening the sense of anticipation. The feeling of transcending slowly infiltrated their blood. Ecstasy leaked inside them, fragmented memories of Gethsemane growing. The night retracted from their fingerprints before spasming.

Finn's hands relaxed on the wheel; his colour was returning. His green eyes were glazed. His checked shirt's collar was damp with sweat. Emilien began to chant, softly at first, like a lover's caress released between them. Azacca, having fasted for two days, gently pounded his chest, opening up a channel.

'Bone as talisman,' he muttered, while an ancient pale bone trembled in his mind's eye like a thunder, spilling pink marrow into his vision as though it was new-found land. The left side of his face was pressed against the window ready to ebb away through glass in collusion with memory and marrow to find new talismans in the warm crevices of Gethsemane's mountains. Therese heard the voices of the women from Jeronimo Dorsey's recording building in her eardrums, rising like a thrashing tide she could enter. Those cries rustled through the trees, spilled from the mouth of a golden goshawk that travelled through time to shadow them, emanating from the flap of a blue tent on the periphery bearing the fingerprints of their shaman god Oni. And the shards of stained glass in the mouths of amorphous ancient hounds dispatched as warnings. She undid her seatbelt, arched her back, stretched her arms wide, closing her eyes. The windscreen trembled. Her body edged forward. The night spasmed again.

They drove for three hours to Pontypridd. Awaiting them was a darkened woodland replete with shadows, a hushed space anticipating their quiet invasion. Every location for their ritual was different, each point of entry to the other planes its own mercurial gateway for bodies in transition to slip through. Finn led the way, having scouted it weeks back, approving of its off-the-beaten-track feel. They sensed their hearts pounding in the ground, conversations with the bloom and decay of nature, their heartbeats were small bombs ticking between leaves, pale signs, damp wooded gates with moss spots glimmering. They passed a small, golden plaque on one wall commemorating a nature reservist who had departed this world, a statue of an ogre that had lost its mouth. Misshapen trails of conkers scattered in every direction. They chanted, wandering deep into the woods; the spill of Ovida's wild marrow berries on their tongues punctuated their movements. Intermingled scents of wildflowers, plants from multiple planes filled their nostrils. The circumference of soft points of earth called to them. The axis had moved again. Golden circles hovered within the circle, symbols that had manifested through breath, claw and umbilical cord.

They formed a ring by the axis where the trees watched from a great height. Their chanting intensified; the speaking of kin's tongues filled the air. Finn's injuries shrieked. Azacca's chest was contorted. Emilien's irises gleamed. His hands went limp. Therese's head was flung back, her fingers danced against multiplied circadian rhythms. The air became thicker. A splinter of static shot through their brains. The woodlands contracted. The temperatures of their bodies increased. A thundering occurred in their blood. The distant ancestral cries of carriers echoed. Liquid ecstasy was spreading through them. Their tongues darted out, quivering with Gethsemane's secrets and sights. A dense blue light emerged from the heavens, bathing their limbs, light so blue as to be the hue of a Tahitian wave meeting the skyline. Shapes appeared inside them, twisted, pressing against their skin, rippling sporadically. The power and feeling of invincibility was intense, addictive. They hovered off the ground. Their expressions were of wild, contorted faces leaving one realm. Architects of change and rebirth, they catapulted through the blue vaults of light, crashing past a ceiling of stars. The static sparked. Their tongues swelled from the collision of languages. The axis realigned. Those shapes within them screamed, incandescent, begging to be released.

They arrived in the other realm to find the valleys bathed in sunlight, warm air potent with new bloom and a sense of discovery. The ground undulated. Golden blades of grass bent under their feet. The aqua-coloured sky shifted slowly, stretching endlessly, turning over bits of scattered windscreen glass. Pockets of bees had short silver lines shooting between them in an electric dance. Bulbs of plant life were covered in iridescent dew. The rivers and creeks glimmered, humming a watery welcome. The sun was fractured, blindingly bright but barely circular. A procession of water bulls with heads made of congealed blood vessels crossed their eyeline, walking on air towards a tree of tongues on the opposite end.

Finn reached out to grab one, to know its movements, but just missed its leg. Therese threw her arms out to embrace the wonder of it all. Emilien moved gingerly between patches from gnarled gum trees which doubled as windows reflecting other planes. Azacca's breath caught at the magisterial headless gulls assembling and reconfiguring into other entities in the skyline. Valleys dispatched orange orbs with runny centres that were scenes of Gethsemane's lives thinning into rivulets as the orbs cooed above them in recognition. A group of one-winged ducks sporting bloodshot eyes as though they were drunken antennae flew at Emilien, squawking so loudly it prompted shadows attached to each other in bundles of threes to move from their hiding places. The frequency throbbed. The shapes inside them strained against their skin. They ran through the demented paradise, absorbing it all, making each new encounter with hybrid seemingly impossible, creatures indelible in their brains. Their hearts pounded in excitement. Their nerve endings wailed. Rhythms in their temples sped up. Their moist tongues darted out before curling in anticipation, touching the flights of ancestral carriers.

The group were incubators, carriers building a new utopia in this realm. The sound of a thousand births splintered in their eardrums. Pale axis lines unfurled in their peripheral vision. They smelled the sly strands of smoke from the three white feathers of Gethsemane, the drops of rain due before they would arrive, a young girl's carcass on one valley the orange orbs circled frenetically. Therese, standing by a creek with the light dancing on it, felt her stomach burst. Pink octopuses with scars inside them shaped like ridges limped out of her entrails, hopping at her feet before trailing into the water, while her mouth murmured softly in pleasure. Finn sat against a large, bulbous rock surrounded by black mushrooms, his breaths ragged. The injuries inside him escaped. Of course, new ones would sprout within him again but for now, these injuries became chameleons bearing mouths lined with gin, the varied greens of their rough skin rippling as they floated away. Finn reached out feebly, mesmerised by what came from his body. They all chanted Oni's name in praise repeatedly, merely architects for her visions and desires. On the north side, Azacca was crouched over four empty nests that had been waiting for him. His throat bulged as peacock heads with his mother's eyes sprouted through the skin, landing on the nests while he roared. The peacock heads shook. Their eyes reflected the gleam of the blade which had severed their throats.

Emilien kneeled before the young girl's carcass protruding from one valley, worshipping its erosion, its innards a blueprint on the passing of time. His hands became long roots shedding its lines into the carcass, which absorbed it like food. It's body spasmed as though a breath had run through it. He stuck his arms into it, moaning in ecstasy. The symphony of their hatchings rumbled through the plane. The air was charged with the language of birth and creation, of bodies unbridled, unrestrained, unmoored in this twisted utopia.

Therese crossed the path leading from the water to the back entrance of one valley. Along the way, she passed large, mercurial cacti dotted around like gatekeepers marking the looming incline, a series of chasms leaking nectar that smelled so sweet and forbidden she wanted to dip her tongue into it, a wall of drooping women's faces exchanging mother tongues, a line of golden moths circling her head before swooping away like utopia's boomerang. Everything felt connected, every element a reverberation within her, every echo a new, limbless disciple. She made her way into the enclave, the soft crumbling of earth warm in her fingers as she hoisted herself up. Drops of dew were cool on her forehead. She took a breath, having followed her body's intuition. Sure enough, there they were: clusters of wild peyote, globular, spineless, strange entities growing in the cracks. Hunting for wild peyote on the planes had become a ritual for her, euphoria seeping into every cell, gateways allowing them to travel, procreate and see the impossible. She edged closer, reaching for those hallucinogenic globes, feverishly rummaging for their seeds as passageways.

When the group arrived home, the house shuddered from the static of their bodies. Finn recognised the familiar soreness of new injuries growing inside him; the underside of his tongue wielded the bright green of a lost chameleon. Azacca felt separated from his body, lightheaded, his throat sore while he mumbled one dialect from the wall of women's faces, tremors of pain filling him from his lost heart that Oni hadn't returned. Emilien couldn't feel his hands, they smacked limply against thighs covered in dragonfly wings. The residue of the other plane was imprinted on their bodies, in the air. And another still, Gethsemane's living archives catapulting towards them. Therese felt the woman from the distant land was closer: an ache winding its way through her stomach, their intermingled hunger, the denseness of echoes expanding in her eardrums, the woman's intensity of movement in her dreams.

The basement door had been left ajar. They stumbled down, needing Ovida's fruit to replenish. Ovida was out of the tank, hovering above the glass cubicle. An unmooring had spilled over into this realm.

Breakings on Ovida's bone were healing. They flanked the tank, one on each side, two at the front to contain it. Ovida had travelled too, but where had it come back from and what memories did it harbour now? Therese plucked two berries from the ribcage; slipping them under her tongue, she left the men and headed to her bedroom dazed. While enjoying the sweetness of the berries, a name filled her mouth under the soft glow of lamplight that took on the burnished hue of Gethsemane, her mouth flooded with the fullness of the name spilled from fruit blazing inside it.

Zulmira.

As though it had slipped through the thin, bruised purple skin of fruit into its new awakening, blooming on her tongue. *Zulmira.* She turned the name over in the darkening underside of her mouth. Instinctively knowing this was the woman whose spirit and desires were growing inside her, whose flickering face felt like a reflection. Pins and needles spread through the right side of her body as a static.

And in Gethsemane, Zulmira's marrow plants began to sprout purple and red berries like small awakenings glinting in the folds of dawn.

Eight

On the night the thunders come, a distant wind reveals its secrets to the pale horn travelling across the rooftops of Gethsemane. Moonshine seeps into the hooves of animals, marrow weeps against plant root, crown refashions into a woman's face doused in exotic scents in the half-light. Pockets breathe against skin. Sueli traces the circular patterns from the cave walls in her sleep. And the clay heart turns in the soil, cracked from borrowing my hunger as inheritance. Domingos disappears again, wandering the wilds of the land, an occurrence that never ceases to worry Marguerite, who fiddles restlessly to keep her hands busy to stave away bad thoughts leaking into the homestead's charged atmosphere, where unruly things grow in the dark.

'You would understand my fears,' she says one day, standing in their bed-chamber doorway, shoulders rising defensively, face tightening, mouth quivering, 'if you were in my position, although you do not strike me as a woman who has ever had a husband. You are too spirited, too wilful, but I can see you understand the ways of men, their needs and desires. This illness has ravaged parts of me, areas he used to know. I fear he seeks those comforts elsewhere.'

'I have not had the need for a husband this time,' I say, hearing the shudder of the mountains, kin breathing over the bone hidden in my wall, the shape of their petticoats swishing above the garden's vegetation, the hum of bees on the split pink melon acting as a trap, the breathing of foreign footprints on the pantry floor. 'The ways of men are many and deceptive. Do not get yourself into knots examining them,' I tell her. I listen, braid her hair, pressing my fingers into her skull like a newborn in my hands. I do not comfort nor persuade. I watch her shoulders steady, the smooth skin of her throat, the incline of her neck in my hold. I savour the trust of it. Her sickness is spreading inside her. Her time as mother and wife is waning. The homestead knows it. It is written in the air our bodies consume. When a man cannot name the illness that ails his wife, he becomes restless, frustrated, seeking answers beyond the valley they built with their bare hands.

'He will return,' I add, holding her head gently, blinking against a sudden desire to mount it on a wall made of kin's shadows. Of course he would come back, even if he is part thunder, rumbling in our rooms with new truths in his mouth, he would return to the three of us.

I set off at first light with Rowena the following day to mine the sea for its seaweeds – or kelp, as it is also known in these parts by some of the town's women who harvest it for various uses. The call for me came several days earlier, through a woman named Hiyasi who helps run one of the local shebeens. Kelp hunting is an activity the braver women of the town do, away from the eyes of their men, who pretend the weeds simply wash up on the shores overnight. Harvesting kelp for its benefits has been happening in Gethsemane for many moons. It takes me away *from the sadness in our homestead, the gnarly guilt about Baby, the invasive sly infiltrations of kin. The homestead is a carcass without Domingos's presence.*

Rowena and I meet the six women at Piranu Point, tucked behind Noma Mountain, where a few goshawks gather, streaking above our heads, squawking as we make our way down to the beach, light guiding bodies eager to embrace the day's adventures. The sky is subdued in the absence of thunder. A fangled creature limps on the shoreline, bearing the injuries of weather before leaving my eyeline. Murmurs of the sea reach sand, stone and rocks, its liquid hatchings keen to burrow in the morning.

We hunt for green and red kelp. The waters are cold against our dark skin. We swim like rare butterflies given ocean wings, holding our breaths. The seaweed undulates, curling between strokes, the water's entrails in our fingers. Red kelp gleams like blood plants, iridescent. Pliable. A piece of flight caught in the hand.

We pluck, gather and uproot streams of it. As we break the surface of water to get our breaths back, I see kin in the skyline, wearing dresses made of seaweed, dripping rivulets to make rain above, wielding the cries of Baby as cruel echoes above my head. My body trembles, the breath leaves me momentarily, a pain throbs in my womb. The women cannot sense my quiet dismay.

I am swimming under, deep in the belly of the sea, when I feel something tugging sharply at my feet. My legs feel entangled within a bloody tide. A splintered pain fills my head and chest. I kick furiously, looking behind me. The currents of rough waters make it difficult to see clearly but I am sure I spot Rowena tugging me down further, her face twisted in the current, body agile in the vortex of water threatening to suck us both into recalibrations.

It feels as though we are entangled in a fight to the death, that she is the architect of this battle. I pull away with every ounce of strength, kicking determinedly upwards towards the perilous ceiling of water. After we break the surface, Rowena's voice is full of concern. 'Are you okay? Your feet got caught underwater, I tried to untangle you.'

I nod, breathless and alert.

We place long lines of weeds on large rocks, examining our batches before the men arrive. Our fingers are numb from cold ripples, hands temporarily infected by the shiver and unpredictable exits of disturbed sea urchins. The weeds, slick, damp and furrowed, are alien-like creatures shorn from water, patiently breathing on the rocks waiting to be swallowed into crevices within nature's formations. These women who know the pain and sacrifice of toiling the land seek in the sea, the body's incantations uttered as ritual, comfort, a way to break bread with themselves. I keep my ears open, watching carefully. They are unguarded before a stranger's eyes. The steady pulse in their temples a sign of bodies in comfort around each other, familiarity, community. Sharp pangs of longing hit my chest. My tongue curls, releasing the memory of travelling with kin; being, re-forming and then being again. When you have abandoned your child to fulfil a destiny, what is the weight of breaking away from the pack?

Oni chatters in kin's ears. And they in turn whisper in me to heart, to lung, to loins; asking for barbed desires to grow. The women's talk seeps into the distance. They wait for their mottled skin to calm, squeeze water from their hair, adjust wet garments, roll sleeves up. Rowena shares a joke about the town cobbler who keeps losing tools walking in his sleep. 'Perhaps you can help him?' they sing teasingly at her, offering suggestions that cause their mouths to curve in amusement.

I laugh softly at their veneer of camaraderie; the internal bruising they cannot see coming. A swarm of ravens appear from the swell of the mountains, circling us, wanting to feed from our hands before swooping towards the lure of the sea. We gather the kelp from the rocks, new again in our fingers. Rowena beside me, fatigue in her tense shoulders. She flashes a subdued smile. The cold air intensifies; we walk towards cloth bags on the sand, like sunken, collapsed mouths waiting to be filled. We sit by them. The women exchange more stories of the town's inhabitants, gesturing dramatically when the tales call for it.

'You must come for Montero,' Delphina announces brightly, eyes sparkling with warmth. 'Should she not, Rowena?'

'What is it?' I ask, stuffing two violet seashells into my bag. They are rough in my fingers, leaving traces of sand, carrying sounds of the shore.

'It is the night of the half-moon where we exchange meals and drink with our neighbours,' she explains. 'You should attend, Zulmira! Domingos has spoken highly of your soups. They are unusual, he tells me.'

Rowena busies herself with her pouch, stuffing glinting cowrie shells inside it.

I flush with pleasure. He carries my name in his mouth, spreads it among his folk. I am in the blood, under the tongue, slipping through the veins.

'You will be entertained!' another woman called Selina encourages, drawing her bag to her as it flutters. 'Memorable things happen during Montero. Once my husband claimed his own *reflection tried to drown him. I said it was too much drink playing tricks on him, even without these gatherings as an excuse!'*

'Let us exchange husbands,' Hiyasi jokes. 'I would slip the coins from his pockets, claiming they were lost on half-moon night.'

Rowena throws her head back laughing, her bosom full and bouncing. Today she smells of a lingering jasmine scent that even seawater does not fully wash away.

I smile at their ease, their openness, the presumption that a stranger wants to know their ways, to be a force for good in the community.

These people.

They have let me in.

They know not what they do.

Our bags are fit to burst with kelp each will mine in a different way.

Rowena plans to sun-dry her batch, sell it on her stall as a natural condiment.

Hiyasi will use it to make candles, soaps and shampoos that she will sell in the town's main shopping strip. For Delphine, it will be a dying agent on lighter clothing during the summer season. Selina, who runs one of the shebeens, will make beer foam from it. Another woman will feed her livestock with it. For another still, it will be fertiliser in her land. I will draw on its properties to make natural medicines, cook healing broths. It will act as a stimulant for my wild marrow plants outgrowing their potion bottles.

For Montero, preparations start days before, they tell me. The goat and lamb meat is soaked in variations of herbal juices plus cumin, crushed juniper berries, woodsmoked Malagueta chillies. Dorade fish is sliced then stuffed with yellow onions, wild sweet peppers and bay leaves. The hog portions are glazed with honey, sesame oil and butternut squash juice. Mussels are slow cooked then served with a garlic sauce. Strings of red onion, fennel and amaranth are wrapped around sticks of sweet bamboo, steamed so the scent escapes through doorways, out into the open where the livestock become restless, sniffing appreciatively. The wine, like the ones produced on Fogo Island's volcanic soil, is made from grapes crushed beneath the naked feet of women in large, wooden drums with holes. Laughing and exchanging gossip while they raise their skirts above bare ankles where a gentle breeze caresses their skin. More women partake in the ritual pulverising of corn in a big ceremonial mortar, wielding pestles, pounding the corn accompanied by singing and drumming. There is plenty of Grogue, a heady drink distilled from sugar cane mixed with molasses, cloves and citrus fruits. Warm hibiscus juice is also copiously consumed. Fried capers are served with freshly made bread. And on the evening itself, the women light juniper-scented candles to conjure smoke-lined dreams, wear their fine dresses, dab their throats using musk from vanilla pods.

The men soften their hands with shea tree nut oil to stroke their wives more tenderly when the night ends. As the evening begins, people all over Gethsemane carry platters of food for their neighbours across the mountains' misted spines.

It is a tradition of Montero for folk to leave gifts in trees as a way of bringing good fortune to another's life. And so they place the offerings in the ones they come upon, tying ribbons to the branches, fold strips of silk in hollows, pin notes of undeclared *love to weathered trunks. And sling the downy coat of antelope fur over a bird's nest. Sometimes, they say, a strange light floods those trees, a red golden hue. Light from a cross between a dawn and a sunset illuminating branches, spilling treasures like rare sightings.*

The women and I part ways. I cut through a path into Sipu Mountain, walking down as the morning continues to be loaded with promise, thinking of Rowena's hands pulling me underwater, her cowrie shells jangling in my eardrums, the scent of jasmine becoming a cloud over a woman's face. Small shrubs sing with movement as I pass. Pebbles rumble under my feet, cast from the shores by curious hands. The violet shells rustle amid the kelp while my bag drips, their bodies ridged, hollow, spilling the murmurs of underwater colonies. I tighten my grip on the bag. My bounty glistens. It hums with the possibility of transformations beneath my fingers. Moss, crevices, rock formations, the mountains' lines are coated in dew, warm to the touch, giving Gethsemane a luminous quality. Figures dotted around are small miracles from the changeable earth, heading towards whatever awaits them. I press my palms against their hidden depths, gaining power from it. A family of sunbirds shrouded in black smoke fly above, wielding bodies flickering from a vanishing island. I think of Domingos filled with thunderous roars, searching for guidance from the land. I think of him turning his back on himself once upon a time. Tears sprout from the corners of my eyes. I push down the feeling of mourning in my blood. Rage fills my body; jagged, rough, multi-headed and ferocious.

The pale horn on rooftops swells, splintering at the edges as I whisper. My throat fills with stony manifestations of doom.

Arriving at our dwelling, the homestead is forlorn, etched against a backdrop of tumultuous weather. A lilac cloth ripples at the entrance like a celestial entity. The rooms feel bereft, excavated of laughter and life. A nettle shrivels in the pantry. Juice of berries stain blades. Kin's treacherous belongings clatter in the void. The pale horn on a rooftop somewhere in Gethsemane leaks droplets of the mountains' secret nectar. Marguerite reaches into a cut for a blood jewel.

Sueli is away from her bed. Marguerite the fading mother clings to her ramshackle crown, howling into the faces of kin invading it.

Chapter 8

The venue, Sarabelium, was tucked behind two railway arches in Deptford, where a strip of other buildings stood, an enclave of south London subject to regeneration, upwards mobility with an artsy edge. It was a combination of workshop spaces, bars, galleries and restaurants. By the time Azacca arrived, the two black security guards with matching dark bomber jackets, earpieces, yellow armbands and fluctuating cynical expressions were debating the merits and cons of AI. A distressed, gaunt, flame-haired woman who'd spilled something on the skirt of her silver dress was talking tersely into a mobile phone. A dishevelled homeless man sitting on a doorstep mumbled into an empty Jack Daniel's bottle, glancing around nervously. The skyline had smatterings of gold, a cartography of travellers leaving their imprints as they passed.

Guitar case strapped to his back, Azacca nodded at both men manning the door. 'Yes, boss,' he said casually, offering his wrist for the stamp that would follow after they searched him. A trace of his Haitian accent lingered. It got stronger when he was angry or in situations of emotional distress. He swept past them into the packed bar and seating area. The din rose, a sea of sound luring him in. Heat enveloped him. Glasses clinked at the bar where three staff – two men and a woman – were poised like alchemists filling byzantine-style tumblers and cocktail glasses with curious concoctions. He blinked. Food in the display unit became rows of hearts, alcohol infused into a catatonic state, beating against the glass. There were bodies everywhere – slouched at the bar, leaning against the walls, standing on one rouge chair of a couch, angled over small plates of samosas, jerk pork, risotto, gathered on the tables – compact, buzzing colonies waiting to be dissipated by the rhythms of music. Azacca wound his way through, sucking on a pip, tiny and sweet in his ravenous mouth. Lately, he'd been eating the marrow berries from Ovida's ribcage before gigs. He knew the others were doing the same. *Berries. Ribcage. Sustenance. Travel.* He ran his tongue over the words as if they were hatchings on a pink fold. He pushed forward, felt feverish, excited. Fluorescent lights swirled. The strange weather from Ovida's tank was etched into his retinas. He got into it with a guy named Spike. Two glasses of whisky and they fell into a conversation about early memories and loss at the far corner of the bar. The flames of small candles on the glass top flickering from the volume of voices. Spike played keyboard, harmonica and the flute for three different bands, depending on whether he was getting on with them or not. He was gangly, the kind of guy who became awkward without the music to lose himself in. He had a blank-faced look that masked an intensity. There were bags under his eyes. He sniffed between sentences, smoothing down the crinkle at the bottom of the army-style green shirt he wore that hadn't seen an iron, possibly ever. 'You know that fucker responsible for my existence?' he asked like it was just semantics.

'You mean your father?' Azacca said, feeling his tongue loosen a little more, a warm sensation spreading through him as alcohol and sweetness from Ovida's ribcage, the nectar of strange fruit, settled in his blood.

'Yeah, him,' Spike continued, drumming his fingers on the countertop. 'He drained the joy out of everything man. My god, anything he did with me was done begrudgingly, even teaching me how to ride a bike. What kind of cunt ruins bike riding for his son? I ask you?'

Azacca slipped off his jacket, placing it on the newly vacated stool to his left. 'You're the son of a son of another son.'

'I don't follow you,' Spike said, head angled to one side.

Azacca watched him through hooded eyes. 'Man is ruinous. Man has always had the default setting of destruction. And they instinctively start ruining their sons early, inevitably.'

'When he was teaching me how to ride,' Spike continued, a grim expression on his face, 'he would hit me if I made a mistake then laugh. One time he bloodied my nose. Called it character building. I learned how to ride fairly quickly so he could stop teaching me. If that fucker were around today, know what I'd do? I'd lure him to an alleyway at night then punch him there relentlessly, trapped between the possibility of escape and the onslaught of physical violence. Then I'd play him some Coltrane on the flute,' he added wistfully. 'Car accident, took him out. Denied me retribution.' He knocked back the last remnants of whisky.

Azacca nodded sombrely. 'Sometimes a little Coltrane is needed. A necessary act then a bit of masterful instrumentation.' He raised his glass. He was handsome, unquestionably so under hazy lights. His eyes shined mercurially, on a frequency removed from everyone else. Spike went off to chase band members that hadn't arrived yet.

Azacca wondered if Finn was back at the house. His chest tightened. It wasn't that he disliked Finn; they lived together, after all. They were bonded after that night he and Emilien pulled him out of the sea, the night Oni punished him without explanation by taking his heart. They shared something greater than the friction between them. All four of them did. It was that he and Finn mistrusted each other despite everything. If not for Therese and the shamanic connection that bound them together, Finn would fuck him over if he needed to. He had that streak in him. He'd do the same to him. And they weren't so much uncomfortable about the knowledge of this unspoken reality, just clear on it. They all needed each other, regardless of tensions. He stashed his coat by the pile next to the sofa which was unbridled, constantly spilling from people rummaging or brushing past. The space for performances was cramped. Several couples threaded their way in and out. There were no windows in the room and the lighting was intimate. A few drink cans and bottles were left in corners by those who couldn't be bothered to return them to the bar. One security guard was eating a plate of ribs and plantain on the sofa, the armband on his left arm gleaming. A garishly made-up woman in an orange tutu gently shaking a tambourine was singing about transformation.

Azacca leaned against the wall absorbing her sultry rendition, the guitar between his legs. The room had got so hot people were removing top layers of clothing. Four bright nebulae sprang in his mind's eye. He, Therese, Finn and Emilien emerged from the slick folds, each one eating pips from pink marrow like communion.

He hadn't told Spike that his earliest memory was being inside his carrier, his mother Veronique D'Aguar, a tall, elegant woman who sometimes wandered the hot streets of Port-au-Prince offering to tell those who were curious enough about their past lives. On other occasions, her restless hands, fluttering like messengers wielding thoughts of their own, curled over the tiny stall of craft jewellery and random items that filled her table at Galerie Market. There was the chatter from visitors searching, turning items before dabbing their foreheads with handkerchiefs. The odd hallowed dog minded a stall or skulked between them, catching other currencies with their dangling tongues. The scents of joumou, griyo and conch lingered in the air. Stray Coca-Cola bottles littered the ground. At first, the other stallholders, fanning their sweaty faces while perched on makeshift stools of ice boxes and empty paint cans, thought there was not much use for the things she sold. They were decorative, frivolous, even, hah! Who wanted pretty items when there were mouths to feed? But Veronique had a way about her which drew people like fragmented sunrays over the Artibonite River. Her strikingly pretty face; her dark cocoa skin; the knowing golden eyes that had a wildness to them; the proud arch of her back when she walked, as though she didn't understand she was deemed merely a poor stallholder, as if she reached for rewards beyond her station. And that walk! The natural swivel of hips, the alluring rhythm in it, the confidence, the walk of a Haitian queen. Why Nefertiti must be crying in her tomb with envy, the other stallholders joked. Veronique paid them no mind, rising at dawn to make her items, ignoring the pain in her fingers at times when she weaved bright baskets with lids like hats, puppets, colourful bracelets for good fortune, with the early rumblings of the city swelling around her, the row of bright sugar-cube-like houses across the way from her kitchen alive with activity. Their faded paint peeled like deteriorating signatures in her eyeline. One day, Veronique arrived at her stall clutching a headless peacock, the blood running over her fingers, dribbling on the ground. Its head was wrapped in green netting inside her pocket, its dilated gaze trapped in cotton material, her fingers brushing against its azure breast. Restlessness filled the crowd. She announced that she had visited the highest peak in Port-au-Prince, where she'd inherited the peacock's last vision, after it followed her all the way there. And that she would become a vessel. Afterwards, the crowd dispersed, their heads and throats full of Veronique's strange declarations as though she'd passed it on.

Two months later, Veronique became pregnant. Six months into her term, she was certain it was a boy. And that it was special. She was sure the baby possessed an awareness beyond what was possible. If there was any incoming danger from thieves who lay in wait for victims after the market closed, once she'd packed up her portable stall, he'd kick her three times to warn her. And she would change her route home, picking her way through the winding streets in the cool evening air, left hand placed protectively along the curve of her stomach as though he might accidentally drop out and crawl through the night's crevices only to land in her crumbling doorway, his umbilical cord trailing behind him, coated in the glimmer of stars.

When she felt sick reaching for things to lean on: walls, tables, street lamps, the ghost of a lover who disappeared, anything to steady the wave of nausea hitting her, the baby would clench its fist then release it, sending twinges rippling through her body that seemed to absorb the sickness. All she had to do was breathe through it. Some nights, she lay in the small compound outside her home eating soursop, looking up at the sky, curling her sore feet, dreaming of multiple lives. She was sure the baby enjoyed the sweetness of mangoes, too, because he moved a little when she ate them, murmuring into the lining of her stomach. One night Oni appeared to her, majestic in the shadows of her room. Stunned, Veronique sat up in awe and fear that the shaman god she had been praying to had come to visit her, a heat blanketing her whole body as if she'd become molten through a powerful force. The peacock she had sacrificed had been no ordinary cock but a vessel for Oni. There would be a price to pay not from her, from her child.

And so Veronique watched him carefully over the following years, they continued to communicate in unusual ways. She started leaving Azacca gifts unexpectedly for the punishment he would face one day. As a child, he would wake to find lovingly hand-crafted puppets in his bed, a Hawaiian hibiscus flower for prosperity in his bowl of bouyon poul stew. Trails of gold-trimmed peacock feathers lined with mountain dew spilled from his pockets as he ran through heat, smog and rain.

By the time Azacca came on stage – a small area naturally cordoned off by the mic, wires and instruments – at least three warm-up acts had performed. He did a few Hendrix numbers: 'Foxy Lady' got the women in the audience swaying hypnotically, digging their fingers into the arms of hovering boyfriends who kept one eye on him and one eye on their women. A kind of release filled the air. People dripped in and out from the bar, collars were unbuttoned, a few ladies took their shoes off, padding about barefoot in sporadic patterns of movement, arms thrown above their heads. A baby-faced woman handed her blue-checked scarf to one of the doormen, who smiled with amusement before handing it back. Another woman started gyrating on the sofa, a red-tinged drink in her hand sloshing over the side of the glass, haphazardly anointing her in a trance. A scraggy-haired Spike in his Black Batman T-shirt randomly leapt at his windbreaker as though there was a body in it, clearly inebriated. The bar staff craned their necks to watch, the till zinging intermittently. Azacca's raw tones saturated the space. He had that natural quality the best artists possessed which was to give of himself, to draw you in yet maintain a little mystery too. Next up he sang 'All Along the Watchtower'. This time, it was the men whose faces contorted in quiet pleasure, whose fingers fluttered at his guitar riffs. Finally, he delivered a song in Creole about a man who loses his lover in a storm. It was soft, intimate. In the bar area, a third fluorescent armband was being passed around like a travelling nymph. Just as his last notes faded, Azacca spotted the familiar, languid figure of Emilien casually leaning against the back wall by the speakers. Hands probably still sore from a day of cutting trees, raising a glass of Kronenbourg beer in salute. His lips curved into a sardonic smile. His hair was ruffled. There was a glint in his eyes, an electric energy about him. The secrets between them vied for other warm bodies. And true to form, he hadn't told Azacca he'd be coming.

*

On the journey back home, a darkness in his expression, Emilien said, 'I wanted to be there in case the hunger got too much, stopped you from performing. Here,' he offered, slipping his hand inside his jacket, pulling out a white scroll of paper which unfurled into a drawing: an image of Azacca's missing heart angled in the static.

It was the carer, Mariella, who found Jeronimo Dorsey. His intention had been to go for a late-night walk, down the hill, over the road and through one of the side streets into the nature reserve discreetly tucked away. Like he'd dreamed of doing for months, right through the tilted axis which had held a power over his limbs that he couldn't explain. He'd woken up that morning feeling it was possible for him to cross the boundaries of his home, finally after that visit from Therese, which was unlike anything he'd ever experienced with anybody. He was more optimistic, envisioning all the things he'd missed out on over the years he'd been held captive by his own body. Perhaps he could even dig out his camera again, photograph more old bomb shelters and bunkers around London, take a trip to the coast, travel to Sicily to visit the vineyards there, eat olives in the sunshine in a suitably old town watching people amble through life at a slower pace. He'd spoken to his son Finley that morning; a spontaneous call, really. They'd talked for an hour. He was surprised by that, a little touched, too, that Finley had laughed at a joke he made about fly fishing. He hadn't heard him do that in a while. He hadn't tried to rush him off either. Heart racing, Jeronimo had put the phone down gently afterwards. Several hours later when Mariella spotted his body, a sudden lightness hit her legs. Her mouth went dry; a scream was trapped in her throat. Her hands trembled as she reached for him, then she stopped on instinct. He was floating face down in the pond. His blue kimono dressing gown billowed around him dramatically like a parachute. There was blood in the water, the chairs at either end tipped over, half a page of a map stuck out of his pocket. A lymph gland had been cut out of his neck; a last memory stolen. The bloody trail from it temporarily sated the house on the axis. Jeronimo Dorsey would never dream of travelling again. There were red marrow berries in the water, skin broken spilling the chaos of a night from a past time into this one. And those dark-eyed watery figurines had risen to the top, a small headless origami woman in the centre, surrounding Jeronimo in the glimmering folds of liquid in a circle of dismay.

Nine

I dream of births in driftwood shrines. Baby has not forgiven me in the arms of kin. Montero passes. A woman named Seraphine leaps to her death from the top of Sipu Mountain with a mouth full of Rowena's seaweed condiment. Plagued by visions of her own demise for days before, then walking barefoot into the mountain's hollows in search of a silhouette she called Candida, which escaped from shards of stained glass under her tongue. Afterwards, those pieces cutting her fingers, her body heaving, her legs folding, kin appearing through the broken glass giving instructions. 'The mountains are talking,' they urged, 'their crevices weep in sorrow. They need your sacrifice. Gethsemane suffers then and now. You must soothe the mountains by going on your own pilgrimage. Listen to the spillage of memory between your heartbeats. Hear the travelling tusk. Mimic it. A woman in flight is at her most beautiful, her most dangerous, her most knowledgeable. A woman in flight can become anything when she surrenders to the will of Oni. Oni selects her brethren. She makes their bodies all seeing. She gives them weapons of pip, thorn, stone and shadow. She hands them cold bones to worship, confess to and grip when the marrow begins to talk.'

I speak these words aloud in my bedroom, the kitchen, other rooms of the homestead. Marguerite withers in the background. They are invitations carried by the cool air to different parts of the town. One cannot stop what is destined to come. Sharp pains shoot through my neck from being angled in positions weighing the burden of a darkness to come. Tremors fill my thighs. My throat becomes parched as though a dry season begins there. And sure enough, the day she sets off on her wanderings, Seraphine's body arched in flight appears in the homestead's doorways, a series of reflections spawned from shards of bright glass.

Ewes from a neighbouring homestead north of Piranu begin to wail at night, stuttering within their gusty enclosure, kin's silhouettes trapped in their irises, their bodies shivering, noses damp, a sense of alarm among them. They are startled by noises nearby, as though something has been reset within them: water dribbling from a bucket, the chopping of wood, the rattling of the fence, the comings and goings of carts loaded with iron, tar, cloth. One evening, they breakthrough the gaps in the fencing, running in a fractured procession, winding along the paths of Gethsemane, the sense of freedom euphoric. They dash towards the waterfall at Noma Mountain. After jumping in, crying out ecstatically. The dark sky rumbles, exposing spots of oddly shaped symmetries. The water foams. The shapes of belongings from the vanished island wrap around the ewes' legs, pulling them under like doomed threads. I am holding a knife to a bloody wound which appears in my room speaking Domingos's name when the ewes wail one last time before their tongues are silenced. They wash up on the rocks the following day, gutted, pale carcasses bereft of their memories, the lymph glands removed from their necks, bathed in broken light, waiting to be reclaimed.

The feathers travel too, carried by a feeling of anticipation in the air. One slips through the window into the homestead of a deaf bread maker who does not hear the sound of distant ruptures taking refuge in his home. Another flutters into the dressmaker's store, lingering in smooth, soft piles of material, catching stray stitches bending in submission. And people begin to spot the geologist from Madagascar who went missing in the caves walking along the back routes of the town, clutching the third feather, drawing the maps he lost with its tip, as if conjuring his release from Gethsemane.

Sueli goes missing playing on the stony path leading to the homestead, tossing her chalk sticks in the air with a flourish then vanishing when my back is turned. Four days go by and still no sign of her, although I feel the movements of her beating heart, the rush of air to her lungs, the taste of a dandelion wilting on her tongue, her frayed smock caught in brushes of nettle, between the movements of night creatures who like the hounds bear the mark and have the offerings of driftwood shrines disappearing inside them. Humming from Oni's blue tent deepens. Kin dance around it. It is a sun to them, a teller of ancestral stories, a keeper of moments which change to dusk in their hands. I am caught by it, this ritual of dance and awakening. I feel it doing tasks around the homestead, sweeping the front path, changing the bedding in Sueli's room, carving other meanings of my name on a papaya carcass, comforting Marguerite during periods of panic. She looks at me with sad eyes, her slack mouth mumbling, pressed against a sly opening that lured her loved ones away. The wound speaking Domingos's name appears again; rising between rabbit heart and stone, crawling towards the hiss of bubbling copper pots, the *cuttings of knives, moving across the ceiling in my room as the wind howls, the soil softens, the garden rumbles its own contained thunder, foreign fruit breaks in the mouths of kin. The wound is one of the scattered brethren. It wants a body, a place to claim. It craves the cracks of discontent to call brother and sister. It floats before the mirror Rowena gave me, reflecting back a woman who is my likeness from another time dressed in odd clothing eating marrow berries greedily from a misted tank. Future kin. I do my shamanic dance, bare my teeth. The wound quietens in the gap.*

Marguerite and I drink the latest brew from one shebeen on Tepela Mountain. We sip from clear, thick-necked bottles, small bits of kelp turning in the mixture like a thousand flakes of comfort. We stumble around in the dark, laughing, talk to our shadows, warm ourselves at night by a fire. I send a stray, orange-tipped flame out to hunt. The loneliness of the homestead is unbearable.

Some women from Tepela Mountain come to visit. The furthest of the mountains in the western region, Tepela is known for its campanula, fel-da-terra and lavandula plants. Its harbouring of five rayed sea urchins now underwater dwellers gleaming silver, purple and gold on nights when anything seems possible and the mountains feel alive, newly mysterious, displaying their power to shape the fortunes of Gethsemane. At the end of the cold season, flocks of lago sparrows land on the mountain's base eating grains twilight spills for them as food, as warning that there is more hunger to come in the skies. The townspeople call Tepela the back-to-front mountain because on rare days when the whole of Gethsemane is blanketed in a dangerously thick mist, the back of Tepela is reflected instead as the mist curls away and people walk into nothingness feeling that they have been tricked.

The Tepela women are strangers in our midst. They glow with good health; their dark skin smooth, their teeth white, pretty faces buoyant, their afro hair braided into intricate, distinctive styles. Their heads are rare jewels bobbing before us as they speak.

Marguerite wears her crumbling crown to see them, her hair in disarray. I notice with interest a hint of madness in her eyes, her thin voice, her unsteady hands.

'You are not alone,' the women cluck. 'You must take comfort in that. What is yours will manifest again. It is the land testing us, my dear. Gethsemane can turn the minds of some, especially if there is unhappiness in the household. You must not blame yourself,' they console. Her pain is evident, raw; she refuses to mask it. Their concerned expressions stretch to fill the room. The fire crackles. The three women – Branca, Edwidge and Carmella – place items they pronounce luck bearers in her hands: a blue amulet, a small bottle of lavender oil, a multicoloured wing. They crane their necks to look at her as though studying a centipede contorting beneath an eyeglass. Drinking their beer with a strange merriment, they sigh and harrumph when Marguerite becomes listless, withdrawn. They watch me with furrowed brows, distrust in their narrowed eyes while I fill their cups. When they leave, their proud backs fade in the distance, a stunted army of busybodies. I imagine the hems of their skirts singed, then engulfed in flames.

It is the early hours of the following morning when I hear stones crunching coming towards me like the ground's clarion call. My mouth is dry. My thighs ache. My thoughts swim from disrupted sleep. Tiredness of the previous day's tasks weighs on my limbs. A tiny, wingless creature changes its direction of flight in my blood.

The woman with my face is spat out from a distant echo. The rivers lose reflections of the drowned and damned to a god's will. Large, unknown vegetation, bulbous with a red tinge, sprout from soft breaks of earth. A cool breeze mimicking the chorusing of kin winds through the circular signs spreading all over Gethsemane like an infestation. Even the elements work on kin's behalf. The caves swell with secret resurrections. Fallow points of earth attempt to talk back. My heart beats rapidly. Marguerite snores gently in the other room, frail, thin, her centre in the grip of sickness toying with her destiny in the waiting hours. I mumble to the clay heart, a compass slowly disintegrating into the memories of creatures in the undergrowth. Marrow spills into my vision like a lurking trap. The plants cry softly, their tips and stems gleam alluringly, caressing the entry points of this new dawn. I grab a handful of bedding to counter the numbness in my curled fingers. I take a deep breath. The air thickens as if the homestead will uproot to land on another mountain, releasing its unpredictable rhythms and cycles to the inhabitants in exchange for currencies from a stranger's hand.

I stand. The crunching of stones is nearer, proclaiming an arrival. I move through the doorway as the numbness begins to leave my fingers. An invisible entity fills the homestead's entrance. My stomach dips. My neck tingles. Figures from my peripheral vision weigh the sound of departures in their mouths. A feeling of anticipation swells within me.

At the front doorway, I watch the figure of a man and a small girl on the path, drawing towards the homestead with purpose and certainty, a knowledge in their bodies that is not the movement of visitors. I recognise them instantly: the man's tall, broad frame; the slender girl possessing a joyful energy that appears somewhat curtailed due to tiredness. The dim light of early dawn falls over them as though they are a trick spawned from one of the mountain's dips. The murmurs of travel fade into the lines of their shadows. My heart pounds, beads of sweat form between my breasts. I moisten my dry lips with my tongue. My nerves feel as if needles are pinned against them. I lift up the skirt of my smock. The air is cool on my legs. The ache within me rears its pulverised head, its recognition of longing pooling into my stomach.

I rush to wake Marguerite, who stirs slowly at first before seeing the relief in my expression. 'They are here,' I say breathlessly, grabbing her arms. She pushes her body up, then standing, leans on me momentarily to take in the news. We hurry to the front entrance, waiting. They are closer now, yards away. Breath, memory and loss become a fanged retreating apparition. Domingos has a tight, weary expression. His dark clothing is torn. He holds a sack in one hand and Sueli's fist in the other. Sueli's pale dress is stained. She clutches a bloodied hoe like a fated instrument to play with. Then they are two formations inside the homestead again. Marguerite rushes at them, gathering them to her with all her might, crying at the wonder of their return, at their unharmed bodies. She kisses Domingos passionately, who reciprocates her ardour. She strokes Sueli's wild mane, holds her face tenderly, gazing into it. I watch on the edge. A slither of anger cuts a trail inside me between heart and lung. I will the tension in my shoulders away. I too want the comfort of bodies I know. Domingos opens the sack, pulls out a batch of fresh fennel, offers it to me.

'Must a man ask to be given water in his own home? For your latest concoction,' he says, smiling mysteriously, curling his arm around Marguerite's waist. I am rooted to the spot. The faint lines *of scratches on his chest are visible markings from a woman's hand. I turn away, catching my breath, biting down on a rising anger. Under the hazy light, dirt patches on Sueli's dress stretch in an attempt at migration. She moves towards me, watching my expression, spinning the bloodied hoe, teeth flashing, eyes blinking rapidly as though seeing me anew after an unplanned absence.*

I keep the fennel in the kitchen on the small chopping board by the knife where the cool air will preserve it. I wonder whose hands had brushed it before Domingos's, whose voice had spoken to its roots, what vanishings it may have witnessed. Everything is a potential disruption from kin. I will use it to make stew with batatas. The homestead, though temporarily appeased, still balances on a tipping point. Any part of the home can bring the unexpected if I will it: women contorting mid-flight in our entrances; the memories of hounds dispatched, growing as cacti in the murmuring garden; the murky lines of the blue tent's horizon slipping in between the gaps, crawling into the corners of doorways in search of fresh offerings for Oni, and the circular patterns on Sueli's walls talking to my marrow plants like new brethren.

    I pace restlessly between my room, the kitchen and the garden. I hear the distant clatter of instruments I cannot identify yet in my eardrums. I will spend the remaining quiet hours tossing, turning, trying to name them, breathing haggardly through it. This is how kin invades while Gethsemane rests. I think of the scratches on Domingos's chest, push back my desire to trace each one with my mouth. Marguerite pretends not to notice the markings.

    Soon, news of Domingos's and Sueli's return reaches the townsfolk and the versions of how and why they came back spreads like a harmattan wind gathering volume between trees. I hover outside Domingos and Marguerite's bedroom door, listening. My body feels twisted, like a gnarled thing worshipping the dark. Dryness returns to my throat. My eyes burn. Gentle peals of laughter filter through, the rustle of bedding, the weight of bodies undulating towards each other in an age-old rhythm, a tender kiss that is an arrow aimed in my direction. I close my eyes, breathing in their coupling as though it is a scent. I see the hoe rising between them like a third lover, seeking soft points of flesh to claim. I dream of Domingos in those precious few hours before dawn. He is a wreckage moving between the mountains' plains, searching for answers from the land which elude him. He reaches for white pips, confessing their cycles of existence before shrinking in his hold. He gathers fennel roots to sip from when his vision fractures. The roots turn golden in an act of treachery. For one afternoon, he is a man with a golden face before becoming scarred again, the memory of a tarnishing caving inside him. He turns his face to the ashes that marked it, traces the shapes of cinders in animal traps, embraces the five-tipped flame I sent to find him like a lost shadow.

When morning comes there is relief, uncertainty. A current lingers in the air that is neither of river nor of land. We hover in the centre of the homestead, just before the kitchen. Marguerite wears a rose-coloured smock which compliments her complexion. She sits cross-legged, humming happily, lifting more items from Domingos's sack as if they are a bounty from a king's ship: a dagger, a line of rope, a broken bit of oar. Domingos rests his hand on my back, watching me searchingly.

'A man has to feel the wind behind him sometimes,' he says gravely. 'He must leave home to feed his spirit, to know himself

again. You understand?' The imprint of his touch is a tender burn I want to nurse. He feels he owes me, a guest in his home, an explanation.

'You must do what is right for you,' I say, my mouth flooded with the sudden bitter taste from kin's tongues, 'when the body calls you to.' I smile tensely, folding a short pile of clothing between us to stop my limbs from betraying themselves.

He does not tell us how he came upon Sueli. It is a secret between them. She emerges from her room clutching the hoe like a prized possession. Her eyes gleam. There are sleep lines on her cheeks. Her mouth opens softly. Her coiled body springs into action. She starts speaking a new foreign tongue, her face stretching between us all, four suns tethered inside a homestead. She walks to Marguerite, who is sitting, and lifting the hoe, Sueli strikes her over the head. The thud echoes, snaring the twitching of octopuses carrying scars inside them, foreign signs becoming signatures in the aftermath of blood, the crack of the clay heart in the soil awaiting an impatient touch. The suns become unmoored. Air leaves the room. The humming ceases. The patch of sky in the mirror changes to a gathering of smoke-tipped feathers. Blood dribbles into a mother's confused expression. The bloodied hoe tumbles towards the current.

Marguerite falls to the ground.

Chapter 9

Therese found a stash of clothes in a black bin bag when she was rifling through Emilien's wardrobe. Pulling them out one by one, she sat on the cold wooden floor with her hands buried in their crevices, her nostrils thick with the scent of stale material, his small clock ticking on the dresser by the bed. The big comforting wicker chair still bore the fading scent of his aftershave, Emporio Armani. The clothes were a pair of grey jogging bottoms, a dark green checked shirt and a black; they had mud spattered on them and blood on the chest area of the shirt. She recalled then his nosebleeds, the way they'd come from nowhere, disrupting him mid-conversation or activity. On one such occasion, he'd been showing her old photographs of his grandfather: a handsome white-haired, olive-skinned man dressed in a pale robe and clutching a tribal mask. His face all sharp angles; his dark eyes had a wisdom and no fear.

'Ah querida,' Emilien teased, accosting her in the kitchen, his hair damp from rain, eyes dancing, folded white tobacco sheets peeking from the breast pocket of his black jacket. 'Here's the man responsible for my disposition.' He fished the photo from his worn brown leather wallet. 'You think I look like him? My parents thought so; my mother always resented that. I reminded her of him, their relationship was strained.' A flash of pain crossed his face, the quick contemplation of old memories bringing an injury to the surface. The boiling pot of jambalaya on the stove hissing, the lid clattering gently. Steam rising and curling were silent gasps. She pressed her hand over his, feeling the undeniable spark that had always been there between them, a molten thing blooming in the space separating their bodies.

'Families are always complicated; whatever happened, it wasn't your fault,' she offered, watching him carefully, noting he was clutching the corner of the photo tightly. As if it would become a winged conspirator slipping away from his grasp, revealing a secret or two in exchange for its freedom. A trickle of blood spilled from his nose then, splattering onto the photograph.

'Are you okay?' she asked, grabbing a tissue from her back pocket and handing it to him, her expression clouded with worry. The heat between them caused a trickle of sweat to run down her back. It was at least the third or fourth time she'd seen this happen to him recently.

'Don't fuss,' he instructed, wiping his nose then the photo, tipping his head back to slow the process of another onslaught. His smile was fiendish through the blood. 'This happens sometimes when the static in my brain begins to call me somewhere.'

One bitterly cold night, it was just the two of them home. Azacca was out at a gig in King's Cross, Finn was away for two weeks investigating a new ice hotel in Reykjavik. They sat in the living room with the fire roaring and unspoken desires being stoked like parched creatures. The fire crackled, spitting embers nestling against a wintry crevice while she and Emilien drank glasses of Amaretto, the sweet liquid lapping at their internal walls. Between their glasses clinking, her edginess, the musical rumble of his laughter, its own seductive instrument when she closed her eyes, something unspooled.

For a while, there had been that age-old dance: loaded looks passing each other in the hallway, bumping into him as she rushed out of the bathroom when she was running late for appointments. Once, for a talk she was due to give on the circadian rhythms between plants and mammals at UCL. There was an amused smile on his face when he asked, 'Will they be making an appearance at the lecture too, querida?' He chuckled, pointing at clumps of shaving foam on her legs that she thought she'd washed off. The mirth in his light brown eyes was apparent. 'Mock me now,' she retorted. 'Bask in my greatness later!' She sped past him, the blue shower cap barely containing her orange-streaked twists.

He was left clutching the bathroom door handle as though it was an anchor. In that moment, grounding himself when a different echo of flight hit, that made powdery wings with women's names emblazoned on them unfold in his chest. He took a breath, the smell of Therese's jasmine-scented shower gel enveloping him.

'I bet Van Gogh's friends didn't laugh at him during moments of stress!' she remarked, glancing behind her at his figure lingering in the doorway, watching her, one last parting shot while she scurried away.

'Possibly, maybe his friends also didn't hog the bathroom,' he replied, shutting the door firmly.

That Amaretto-soaked night in the living room, the blue-tipped, multicoloured fire's flames swelled and curled, breathing its ambition to claim the hearts of those before it. Emilien told her he was sure something deeply traumatic had happened to him in childhood, only he couldn't remember. It was his grandfather's love that had soothed the chasm he felt between him and his parents, a gulf he traced endlessly with a shaky hand and a hazy sense of self. Somehow, he was chasing this secret monster between accidents. Trying to grab its mercurial shape while being in the crushed metal of a vehicle on a roadside accident, falling from trees or hurtling into thrashing waves from a great height. For several moments after his confession, they listened to the ebb and flow of the night: its absences and revelations throbbing like the faint ache of a missing limb. She didn't ask why a man would repeatedly put himself at risk to find some solace or blame himself for the inherited cruelty that dogged him, scattering its teeth in his blood as defective jewels.

'Whatever it was, it's rarely the child's fault,' she offered, watching him through hooded eyes, picking at a run in her tights in the thigh area.

His face twisted into a grimace. 'That's not helpful. I don't need platitudes that don't change anything.' The flash of annoyance in his eyes surprised her. He took a swig from his glass. 'Is there any bourbon in this house?' he asked, running his finger over the tumbler's rim in a way she found slightly hypnotic.

She uncurled her legs which had been folded locus style. 'Then what is helpful?' she asked, unable to keep the edge out of her voice, an acknowledgement of the tension they both knew had been building. Outside, a car screeched to a halt. The neighbour's cat that often perched on the welcome mat before their front door darted through the surrounding shrubs, meowing at a disturbance. The moon, a resplendent orb, deployed its night disciples to wander through the streets. Therese had deliberately sat opposite him to read his expressions carefully. She was also positioned near the crackling fire, which under the comfort of alcohol had a contained fury, much like the flame-doused corners of the man before her, whose ability to transform elements of himself both subtly and overtly had intrigued her from the moment they met.

He patted the sofa space next to him, the way an illusionist might luring his favourite apparition. 'Bourbon and you closer would help, querida,' he said bluntly, catching her fleeting expression of desire with a knowing look. 'Are you scared? You never seem scared of anything.'

'No,' she answered, swallowing the sudden lump in her throat. Her palms were sweaty, a dead giveaway she was excited. The scent of his aftershave was exotic, filling her nostrils. Her heartbeat thudded like a warped siren. She walked over casually, careful not to allow her body to betray her, at least not immediately.

She was acutely aware of the tension emanating from them. And the clay plant pot witnessing this attraction between two people who initially wanted to resist their bodily inclinations. Both perched on the powder-blue sofa before the glass table carrying the remnants of a failed card game, and copies of his graphic novels she'd rifled through earlier, *Persepolis*, *Fun Home* and *Johnny Bravo*. Their reflections in the glass fragmenting into quiet cataclysms. When she sat beside him, the softness in his gaze returned, his eyes wielding a filmy sheen. He took her left hand in his, not watching her body but listening to it. Having seen it move through its joys, sorrows, its private ruminations with a hidden admiration. Green veins crossed on her skin underneath her fingers, rushing towards a bough, a furrow in the horizon, a chasm of foreign soil. He traced the veins with his fingers. 'Is this okay? Is more than this what you want?' he asked; the edge in his voice was back.

'Yes, this is what I want,' she replied, her body turned towards him, her response an ember crackling in the air. It felt right opening up in this way. She knew that already. They were both heady as his mouth angled over hers, sucking her tongue, his hand on her back guiding her limbs like one half of an equation. They undressed, their reflections in the glass moving in synchronicity. His mouth became a marauding seeker over her breasts, belly button then across her feet, memorising their shape, their arch and dips, as something to be worshipped. He ran his tongue between her toes then sucked them greedily, his expression feral. His arms were sinewy, his head angled over her feet as if they were rare delicacies. He slipped inside her vagina deftly like he'd always known that part of her. His hands gripped hers while he moved rhythmically, watching the subtle changes of her expression as though they were degrees of light. A reflection of her pure pleasure and sensuality. Therese's heart raced. The centre of her exploded. The rhythm between them moved towards a crescendo. She didn't recognise the roar that came not just from her mouth but from her whole body, a molten thing in a hedonistic tryst. His face contorted in pleasure, an untamed stranger once more just as his release followed hers. And their reflections in the glass shattered all over again into a thousand tiny luminous particles.

Stumbling through the empty house alone, drunk off Ovida's grapes, Therese saw Zulmira carrying a bloodied hoe in the distant land. Her slender body agile, a carved statue in a pale costume moving to ancient instructions. Zulmira stood in a crumbling garden washing blood from the hoe where warped fruit sprouted as Eden's counterpart. The ringing in Therese's ears intensified. Their hearts beat as one. The blushing skyline carried murky shapes while it shifted. Restless patches of blue and white hovered above as a ceiling of discontent. Zulmira sang, a song coming from the corners of her being. Afterwards, holding a curved white bone that was weapon and silent companion. The intertwining happened again. The static, white-hot and piercing splintered into points of entry. Therese felt Zulmira's longing in that moment. Their skin was slickened with sweat. The underside of their tongues bruised from harbouring pieces of bright glass, chests unbridled with luminous entities beating beyond dimensions. They shared the hunger, indifferent to injuries following them as if part of the order of things, a secret circadian rhythm to take them where they would be reformed. The din of static rose in Therese's ears. An exotic, sweet taste filled her mouth. Her nostrils flared from the scent of nectar. Her feet began to bleed, temporarily inheriting a future injury from Zulmira. Then Zulmira was in flight inside her, whispering, urging, a hint of sadness in her movements. They were beautiful but there was a bleakness, too. Later, she tasted Zulmira's drinking from reflections in the river, her breath forming circular, golden patterns on bald patches of ground, stand at the top of valleys speaking foreign tongues in praise. Therese's pulse sped up. A slippage occurred. Her pulse slithered into Gethsemane again, reverberating like an echo. Zulmira paused as if to acknowledge it, looking back at her through a misted circular mirror. She followed it as the sound deepened, held it tenderly. Therese began to cry then. Zulmira stood at the bottom of one mountain, surrounding her beating pulse, looking up at a small break containing days of suffering. Reaching inside their stomachs, she pulled parts of a costume from their loins. Her expression was intense, contorted. She arranged the full costume on the warm ground at an angle. Their faces merged into one. Bone raised, Zulmira and Therese started chanting. Marrow spilled on the costume, against the absence of a body in it. And Zulmira's howl rippled through the vacuum into her body.

Back in her bedroom, dazed from the impact of another's movements within her, Therese sensed Zulmira's hands searching through her, under the glow of the bedside lamp. She knew that feeling of things being planted in the body. After all, she did the same, reaching into sick people to really see them, under the guise of comforting with a healer's fingers. She touched long-buried memories they thought had been forgotten, moulding them into a temporary relief, gathering with the urgency of an impatient scavenger of blood and inheritance. Zulmira's humming in her head spread like a colony of bees in her veins. She sat up, touching the damp bed to steady herself stained with blood from her feet, listening for the secret noises of the house which seemed more pronounced at night: the quiet wailing of Finn's injuries lodged in her brain; the rustle of gifts hurtling through the static, becoming white vacuums at the other end; the clinking in Ovida's tank as new fruit emerged, scattering in the waterfall; the glimmering tadpole-like creatures attempting to make their way out of the tank, waiting for other surfaces to bloom on. She heard everything with a crystallised intensity. Zulmira's humming faded. She rubbed her temples then reached for the glass of wine on her dresser. Taking a swig, she closed her eyes momentarily. Zulmira had stopped howling. Instead, she whispered of more births in the new utopia on the plane, more offerings, addled bodies for her to see with her other eye. She sang of hunger, of ways to curb it.

Then Zulmira began to speak through her, like a puppet she found herself mouthing the words, possessed by another's instructions. *You must feed your thirst for using the bodies of others as husks. Move towards your gifts. Do not look away blindly. This is the order of things hidden from the eyes of others. It is how we honour Oni. Do not fear the spillage of lives as part of it.*

Zulmira moved temptingly in the distance, re-forming beneath splinters of light, bone tucked into her pocket. Her tongue vibrated through the space between them.

Therese stood gingerly, went to the upstairs bathroom to wash her feet, listening to footsteps marching in blood slipping through the plughole. When she returned to her room, clothes were strewn all over the floor. Her breath caught. By the door, on a blue-sequinned skirt, laid a two-headed water bull from the third plane. It had bloodshot eyes. Its body rippled. She recognised it as a disruption from that other plane, a manifestation of Zulmira's chanting. Her heartbeat quickened. Her throat constricted. She moved towards it slowly; it pulsated against her fingers as she reached out before it faded into the chasm. After that, she put on a pair of worn, dark jeans, a black lace top. She arranged her twists into a bun, a few loose strands grazing the back of her neck. She felt heady and strange, alive with a secret power. The warm, sweetly alcoholic aftertaste of Portuguese rosé lined her mouth. She stood before the wardrobe glass watching as though it was a trick mirror. Zulmira's figure glimmered behind before merging into her, their heads orbiting towards each other in a kaleidoscopic amalgamation. Therese was curious to spot the wild-eyed, mutated versions of them emerging, intoxicated, throbbing on the wooden floor, grabbing at her feet to pull her under and anchor themselves. Tingles of excitement spread. Her stomach was a ball of small knots. Her palms were sweaty. It was becoming apparent that anything could be an entry point for these disruptions where parts of the other plane emerged, or Zulmira took hold of her nervous system. They could manifest at any time, a fragmented language telling her things. She was sure the others received them too. She pulled on her scuffed suede boots, stuffed a few items in her bag: a purse, a vial of liquid peyote, a tiny bottle of macadamia oil from her apothecary set, a packet of chewing gum. She felt a burning sensation in her eyes, friction in her chest, the lines of cold weather winding through her, the tug of Ovida calling. There were bursts of dew on her tongue like bubbled clingfilm, a showering of seeds passed through her. She felt the prick of sharp objects against skin, the markings of new entry points. The calls of a golden goshawk crumbled into chalk in the distance.

She headed down to the basement where Ovida floated in the tank: a beautifully macabre reality, a tender bait to lure the night's secrets. She pressed her face into the water, drinking greedily as the burning in her eyes subsided. Flickers of a bleak holding on top of a mountain flashed. Zulmira began to howl again in her head, this time merging into the image of a carrier frantically swallowing doomed roots on the brink emblazoned in her mind.

Outside, the night was a duplicitous vacuum, with people carrying the shrunken symmetries of their lives in their pockets. She wandered among them. At Oxford Street, she threaded through the buzz of bodies in search of things to consume, the seductive pull of intricately decorated stores beckoning. At Piccadilly Circus, she passed the window of a bookstore where a rare copy of an Amos Tutuola book sat like an incandescent wing waiting for the stroke from a stained-glass hand. She took it in momentarily, filled with warmth at spotting one of her favourite books that somehow seemed fortuitous. Afterwards, feeling slightly removed from her surroundings yet still connected to Zulmira's wavelength, she absorbed it all in microscopic detail, buoyed by the knowledge that her vision and senses were sharpening even more. On the main road, a ginger cat skulking by in her path had one filmy eye. The billboard of a Hugo Boss perfume advert began to peel at the corners just as the bottle turned into a vial. A set of traffic lights near by shrieked. In the key cutter's shop window on the opposite side, speckles of black rain fell at an angle against the glass, growing in diameter, like bulbous dark nuclei obscuring the view. Oni's utopia's twisted elements could reach her anywhere. She wanted her and the group to know there was more work to be done, more to build from their loins that could cross planes, states and consciousness. She slipped a five-pound note to a ravaged, blank-eyed homeless man shivering under several cardboard boxes. The smell of urine was subtle. His fingers were rough. His clothing had seen better days. His belongings amounted to sets of stripped, tinned cans assembled into coin boxes; an empty kebab container; a keyring shaped like a London bus; a folded map of Machu Picchu, Peru. The man's mumblings were incoherent. 'You left something in there!' he yelled. 'What did you forget?' he asked, spittle at the corner of his mouth.

'An exchange,' Therese offered, reaching for the map and its delicate folds. She placed it in her bag, nodded at him to end their brief interaction. The air crackled. The man slumped back into the night. She tasted black rain on her tongue. Zulmira was now at the opposite set of traffic lights, holding the bright heads of water bulls like antennas, breathing a rising power into her. *Do not be afraid of the spillage*, she mouthed, this time clutching Ovida like a daughter. Therese turned this image over in her head, a puzzle within a puzzle. Her heartbeat pumped frenetically; perhaps Zulmira wanted to take Ovida away from them. Maybe that was why she kept manifesting.

*

Therese headed to Old Street tube stroking the folds, reminded of how static maps held new worlds even within the restrictions of its lines.

Zulmira filled her body with the songs of kin, rhythmic songs that lived in her banished mouth. They came like seekers talking of joy, destruction, of memories left like scattered embers on the planes, of carcasses in need of a gutting, mined to raise excavations to a treacherous light.

Oni has sent us, they cried. *What are the lands if not to be tampered with? They are mere playgrounds for Oni's touch. What is the body but a crooked disciple? What is the weight of a deception under imposter moons? You are breath, instrument, the compass in water, the withered apprentice in the month of July searching for a season of snow. Oni instructs us. She always knows. All-seeing, she is mother, god and being. You are the baby in the valley building a drunken dawn, the severed apparition sharpening its tools, its modes of appearance, the lonely ripple in a crowd of strangers.*

Oni will line our loins again through the ages. We will hunt for blood in the bread, leave signs of dissent when there are none, watch new creatures form inside scorched costumes. We will long for the one who left us, turning the act of betrayal into a prayer. Breathe into pockets that carry the bone, the marrow and the current. We will beat as one with our descendants, leave teachings in the blood, plant seeds in mirrors. Just as a man needs a name, a grain of sand seeks its beginning. The blue tent needs its offerings. Oni expects it. We must always deliver. It has to be fed between the modes of vanishings and resurrections.

The songs of kin throbbed. The vanished mouths soared.

Then they were injuries.

Then orbiting, feathered gifts.

A chorus of infants' cries.

A series of contortions in the dark.

Therese wept silently as these discoveries doubling as songs reverberated through her body.

On the Metropolitan Line, the train, a beast of the urban wild, stuttered along the tracks. In the carriage, the air was stuffy. The smell of cheap perfume lingered. The sounds of revellers, football fans and clusters of friends on an evening out filtered in and away, dribbles of sound punctuating the closed expressions people had. Therese watched her reflection in the darkened glass opposite. Its blackened hue as the train stopped felt denser. Her mirrored image looked like a pattern of warning signs. It was her but she was fragmenting, the lines of a blueprint crossing, rushing through her like an uncontainable infiltration. The haze of revelations from Zulmira and kin, the aftermath of their chant, made her feel discombobulated. Her mouth in the glass bobbed, moonfish in an aquarium of map lines. The train moved for a bit then screeched to a halt. On either side of her, the scruffy man and vacant-eyed, mousy-haired woman coughed and grimaced in succession. Therese drummed her fingers on her thigh. A trickle of sweat ran down the back of her neck. Veins on the inside of her left wrist swelled. Her skin tingled. The chanting of Zulmira and kin underneath it was another layer. Every part of her felt alert, as though a thousand pins pricked her skin, floated in her bloodstream, encountered its secrets in brief ceremonies of awakening. She ran a finger over her bag, a dip in the leather material that caved somewhat. A sense of anticipation flooded her limbs, a slight headiness, the knowledge of her power.

Did Finn, Azacca and Emilien feel this way too? Did they have scenes from other planes follow them, parched and wanting to quell the ache? She glanced up at the carriage ceiling. Kin's shadows danced, shrinking into the edges. She looked back at the glass opposite. The map lines had been reduced to a tiny blue line in the right-hand corner, flickering like an electric vein. Her reflected mouth spasmed.

We are the mammoth, the severing in the valley, the carcass becoming language.

We are the crossings of half-formed memories released from the bones.

Therese's eyes honed in. It was her mouth, but the voices were Zulmira's mingled with kin's. It came again in waves before disappearing into garbled static.

This time, the man, Lorenzo Amante, had a rare condition where the bones broke easily and the body's growth was stunted. In his mid-twenties, it was miraculous he'd lived this long. He was olive skinned, in a wheelchair and frail. He looked as though the sudden movements of things he hadn't accounted for would rattle the core of him. His forehead was elongated. His lips bore an unhealthy blue tinge. His cheeks were hollow. The Nirvana T-shirt he wore was a little baggy on his frame. Behind him, the sparsely decorated hallway with colourful wall mountings felt like a tunnel that would suck them both in before spitting them out as sharp edges. He invited her in. The air was stale, yet the scent of a woody cologne filtered through. The creaking of floorboards above indicated that perhaps they had company. Picking up on her unasked question, his voice was surprisingly grave when he spoke. 'Don't worry, we're alone. It's just next door. Sometimes I think there are people in the house when there aren't.' He watched her through startling blue eyes. And was almost handsome bathed in the shadows, if slightly odd looking. His mouth twitched, moving to meet the mouth in the train carriage window of kin's utterings in an impromptu assembly. His breakable body was poised to create new adventures despite its fragility, its limitations. The rise and fall of his chest was a warped lullaby.

'You look very sick,' she said softly, her bag brushing against his arm.

'Does that make you happy?' he asked, voice rising. 'I hope so, but I don't want your pity.'

'I don't pity you,' she added, slipping her jacket off. The axis bent on the periphery, shimmered. She closed her eyes. Everything magnified. The smell of his sweat mingled with cologne trapped in her nostrils, the flutter of silvery wings trying to find routes inside his body, calling for her touch. His wheelchair tumbled towards the axis in a new fingerprint. *Spillage is a part of the process, embrace it.* Zulmira's voice rang in her ears. And then the accumulated sounds of his bones breaking in the past, gathering, rising, expanding, till it was deafening and the hallway couldn't contain it. It was so beautiful, she raised her arms up in ecstasy, arching her body to sink into it while Lorenzo stared, hypnotised.

*

Later, when she arrived back home, she headed to her bedroom. Her laptop was open, warm. Someone had been going through it. She drew a breath. Hands shaking, she collapsed onto the bed, mulling over the weight of this knowledge amid the chaos in her brain.

Finn's carrier, Tulugaak, was an Inuit who had attempted to set his people on the path to enlightenment. Just after his seventeenth birthday, an incident had occurred that would impact him for many years to come. He noticed that after several days, a majestic golden-crested goshawk had been trailing him across the peaks and troughs of the Arctic region, the Inuvialuit north-west territories his tribe occupied. It had been Tulugaak's shadow at the first rites of passage ceremony; its wings quietly fluttering amid the gathered bodies as though it would multiply into a thousand winged-witnesses. Its black eyes leaked the memories of limbs jostling, circling a shrine doused in black rainwater, the markings on skin that bore a bright luminescence as the coloured imprints became running beads of sweat. The goshawk watched the heady dancing of these boys who howled in the night, ushered into manhood by this tradition from a shaman opening the channels of communication between men and animals which had changed very little over time. Tulugaak, a gangly young man who had appeared out of synchronicity with his body in the past, a daydreaming boy thinking of other worlds outside the ice habitat, was often slow to anger. He had awoken two days after the first rite of passage celebration to see that goshawk, perched on a pile of stones outside the small home he shared with his parents and two younger brothers. Momentarily, he watched the rise and fall of its golden breast as though it carried the secrets of another night. He walked steadily towards it, careful not to startle it, the icy mounds that were homes suddenly fading around him. All that mattered was this creature, poised like a winged heart beating between body, land and sky. The morning light was bright, piercing, the day full of promise. Cold air curled away from his mouth as he mimicked a bird call, his lips pronouncing a deeper sound from the force of the action. 'Caw, caw caw!' he called, keeping his approach casual. He felt a connection to the goshawk he could not fully comprehend yet. But like the best seducers, just as Tulugaak drew closer, heart racing, she took off in flight towards the wondrous blue, conspiratorial sky which was shedding processions of strange cloudy shapes.

Afterwards, he left home, tugging the old trap his father had gifted him, just as his father before him had passed it down, an inheritance to aid him in finding his way through the rough terrain of manhood. Tulugaak pulled the trap as he walked. It sloshed through the thick snow like a giant corroded mouth. He hummed, soaking up the wildness of endless snowy land. The trees surrounding him trembled. Rustlings between their trunks felt like company on a lonely trail.

A young man from Tulugaak's tribe must mark his adult arrival into his community with a catch. Therefore, he had to do the same. He shivered. His brown trousers, shirt and wolf fur seemed inadequate against the elements despite the protection they offered. His thoughts raced back to ensnaring prey. He had always had an affection for creatures, a curiosity about their hidden lives that had made him whisper to fireflies assembling into constellations in his peripheral vision, a seal which had appeared in the middle of their camp one evening, its long tooth dislodged, its mouth a bloody hunter squawking in search of some shared language. A feeling of confusion hit him. He saw a deer's flank sputtering in the trap before it became mangled, then marrow pulp throbbing, vanishing, as though it had come to him feverishly from an opening in the future. He was so lost in his reverie that having walked for a few miles he missed the sign for the ice lake: a strip of patterned orange cloth tied onto a branch, fluttering like the land's dazed oracle. Haplessly, he missed, too, the three warning cracks on the frozen lake as he forged ahead on the slippery surface. He slipped; a sharp crackle filled the air. It was the unmistakable sound of ice breaking. He fell in, the breath knocked out of him. There was a streak in the sky as the goshawk circled above, a whoosh, the shock of freezing water to the body, a frosty enveloping, a pain like hundreds of needles breaking skin, the animal trap becoming an ugly corroded creature in the water tugging him down further. The ceiling of ice was a new terrain to shatter as he ironically found himself trapped in the lake. The force of his fall, the water's freezing temperature, surprising shots of pain in his limbs was at first a shock, then a prompt to fight for his survival. He had been taught to swim by firelight as a child, to wade into springs with groups of boys, catching eels and fish that were slick and illusive using wooden spears, some wriggling away upstream to avoid the points of those weapons. But how could these excursions with the elders of the tribe prepare him for what loomed? An inevitable death at eighteen years of living on ancestral land had not been foreseen for him. There had been no worrying visits from his father or others in the tribe to warn him that this was a son who would bring bad luck or shorten the family line, nor pitying looks at his mother during gatherings, sad glances often reserved for those marked for a bad fate. Therefore, how could he bring about a travesty through carelessness? Tulugaak, who, his mother said, when born had squealed so loudly, bathed in the glow of soft candlelight, it challenged the sound of thunders. In his peripheral vision, the strip of patterned orange cloth from the tree's branch shook as though deciding to lodge itself in his memory. His arms flailed then instinct took hold. He kicked frantically, panicked, tried to let go of the animal trap but it had caught on his trouser leg, pulling him further into an ice-cold abyss. He reached for the knife strapped to his left ankle, sheathed in a leather covering. He cut into the right trouser leg, releasing the trap in the process. His eyes stung, his heart raced. A series of images flashed before him, chasing the sharpened blade like a small insurrection: his mother cutting leaks on a stone slab in their makeshift cooking area, an intense look of concentration on her face, the occasional wistful smile appearing. His father hauling wild boar through the snow on his way home, shoulders rising with the effort, his hands red and raw from the straps. His brothers playing on the path behind their home, laughing while slinging stones at each other in between plans to trick him.

Tulugaak sank further. His body's movements were spasms in an underwater world. He sensed the breath leaving him. He thought he could not hold on for much longer when he heard the call of the goshawk, distant at first, then closer. A sense of calm settled over him. He felt lighter than he had ever been, as though moving through consciousness. Those images from his life mimicked the movements of his limbs before becoming bursts of light ebbing away. He felt an upward surge, a breaking in his chest, a series of wings passing through him, the goshawks cries spreading in his veins like liquid sirens. The trap tumbling in the depths caught past drownings at the bottom of the lake. The orange cloth trembled again, as if realigning the quiet exchange between the land and the water. An internal injury the shape of a calendula bud bloomed in Tulugaak, just below his heart, waiting for instructions in the blood before it roamed. A cold, beating undertow rose to meet the skyline. He had no idea how long he had been under. He could not feel his limbs as he swam back up, reaching for the rusted pole that was poking through the water, grabbing it in relief, his fingers numb, his legs weak, his arms at the point of collapse. Just before he was carefully pulled out by a disgruntled passer-by the last thing he recalled, as though burned into his irises, was the goshawk multiplying into a procession then smashing its heads frantically through the lake's ceiling of ice.

The man who pulled him out of the frozen lake was not of his clan. He possessed one sleepy left eye that made him look suspicious, a long hollow face, and there were large red spots on several of the fingers on his left hand, like someone still recovering from an irritating affliction. They crawled off the ice carefully, back on to the winding path before speaking. The man's beard was shot with flecks of grey. His expression one of concern before changing to incredulity. 'You should be dead, young hunter,' he remarked, his dark eyes gleaming with anxiety it had absorbed from their situation. 'That lake is unforgiving. Many men more experienced than you have been swallowed into its depths, never to be seen again.'

Tulugaak spluttered in response, water spilling from the corners of his mouth. His body was shuddering, his teeth chattered. He felt oddly tricked by the surroundings, as though everything was in disguise: the path-hardened burial ground that gathered abandoned shadows, trees harbouring the last frightened cries of men they would later shed as warbling winds, heartbeats sucked into the movements of creatures at night. And perhaps the man himself, hunched over him, steadying his rising shoulders, was a kind of apparition, a figure his mind had manifested to help him cope with the shock. But the apparition seemed real enough even in Tulugaak's disorientated state. 'I could still be the greatest hunter in all of the Inuit lands,' he croaked, unable to control the anger seeping into his tone.

The man laughed, his face transforming into its full beauty, his eyes filled with mirth. 'You possess a spirit about you; good. I have a feeling that you are here for more than hunting.' He reached out, helping Tulugaak sit up. They gathered their breath for a few moments. The goshawk fluttered above, streaking through the sky in quiet celebration. The man, whose name was Nanurjuk, had travelled through several lands to negotiate over wolf furs, kindling and the rare root plants that grew in the area's frosty plains. He would do this every winter, without fail, for as long as he had breath in him. His clan relied on these isolated trips he enjoyed making. This gave him a certain reverence among his people, he said gravely. There was mischief in his eyes as he gripped Tulugaak, who threw his left arm over Nanurjuk's shoulder. His body, now leaning against him, moved stiffly. The surrounding areas swelled as though harbouring the breath and heartbeats of weary men. The wind dappled their strained bodies. They paused now and again to gather themselves along the way. And Nanurjuk kept talking to hold his attention, to stop his heavy lids from closing. On his way back, when he spotted a hole in the lake, he had been disgruntled from a difficult negotiation. It was almost as if that break in the water had escaped from his mind's eye. An age-old fear had manifested itself, the sound of ice splintering, lodging in his eardrums. His body coiled with tension at the memory. 'Young hunter, you were under for a long time without breathing. That should not be possible.' He slowed down a little, applying a gentle pressure to Tulugaak's shoulder as though to transmit his words through fingers into his subconscious. 'Now you know what is possible,' he whispered, hoisting him up again. 'The elements can work with you. You must surrender to Oni's wishes. She is all-seeing, you are her disciple kin.'

He left Tulugaak leaning against a fence just outside the perimeter of his community's stretch of round ice homes, insisting he was a humble man who did not want to receive any fanfare for his part in the rescue. Tulugaak was hailed as a hero by his clan, despite unwittingly falling to a possible death and losing his father's trap. Men more experienced than him had not survived that lake in the past.

After his recovery, when Tulugaak enquired about Nanurjuk's negotiations with the neighbouring community, nobody had ever seen or heard of him. It was as though he did not exist. He vanished, an apparition chasing dwindling cold tremors. A few days passed. The goshawk returned to watch over Tulugaak, who called to Oni now that the seed had been planted. He knew this creature somehow carried the root of his awakening, the mystery of Nanurjuk and Oni in its watery eyes, its rambling flights crashing into his dreams of underwater worlds with a hundred versions of himself waiting for release from a golden wing. And this time, the ice lake caught a womb at the bottom, pumping before releasing it so it would travel through time to find its reckoning.

Ten

It is the wound which roars Domingos's name in the homestead that warns me of a coming onslaught. I hear the sound of footsteps crunching on stones along the path, the rough urgent whispers between men, their beating hearts tainted with the seawater of pink octopuses. I sit up, the thin white bedding twisted between my thighs, my neck slick with sweat, angled curiously like a creature in the wild gauging what is to come. The silvery, bulbous moon an instrument of kin is full of doomed truth, the unruly garden growing chaotically wields the contorted shadows of men who come to claim some semblance of power threatened by my presence, their instructions to each other haphazard. The whispers are closer. 'She must pay for this latest death!' one says, his tone accusatory, splinters of dark punishments lodged in his mind. Another, whose voice rumbles in my eardrums like warped bells, replies, 'Remember, we take her without causing a disturbance. Do not alert Domingos. I fear he is bound to this woman in ways he does not recognise. He has let a poison into his home. We must save him from her treacherous desires.' I turn this desire over between my fingers like spiked fruit as the men draw closer. There is one among them whose voice is muffled yet seems vaguely familiar. A smoke-lined desire consumes a shaman over time. So much so that she attempts to keep secrets from her kin and the god of all, Oni, which she nurses in quiet moments between various lives. She turns this desire again until the other side of it is a torturous wound, an optical illusion that beats and changes currencies within her scarred heart. The men approach. There are four of them. They pull me roughly from my bed. My heart thunders but I do not protest what is inevitable.

'Bind her hands!' one orders. Their faces are covered with masks from the Montero celebrations. Their eyes gleam through them, cruel, iridescent pools. One slips a sack over my head with holes for my eyes and mouth only. The rope used to restrain me is rough against my wrists. Another speaks quietly, his breath laced with beer for courage. A jolt of recognition shoots through me, I know those voices from prior encounters. They are Domingos's fellow fishermen, the last one to speak with the beer breath is Paolo, the man whose wife Ezadaro thought she was becoming fruit, the woman who Domingos and I gifted a cut to in the slanted orchard. The marrow plants begin to weep as the men drag me out of the homestead. I am pulled along recklessly, barefoot, the sharp sting of stones, glass and the scatterings of nature's barbed vices taunt me on the way. The murky, swirling dark sky on the edge of dawn watches from above conspiratorially. Kin's voices rise through my eardrums. The heat is punishing, the taste of red dust fills my mouth. A jagged line of sweat runs down my back into a hollow that feels trapped between two countries named fear and doom. The homestead reduced to a shrunken force behind me is twisted, bereft without my wound to conduct *it. My new family do not rise nor hear the tempered commotion of my bundling. They are lost in feverish dreams offering no respite. I take note of details about these misguided characters before me, fishermen in arms betraying their leader, blinded by the belief that they are helping him. One stammers and has gout, the other wrestling with a faulty heart whose tremors can be bent or snuffed to the point of stillness. Another has a left wrist recovering from an injury. My crime, they say, is killing the man whose blindness worsened after I visited him, who was no doubt taken by kin as an offering for Oni. 'He was never the same after you saw him. Not after taking one of the concoctions you gave him,' the one with the bad wrist claims.*

We stop momentarily, two hold me on either side while I am punched repeatedly in the stomach by another. The pain of the blows drives me to my knees, my eyes spin and water. I crumple, breathing roughly. Brushes along the mountain path shudder, air between trees hisses, the golden circular signs hidden in the land fracture, dormant shadows start to rise.

I do not tell the men that kin ruined the man who turned blind after seeing them in the field to punish me. They brought his ending into being. A bloodied goshawk's wing infiltrates my eyeline from Oni's collapsible tent. Lying on the ground, the tension is so thick more torturous assailants could be hiding in its folds. I do not scream or protest as the men kick me viciously, shouting obscenities. This defiance costs me. One man removes the sack, his garish red mask flashing before me like an unhinged premonition. There is a blow to the back of my head, blood gushes out. I feel dizzy, things turn black. The rope on my wrists cuts into the screaming wound.

*

I do not recall how I get there but I am taken to the small prison holding reserved for one. A copper, shanty enclosure perched at the top of Sipu Mountain like part of a corroded tower. I am told I will have no trial as decided by the town council of faceless men. Instead, I will face the guillotine for the death of a man I ironically attempted to help due to the urgings of another who quietly taunts me with his sweet temptations. I think of the feeling of warmth and desire as his gaze rests on my changeable body, the softness of his breath on my neck in the homestead's pantry, the promise of the joining of loins that seduces and eludes us. I feel the barbed edge of memories I carry in my throat. My prison is a scorching instrument harnessing the will of kin. I am locked in. It is a suffocating space, at odds with its position high up, shrouded by swirling blue sky. Something dies in my mouth attempting to become a second tongue. The guards leave a rusted bowl for me to relieve myself in the left corner of the holding. Collapsed beside me is the dusty sack that obscured my vision along the route, damp with sweat. On one wall hangs half a pink rosary, an indulgence in this hellish precipice. I smell the stench of carcasses of the individuals who did not make it out alive. It is ingrained in the walls, thick and overwhelming, a form of quicksand for my nostrils. There are no windows, only two slits in the right-side wall that allows in a bit of light. I scramble towards it as if it is a shimmering pool of water in the desert, pressing my mouth against it, taking in gulps of air.

Hours pass, then days. Food is shoved in once a day, tasteless broths and hard slices of bread unfit for consumption. A vast, looming darkness threatens to swallow me.

I have no visitors except rotating guards with hungry eyes that linger on my body. Domingos's fishermen are long gone, leaving me to a cruel existence. I dream of Baby as respite. Baby's umbilical cord glimmers next to the rosary as headaches come that intensify. Rosary and new birth commune with the dead tongue in my mouth. One white feather slips in, bringing news of Gethsemane's happenings. It flutters in the dark, curling and bending above my head in recognition of something momentous on the horizon, its tip poised to inject the lines of a vanished island into my veins like an anointing. Mired in the changeable weather in my small prison holding, I become a spectacle for passers-by who approach gingerly, raising their heads to catch glimpses of the stranger held as the sacrificial lamb for the town's underbelly.

A cloth merchant from the Gambia with skin dark and smooth as a mahogany god asks me to solve a riddle in a song about a man who cannot find his lover in exchange for a dream with a resolution. The man finds this woman in rubble, not river reflection or mirage. I look at the merchant's oiled bald head through one slit, the light coming in as though it is an unfurled atlas. The right side of his mouth dips as if chewing something over. His blue garb with gold edges is foreign in these parts. His expression is open, measured. There is no judgement in it. I am surprisingly touched by this small act of compassion, a kindness that feels heightened in the moment. He listens to my movements as if they possess a knowledge along with the sway of my nightdress skirt harbouring tiny miracles. 'The woman does not want you to find her, which is why she continues to outwit you even in a song,' I say, shielding my eyes against the rising red dust, the restless cluster of flies buzzing in the slits as sporadic harmonies. He is vulnerable, crestfallen and wounded before my eyes.

'How do I reconcile with the weight of her loss? What am I to do in the end?' he asks. I let the silence linger for a moment before answering. 'I am the wrong person to ask about endings,' I offer, watching the flies charging at his mouth in case there is something sweeter there than a dead second tongue. 'Endings become something else entirely in my hands.'

That night, the guard with the lingering gaze rapes me, hitting me in the face with such force he bruises his knuckle. It knocks me to the ground. The injury at the back of my head opens up. Blood spills again like a series of ruptured jewels. My arms are held back. His sweat smells sharp and unpleasant, his breath stale. One stained, chipped front tooth is another mutilation in the dark. He moves inside me, panting when the clattering rosary mutates into my shrieking marrow plants. His penis detaches, coming off within me. He screams, shoving me aside, frantically patting between his legs urgently. It is too late, kin already claim it as an offering for the blue tent in Oni's honour on the other side. He backhands me, furiously hissing and spitting a barrage of insults. Now frightened, deflated, he scrambles away from me. Blood in my mouth is a familiar comfort, a favourite old blanket. Thick currents in the air belong to kin. I laugh maniacally, head and wound dangling from the precipice. Baby's umbilical cord and the rosary exchange confessions, conspiring against shattering copper walls blurring into oblivion in between the sharp pains in my head, flashes of light through the slits doubling as an indicator of time.

The guard who attempted to make my body a desolate husk retches, doubled up in pain, muttering unintelligible recollections to the far corners of the mountains' peaks which flicker *remorselessly, dispassionate in their splendour. I watch from the cavernous slits as he is taken away, faint, his pallor paler, his demeanour collapsed, that feline quality to his expression subdued. The slip of red cloth protruding from his trouser pocket is spotted with dirt, frayed from being an inadvertent witness to his calculated attempt at my destruction. He is unable to speak of his diabolical act, for tampering with one who is part of kin.*

Three weeks pass, the rains come, thundering and heavy, anointing the fingers I stick out to catch droplets. I dance like a mad woman in my shuddering, suffocating prison to honour those rains, the respite of water from unpredictable skies. Kin circle above, invisible to others, slipping in through the slits for my wound. A blunted thorn, Baby's face appears less defined, stretching towards another womb. Food is sparse so I become thinner. A metal bucket with water is brought in for me to wash myself. Rowena comes to inform me of the women's seaweed hunting group's attempt to lobby the town's council on my behalf. This time she smells of vanilla and peppery notes, the scents of Montero clouding my nostrils again making me feel so unsteady that her tempered vibrancy is no form of relief. The throbbing in my temples increases as her scent intoxicates me to a sickly state. I fear I am going mad with unbearable headaches and distorted visions. Advocating on my behalf fell on deaf ears. She tries to lift my sour mood, telling me of her last attempt to make beer which she tested on a few goats at a neighbour's farm who collapsed in drunken stupors. Even this light relief does not ease the tension; marking the days on the wall with a stick of chalk shrinking in my fingers stops the untethered feeling from completely consuming me. Domingos's decayed homestead throbs in my peripheral vision. When its lines begin to spill through the slits of my prison I cannot tell if feather, chalk or the madness in me causes this.

On the day of my beheading, I offer kin more incantations. My songs come from my core, like they did as a young woman many moons before. The air is thick and changeable with tension. The sly scent of prisoners who did not make it out of this hellish pinnacle alive taunts me. My fingernails are lined with crusted earth and chalk, my mouth dry from the dead entity no longer wanting to be a second tongue. There is fear in the faces of the two guards left to tend to me, given what occurred with their fellow guard earlier. This delights me. I laugh maniacally at times. They do not know what to make of my proud demeanour even in the face of annihilation; my strange chanting, my bursts of ramblings pacing back and forth in the holding built to destroy. The guards bring me a final meal of tasteless vegetable broth which seems trite, pointless amid a litany of horrors. I pour it down cracks in the left corner of the prison, fissures waiting to reveal their true power. My body aches, numb and heavy, when murmurs from the clay heart under the homestead come through those fissures. I follow its deep reverberations, transporting my spirit back to my temporary home of dysfunction and hidden cruelties.

Sueli misses my presence, whispering to me before the mirror, confiding to the crescent-marked figures of future kin who flash before her seductively, wanting to lure her to whatever lies on the other side. She waters my marrow plants tenderly, marvelling at their plump, shiny grapes, refracting porous centre, humming to comfort them as she has seen me do in the past. Domingos and Marguerite sleep side by side in a cold existence. I think of the scent of the sea on his skin, the way his gaze lingers on my collarbone as though it is a necklace under the flesh, his desire to linger around me holding catches of the day like watery conundrums. Longing and anger explode inside me in a collision that makes my hands tremble. I weep silently. Outside, red dust rises like a palpable mist just as the guards bang on the door of my sun-stroked holding. The feather is lodged in my nightdress pocket. Since I was not given a change of clothing, I had to wash the armpits with water brought in for me to clean myself, afterwards placing the sack used to obscure my vision over my bare breasts while the nightdress dried in the acrid heat.

They take me outside, the hot weather providing little relief for them. Their obvious anxiety to be rid of me is a gulf between us. The feather becomes a key made of smoke in my pocket. The sound of a fractured drumbeat, slow at first then quicker, rises in my eardrums. The afternoon light feels blinding, illuminating the beauty of Gethsemane, engraving it into my memory. Its lush mountains and peaks are tempting illusions to lose myself in. We walk down the mountain, cross the river, heading towards the town square. The drumbeat disrupts my heartbeat. The wound at the back of my head opens again. Kin's whispers rise like a fog. I am parched, touching a void with dry fingers. At the town centre, the streets are lined with people who have come to sneer and gawp at the woman accused of sorcery and murder. Their accusatory gazes pierce my skin. A few throw sticks at me shrieking, 'Murderer, finish her! We must root out the bad eggs from our town.'

Their chants become a blur. I turn away, my gaze is fixed ahead; a calm washes over me. On the raised circular area of the square at the far end of one street where more crowds gather, a man awaits with a guillotine. We walk towards him. The guards deposit me on the raised area by the executioner, who does not look me in the eye. I am left there, a doomed creature awaiting a brutal ending. The executioner places my head in the guillotine carefully. The tightness around my neck is swift, the feather as key of smoke slips from my pocket. I start chanting to kin. Blood trickles into my eye. The executioner, a fairly large man, is unable to work the guillotine. His eyes are completely white, his irises gone. He is blinded, falls to his knees screaming. Kin take his irises as an offering to Oni. The smoke key unlocks the guillotine. The crowds are stunned into silence. I slip my head out from the heavy circular construction, throat hurting, fingers numb, eyes strained from the blood inside them, wound exposed like gnarly mouth. The shattering of the dead thing trying to be my second tongue now shards of light. I dodge my own beheading before the guillotine snapped in the greatest sleight of hand the people of Gethsemane witness. Stepping off the raised area into the crowd, my head throbs, the executioner screams behind me. The crowd parts, forming a path for me, the mad shaman sorceress with blood in her vision. They are stunned into a quiet state mingled with shock and fear. One woman steps back from me, holding her baby a little tighter. A haggard man with a fading hairline clutches his sugarcane stick. The fury manifests in me again. Domingos did not come to visit me during my imprisonment, nor did he advocate for me. This second betrayal burns a hole of cinders into my body as I make my way towards the homestead, scarred, bruised and bloody.

Chapter 10

Finn rose to the sound of his wounds migrating in the blood, an internal chorus prompting his body into action with their mutating shapes. These architects were a galvanising force within him searching for secrets twisting out of his reach. His wounds communicated at impromptu moments; he felt the sharp sting of them during sex. They were intoxicated pockets when the whisky seeped into his bones, reduced to wailing repositories while he weaved his body through urban landscapes punctuated by quiet warfare. He imagined these wounds he'd traced many times after the mutations that occurred on the other plane as if they were small meteorites seeking sources of sustenance. He moved gingerly, throwing the rumpled duvet aside. His head throbbed; his limbs were stiff, as though they'd been put through intense activities. His mouth was salty.

The memory of mist from Ovida's tank clouded it then faded into the air. Finn took several deep breaths, eyes sleep speckled. The blare from the radio filled the room. The space pulled him into an undercurrent, a fracturing of a scene from

Gethsemane. He heard the clatter of wind in seashells colliding against a spill from the tank, unleashing those tender sweet berries into light-studded throats in oblivion. Ovida had visited another plane when they departed for their ritual. He was sure of it. He'd been plagued by curiosity since that night. He knew it was all connected. The four of them, he was certain, had turned over versions of that thought like a small corrosive memento as the night faded away. He remembered the white seeds left out in the bowl for him in Gethsemane, the octopus wound like his that he'd touched as though it was a star, a feeling of recognition in his limbs. He thought of Ovida spilling marrow fruit into their lives, and that strange feeling of recognition hit him again. It was hazy, like the lines of a memory not yet ready to reveal itself. He grimaced, an image of Emilien flashed, hovering over him, spilling wounds from his mouth in an anointing which filled him with dread. But then the image vanished, sucked into a crack on the fringes. Pain shot across his back. Grabbing the towel slung over a lone wooden chair, he left his room, whistling *The Addams Family* tune.

He crossed the stairs awkwardly, conscious of being too noisy. Emilien pacing back and forth in his room rang like a stifled alarm. The floor creaked in response. He paused at the top of the landing, hand gripping the dark banister tightly. He released another breath. The pacing paused as if Emilien, poised like an unruly hunter in from the wild, had picked up his signal. Finn considered knocking on his door to check-in but decided against it. They had their ways of coping, of seeing and reaching into each other's rhythms. The unknowable parts they bore formed a concave of darkness inside them.

Some days, Emilien was a charismatic soulful man, keenly observant, shrewd, but he had a restlessness that Finn found intriguing. On other occasions, he seemed like a stranger. As if some configuration in him had recalibrated, matter made malleable in the quiet hours. He'd been disappearing quite a bit, keeping himself separate, not being as involved with the group except for Therese and when they did their rituals of flight to the other dimensions. The other day Finn had rummaged through his room while he was absent. He wasn't sure what he was looking for but he was curious about why he seemed more distant. His room was in a reasonable state. And there were the nosebleeds. Increasingly Emilien experienced frequent nosebleeds, something that rarely ailed him in the past, the blood gushing out at impromptu moments including when they gathered. From certain angles, it looked as though Emilien's right nostril was eroding, turning darker at the bottom edge. That day in his room, Finn came across his sketchpad resting on the large wicker chair. He flicked it open; halfway through, his breath caught. Emilien had sketched a girl clutching a bloody hoe. He had a strong feeling of familiarity. Her eyes were distant, her expression calm, as if whatever act the hoe was used for had been an inevitable occurrence. Her dress was made of cotton and flames, the blue- and orange-tongued flames ascending from the hem, rising upwards, yet she seemed removed from it. He staggered backwards, a throbbing in his temples, his mouth desert dry. He was certain he'd seen this girl in Gethsemane.

He ran to the basement to sip the misty waterfall from Ovida's ribcage, something he now did regularly when the pain and haziness flooded his body like a cursed dam. At first, he'd done it to investigate. Start with the fruit then the liquid, the thrill and sense of wonder felt like divinity. This was communion in the kaleidoscopic vacuum while shadows broke like disrupted bats. He had tasted sweetness in the water, an earthy depth to the flavour that was also herbal. Sometimes it helped ease the stinging of his wounds, but it was lodging other things inside him too, the memories from the white seeds in Gethsemane. He saw the heads of children disintegrating into crop signs in that faraway land, heard bones rattling in the front hallway like nature's chimes. A tilted axis was covered in spots of blood. In a separate traffic, the azure sky had crashed into gleaming, spilled fruit. Kin's hand deposited fistfuls of pink mass into his wounds.

For Finn, the game was not losing your courage in the dark. Its nooks, hollows and folds, its unquantifiable might. The hold it possessed which could engulf you, if you let it. But boys would be boys. Aged twelve, they wanted to test themselves in these slipstreams and barbed spaces to experience some parochial idea of thorny teenage life. And teenage life in Runswick Bay, Yorkshire – as scenic as the village was, with its beautiful bay and charming red-roofed cottages – didn't always offer enough to do. So the boys, Finn and his friends Topher, Arlo and Grayson, would create excitement in the form of dares. They would conjure up challenges huddled over copies of *Playboy* magazine that Arlo had pilfered off the top shelf from the local newsagent while browsing for crossword books, or sitting around the back table in the school dining hall, or passing notes in RE, or knocking the curved heads of their hockey sticks after a game. And the sticks became wooden warriors in conversation, slick with the sheen of sweat from boys in competition on a field.

I dare you to leave a condom full of phlegm in Mrs Winters' handbag. Mrs Winters was their hard-faced tiny dictator of a maths teacher who didn't look unlike Margaret Thatcher, fondly nicknamed *Maggie Baby* by Topher. Occasionally, she'd make the sign of the cross sarcastically in class, her beady eyes watching them attempting and failing to solve equations, her mouth a flat line of disapproval while the boys displayed their comic antics before bursting into fits of laughter.

They could each instigate or suggest a dare to another member of the group. If you forfeited, there was no offering of truth instead as a compromise. That was for amateurs. You had to do two dares the next time. *I dare you to leave one of your father's model aeroplanes from the air show on a school rooftop.*

What? He'll kill me if he finds out. (A sullen Grayson, pissed at drawing the short straw.)

I dare you to put some of the frog we'll be dissecting in Supplementary Science into your mouth. (Finn levelled this at Arlo, who he knew had a sensitive stomach.)

That's disgusting. I could catch salmonella or start having an itch on random parts of my body. I could develop leprosy in my dick. Pass!

You can't forfeit asshole; you know the rules if you do.

Yeah, I get it, but Finn came up with that, the deviant.

The other rule was at least one of them had to be present to witness these acts. The dares became ritualistic for boys who'd seen blood on the horizon but didn't know why.

*

Finn knew he was different although he couldn't fully understand how. There was Inuit ancestry on his mother's side which he found fascinating. He kept it to himself, not out of shame. In fact, he was proud of it. His mother Adrienne had revealed this to him one night over a dinner of chilli con carne, her pretty, heart-shaped face ashen as she filled his plate with a trembling hand, glancing longingly at the absence of a body in his father's chair. It was a moment of quiet joy for him despite the circumstances. The table was immaculately set with a rose-patterned cloth, her good silver cutlery on display, a large vase of fresh chrysanthemums in the middle. Two other places were marked with warm plates, as if unexpected guests would breeze through the dining-room archway wearing the clothes and bearing the mannerisms of a bad husband. It was Finn's secret to cultivate, the power of ancestry, what it released in his veins, subtly stoking his curiosities, wilful embers hungry for fires yet to be claimed. Already a strapping, green-eyed force, Finn had a mischievous coolness other boys were drawn to. He could happily participate in the shenanigans of boyhood; it suited his thirst for adventure. There was a darkness swirling in his eyes, storms gathering then made to change direction. He wore his intelligence well. He could quote Voltaire in a conversation then round off with a lamentation on Russian Marxist philosophy followed by a segue to Stuart Hall while the other boys looked on blankly. He was smart enough to know he had to meet them at their level most times in order to not cause jealousy or rattle the cage. He had an interest in other cultures. He knew, for example, that at the Holi Festival of Colours in India, which had been celebrated since the fourth century, people painted their bodies during the celebration, offering coloured limbs in joyful abandon. He loved the story behind its origins. He liked geography, English literature and the sciences. He adored old maps – the feel of them in his hands was special, the scent of weathered paper filling his nostrils made him feel he was on the verge of discovering something exciting. A telescope in his attic room collected the memories of stars in sporadic instalments. Wandering the school hallways, often whistling absentmindedly, there was usually a rolled-up map of the byzantine era in a pale plastic tube along with a copy of *The Adventures of Tintin* languishing contentedly at the bottom of his rucksack, leaning against the zipper in a state of reciprocal confessions. He had an appreciation for folklore, myths and legends, for individuals who possessed the ability to reinvent themselves. The stack of books on his compact single shelf above the chestnut set of drawers in his bedroom were on explorers who dared to venture into new or hidden worlds. There was a copy of a book about the great Black arctic explorer, Matthew Henson, the first to reach the North Pole, which Finn inhaled with real interest, as well as biographies on Nan Shepherd, Roald Amundsen and Pedro Alvares Cabral. The escapades seeped into one another while the books' spines took on a luminous quality. Sometimes, on nights he felt lonely, he listened to a recording of Johnny Cash at Folsom Prison on the stereo. Afterwards, it felt as if a constellation had slid into his brain.

Finn had a secret he could not tell the other boys. Oni the shaman god had begun to appear to him through the cracks of his existence, a dusky-skinned, long-limbed beauty who whispered about powers that would be his, waiting for him to claim them. She instructed him to fill the blue tent with offerings from the dares. He would recognise them when they came. His teenage masturbations were to Oni's voice, the thought of her unfurling her tongue over his body, her hand reaching through voids into him, stoking him to keep daring to do dangerous things. When she visited him in his room one night bathed in an incandescent light, she was made mighty in his mind and soul. He vowed then she would always have his heart. It ached for her incessantly after that first encounter. She was cruel at times, ignoring his calls to her, after refusing to manifest when he cried for her in the dark sometimes she ruined him for other women down the line, denying him the desire to be truly intimate with lovers in the future. Despite this, she whispered in his ear that he must do something for her: an act of retribution for his failing in a past life, a spill of blood offering was needed.

One night, he dreamed of a wretched earth where the cactuses bayed like wolves, the sky swirled the heads of goshawks in a bloodied backdrop. Oni's north wind conspired on his behalf. In the morning, those images filled his throat, awaiting interpretations in the light. And so when Finn's latest dare was issued, thrown at him by Arlo after an argument over a missing signed copy of *1984* in the science block hallway with locker doors slamming, the bell ringing loudly, the fracas of other bodies ricocheting as though contending it, Finn wasn't resistant. That was the whole point of these feats, to take them on even if it was out of their comfort zones, which they usually were. The boys had a mantra when there were hesitations: *What would Evel Knievel do?* Exceptions were made if a dare could potentially result in serious injury or death. This dare was being buried alive in a cavernous, gutted space in the old windmill area. It had a makeshift covering of an eroded wooden board marked with smeared words from felt pens that had lost their definition. Worms wriggled through small holes in it. The powdered wings of butterflies made it nature's derelict trapping. What sort of boy would want their friend to be buried alive? And what kind of boy would accept the challenge without batting an eye? If there was a dead body in there already, he'd have company. What if he was claustrophobic, asthmatic or panicked in the dark? Ironically, Finn had none of these issues, but he was irritated that it fell on a weekend, a Saturday, which meant he'd have to do it after his morning paper round. Post his hands sliding rolled-up newspapers into door slots waiting to be fed.

On arriving at the field where the white windmill stood at one end like an arch-nemesis, a feeling of anticipation filled his stomach. He pictured the windmill catching costumes as if they were skin as it spun. A fine sheen covered blades of grass from earlier light rainfall. The scent of scattered dandelions lingered in the air, a cluster of wasps hovered above, fat with the lines of other weekend afternoons, perhaps dispatched from the future to follow his progression. A gold cat's cradle fell from his pocket, multiplying into temporary cotton plants bending restlessly in the field in a trick of light. As he made his way towards that grave, he saw the cat's cradles reshaping into unidentifiable things. In the distance behind him, one of the boys paced back and forth, true to the agreement of bearing witness although he couldn't tell which one it was.

The snake of concrete behind that figure was a road leading into the back of town, a highway of twisted dreams becoming passengers in vehicles that crossed it, the sounds dwindling into a series of thinning echoes.

At the spot, the air seemed thicker, as if the tension and excitement in him had spilled out, transformed into particles. He moved aside the long, gnarly branches then the wooden board. He climbed in, creating a temporary ceiling with the branches. It was at least five feet deep, a hollow muddy crevice bearing an assortment of items: bottles, old crisp packets, shoes. It was a chaotic assembling of unfinished miniature tales. This grave the earth had spawned waited for his discomfort, his heart beating like tiny breaks inside it. He lay on his back looking through the darkness, breathing through his mouth to tolerate the stench around him. He'd have to haul himself up. One way or another, his upper-body strength would be a factor in getting out of there. Otherwise, he'd need to rely on the boys coming and seeing his humiliation if he ended up stuck. But who knew if they'd turn up early enough or allow him to sweat there for a few hours. Whoever issued a dare had power. If you completed it successfully, you took back the precarious crown that toppled off their heads weekly, at least temporarily. Little Mussolinis all of them, waging secret wars against the perceived leader of the pack. The shadow in the distance still paced, ready to be consumed by an accident.

Finn tried to lie still. Beads of sweat formed on his temples. His heart rate increased. The thrill in his bloodstream splintered like tiny flame-filled fissures. He reached for the light through the branches, his ceiling of companions. He touched the shapes of others who had deposited items into this gutting. It was cold and dank. A few rats scurried over his legs before making their way to his ears. The bottles jutting out from underneath him made it even more uncomfortable. He closed his eyes as though trapped in a requiem. A wing flapped in the air, almost brushing his face. He listened for it again. Sure enough the sound repeated then multiplied. He reached out, touching what felt like a procession of beaks moving. His eyes watered in the dark. His tongue loosened, floating in his parched mouth like a pink defector angling to reach the multiverse. The ground trembled. The rats started screeching. The wind became a chorus of whistles passing through squashed cans, casting some branches aside, scattering his temporary ceiling so the aerial view was of his body spasming in an angle of blue light.

When Finn emerged from that trap roughly two hours later there was a filminess to his eyes. He was achy from bodily contortions that were misshapen stars in the dark. He appeared high from the cold, the muddy earth, a vast sky that was cloudy blue glass in his vision. Acting as an antenna, his beating tongue tried to locate items he'd lost from his pockets, swallowed by the chasm in an unforeseen exchange. He was disorientated. Later, he'd try to process what had happened to him. He limped towards the shadowy figure beckoning in the distance. He still couldn't tell which one of the boys it was, pacing out of reach in a brink of their own making, where the sky had colluded alongside pieces of a puzzle they each held with shaky fingers. Maybe the boys had merged into one for this act of bearing witness, wielding the innards of something dangerous, the inky hue of discontent, a fangled tooth from the abyss, and just outside of them on the periphery, Oni's hand stoking the tension between boys on the cusp of something magnificent.

Finn laughed as the figure came into focus, a fleeting apparition, grappling with the first wound that had formed inside him in the cold hollow, blooming through a dare. The apparition of boys seemed to be made of blinding light. He raised his arms, bracing against it. The first internal wound opened like a mouth born from a bloodied edge. He knew then that the first offering for Oni would be one of his friends. Later, the pain from that, which spread to future wounds, was unimaginable. And after leaving him with that pain, brutally, Oni never offered healing for his wounds, holding the debt over his head each time he thought he'd paid it.

Eleven

Upon my return to the homestead, Domingos is shaken to see me. Pleasure and guilt intermingle in his expression. His mouth opens in shock. Sueli rushes to greet me, shouting, 'Where have you been? Papa would not say.' She tugs at my skirt. They each take on a new dimension in the battered homestead. I walk towards Marguerite, who stares at me with fear in her eyes, her expression crestfallen. She raises her arm towards me as though I am an illusion before her, grasping for threads collapsing between us. 'I am sorry I could not come in your hour of need,' she says as a peace offering. Domingos rushes to embrace me. I tremble with anger in his arms, watching a hollow hare spin on a hook in the pantry like a silent arbiter of chaos.

Later he washes my bloodied feet tenderly in the garden. His head bowed over them in contemplation, gently rubbing his finger along a throbbing green vein on my left foot. His mouth hollow then curved down in regret. It is as he washes my feet gently that I wonder if he instructed the fishermen to remove me from his homestead. After all, a betrayer loves you with one hand, guts you with the other.

Frightened of my abilities, the town let me be. No more henchmen are sent to take my brutalised body from its temporary home. Word spreads: the foreign woman has an unholy entity on her side. It is past the witching hour when the marrow plants start shrieking quietly. They are nature's sirens, poised to sense a disruption. The clay heart turns slowly in the cold soil beneath the homestead, crumbling a little more, a break appearing across it, a bolt of lightning shooting through. I sit up in my bed shivering, listening for my marrow disciples in their hiding place softly breaching through walls and barriers that manifest, that dare to test their resilience. The bone hidden in the wall keeps the secrets I carried with me to this town, this time and the life due to come. I trace its shape in my mind's eye as though it is a comfort, running my fingers across its length, feeling it swell, a call to my blood in soft murmurs. A language only kin can interpret. I am restless on this hallowed night. I cannot fathom why. The air is charged, cold, and mottles my skin. Dark bedding is tangled between my legs, the blood rushing to my head. Through the window, I see a fine mist unfurling from Jellah Mountain in the distance, breathing its intentions for the coming day in gentle weather-shrouded proclamations. The homestead is at an angle. I am certain of it, as if creatures burrowing below have been instructed by an invisible axis leaning to one side. The creatures eat tiny bits of clay as fuel. Swallows circle the mountains' silhouettes after losing their heads momentarily in the smoggy skyline before regaining them again. I know this illusion from watching it of a morning or two, slipping it into my frayed nightdress pocket, willing my skirt to trap the skyline.

My mouth is dry, my tongue loose, floating in its own unmoored moist cavern where the potential of what it could become in the dark are endless. The dead thing from my prison holding no longer resides there. Miracles await it, shaped by hands not of this world. The sounds of movements in our rapturous, dilapidated garden filter through, assured rustlings, as if the visitor already knows the homestead's corners and bodies by memory. The visitor is rummaging. My bone pulses in the wall, its heartbeat mimicking mine. The circular markings from the cave glimmer on the wall. I raise my knees; bend my head towards it, feeling out of my body. They say the witching hour can bring the ancestors out. Perhaps one has come to search for something. When the homestead feels precariously balanced, its rhythms and confessions intensify in my eardrums. I hear Sueli tossing in her sleep, attempting to make sense of the language kin placed in her spritely, small body at its most vulnerable state, the expressions on her face fleeting, faint as if hand drawn, the soft release of breath through her parted mouth. Domingos's snores rumble in the bedroom across from mine. The shadows of their daily disappointments want to wear their clothes. They are unaware and sickness spreads within Marguerite's frail body seeking the origins of a desperate metamorphosis. My hunger cannot be sated in the hold of this yolk night where longings spring forth. The visitor in the garden is future kin, searching for sustenance, scouring unearthly planes for relief. Later, I find a small headless paper woman lying in the vegetation, a malevolent calling card.

I command Marguerite's limbs after spotting her stumbling from their room at dawn's light, her face paler and sweaty, heaving over a metal bowl, her curly hair a frizzy halo, her breath short. My commands find a home in her body, playing its part in what cannot be undone. A knot of anxiety settles in my stomach. I turn my body towards Domingos's rumblings, wanting to rest my head on his shoulder for comfort or blow air gently on the dip in his back where a tension gathers, or run my fingers knowingly over the rougher, tighter skin on the burnt right side of his face, holding his gaze. Some days, I sense a thawing in him regarding my presence. When he brings the day's catch home there is a growing curiosity, the lingering of his fingers passing daily offerings between us that I cook, including a surprise ingredient in each meal for the family to guess. Moments of wonder and lightness in a homestead where the traps left by kin's hands never announce their arrival. There is more than one foreign entity in this house. I reach for a worn brown shawl, throwing it over my shoulders. A memory rushes towards me, a horizon filling my chest. It is Domingos sipping from a woman's new wound with me, the cut in the orchard, his mouth bloodied, his eyes drunk with a desire he dare not name, his hands shaking in anticipation.

And my mouth,

my eyes,

my tongue becoming all he sees in that momentary surrender.

Gethsemane in its corner of Cabo Verde is a god's vision. The night air is loaded with possibilities of the coming day. The mountains shift seductively. Creeks sing with the cacophonies of underwater wanderings. Waterfalls house the bright-eyed infants of ghosts. The trees shimmer. The soil possesses the hue of dunes. The pulse in my neck hums as though a hornet found its way there, set on feeding from the throbbing inside me before finding itself in a dazed state. I untangle the bedding from my thighs, head to the golden circular patterns beckoning me from the wall to the left. I trace them with an unsteady finger. They are delicate manifestations waiting to be airborne, to play their part. These *patterns have begun to appear on farmland across Gethsemane. News of one farmer, Mirelo, walking back and forth over the enlarged patterns under moonlight as if crossing parts of a map he does not understand has trickled through the town. He may fall into the golden circle's molten centre, innocent to the methods of Oni. The true penance for one who betrays their clan is hidden in the harmattan winds. Kin will keep enacting punishments for my selfish act, my break away from the pack, to be led by one's desire to harness the possibilities of my power. The hunger in my body finds ways to resurrect itself when I think it is sated. Rustling in the chaotic garden deepens. More visits from future kin occur. It is a rustic oasis nurtured by my hands growing yams, vegetables, herbs, and an assortment of cooking and healing necessities. The hornet pulse multiplies its wings in my neck. I follow the sound coming from out back.*

I remember that original passage in the womb.
  The first birth.
  The cocoon of water and foreign organs. My tiny limbs growing, the sounds of ritualistic chanting in its walls, voices of several women singing to me, blessing me, guiding my travel through that vessel of cells, blood and matter. Kin marking it, claiming bloodlines as my limbs grew to that celebration of an imminent arrival.
  I responded in kind, kicking, turning to face the opposite direction then back again, as though mastering the art of movements. The study of learning to walk in different lives began then, in the marrow. This is how I come to carry my own marrow from that first birth in the bone where it regenerates to provide sustenance when needed. It is a source of danger and unpredictability in the wrong hands.

My marrow bone's shadow, the pale husk that scales the rooftops of Gethsemane, operating as a compass of misdirection to unwitting households, catching tiny breaks of light as a quiet inheritance. And the birds of the town are heady from attempts to carry these secret revelations brimming beneath the surface of daily life to the sky.

And so the first birth. And Baby who I still dream of.

That emergence from a moist, retracting hole, the slippage of manifestations growing over seasons, the body slick with womb-lining liquid, tiny fists curled, mouth mid-scream. Baby came into the world to a trickle of rain falling on my skin, a light between the trees splintering, the swirl of forestry as my surroundings. The safety of a womb was gone for now, at least temporarily. The cluster of kin were a series of dusky moons surrounding a startled expression. Their breasts were slick with sweat, their tight ringed curls damp, mouths upturned at the corners. They bore satisfactory expressions, gleams in their eyes. Exchanging looks of confirmation, their mauve-coloured dresses billowed at the waist while they leaned in, reaching for a tiny bundle. They had all given birth to Baby with me at once.

Here in Gethsemane, several nights before, kin show me where the three feathers from the vanished burning island have lodged themselves now, carried by a marauding wind that argued with their tips. The feathers are instruments always ready to be dispatched; wielding traces of smoke, hallowed screams and the crackle of fires with blue- and orange-tongued flames rapidly engulfing inhabitants. For now, the feathers observe quietly before dispersing to their next dwelling.

One feather is situated in the lock of the animal pen at the Divallo farm on Piranu Mountain within a reasonably sized homestead of six acres. Nobody knows which member of the family placed it in the lock, perhaps one of the two boys. But the feather itself landed on the farm on a bright breezy morning where the delivery of deerskin was taken to the dressmaker's store in town. It flutters into the pen, white and deceptively delicate, landing on the moist trails of bulls. And the bulls, increasingly drawn to it, circle while it pulses before them. After two days, the bulls have smoky silhouettes, becoming restless as another day passes, as Domingos and his band of treacherous fishermen haul a chest full of jewellery from the waters. Lying amid the bed of winking jewellery is a finger as though it slipped from one of the rings in turbulent seas. It is an ironic confirmation that nobody knows what the waters will bring to the contraptions of men who foolishly think they can outwit them.

The feather in the company of bulls continues to make good on its promise to kin. Soon, the pen is filled with smoke at unexpected moments. And yet, there is no fire or wood or kindling starting it a person can physically touch, no flames stretching in lofty intentions to commune with women who glimmer like spectral ghosts. Soon, the Divallos are throwing buckets of water at fires that are impossible to trace. Their roughened hands shaking, clutching clinking handles. And the bulls rush from the pen, startled by the chaos, inhabiting screams in the dark, perilous disruptions that do not belong to them.

The second feather lingers in the dressmaker's shop inside the crevice above the door where a pair of small brass bells chime on people entering, bringing bits of weather, gossip and footprints of soil, evidence that certain grounds are softening in Gethsemane.

The feather propelled by a gust of air from the door swinging open lands on the shoulder of Marianna Galepo, a tall, handsome woman with surprisingly elegant hands who often bears a deceptively stern expression. A seamstress producing clothes for the town in her tight back room under the gaze of kerosene lanterns. Often with slyly flickering flames and swathes of materials spilling from a table hewn from beech wood, tiny white orchids growing on it. Marianna sets aside a day every month to treat herself to something unexpected. On this day, when the feather lands on her in a swift baptism, she does not think anything of her heart thudding, her eyes widening, the keenness of her fingers grazing various materials. She notices this alien thing on her person, plucks it off her left shoulder distractedly, unaware of its power. Briefly, she looks at it curiously while the bright cloths beckoning swim in her peripheral vision and the jewellery winks in glass cabinets like beaded insects. It is merely a thing in her fingers. Comically, she thinks it could just as easily be a coin, a ball of cotton, a dart with which to poison one's enemies. Marianna possesses a caustic humour she relies on when the world closes in on her lonely homestead. She cultivates it over seaweed beer made by the hands of other women in the town. The pots of fresh flowers hanging from the corners of the shop are gathered off the bottom of Noma Mountain. They glisten with the dew of new dawns. Marianna moves away from blocking the store entrance, snapping out of her reverie, thinking that the feather is the first surprising gift she should embrace in the store. She slips it into her skirt pocket. And the feather lies nestled in a slit of silken darkness, waiting to stir the echoes of dissatisfaction with its dust-covered tip.

*

I think of kin circling the skies of Gethsemane; plotting, tracing the silhouettes of soft infiltrations. I see the curve of their spines in flight, releases of measured breaths, the fluttering of tiny wings scaling their throats like stunted towers, a filminess to their eyes as though carrying the beginnings of rainfall in those irises. I miss the beating heart of this sisterhood which grows in depth and dimension, pulsing in the rugged surroundings between the mountains, filling the driftwood shrines with its own form of thunder, grazing the mountains' crevices in a tumultuous dance to rival the omnipotence of gods. I must reconcile with letting one of my births go, leaving its absence to the grasping hands of future kin, breaking away with a fervour destiny witnessed. Flashes of my feet bleeding in frothing white waters come to me. The ache of hunger within is problematic again. Now that I have planted it in Domingos, I can sense his body dreaming of unspoken desires in the dark.

Sueli groans, tossing and turning. One arm flails in resistance to something. The ache in me is spreading. I push it down, trying not to fathom its meaning; blinking away the image of offerings in circular, golden patterns, the souls gathered from robbed carcasses left behind like derelict outhouses. I stand awkwardly, body disconcerted; I head towards the ripple in the garden drawing closer.

I stand still in the back doorway for a few moments. Cool air grazes my skin, my clammy blue nightdress billows, as if planning its own reckless departure. I spot the shape beside the vegetable patch then, low on its hunches, snarling. One of kin's students, a dog from the pack, having broken away begins to shatter the shard of stained glass in its mouth against a blushing, plump beetroot jutting out at an angle in salvation, like a shattered mirror in an unyielding grip.

*

After the ruinous crown I fashioned for Marguerite catches an umbilical cord, dog teeth and moonshine within its gnarly folds, Domingos releases it into the scowling sea. He is dismayed witnessing Sueli pierce her finger crowning herself in Rowena's mirror, raising the cut over her right eye then chanting that foreign language of kin's while flinging her arms up in triumph. The crown floats in the sea after departing from Domingos's hand, pulled in by a ravenous tide wielding fisheyes and stray branches. I watch Domingos from my vantage point, hiding behind a crumbling crevice on Jellah Mountain. The surrounding homesteads are perched precarious watchmen. The high tide is a precipice. Faces etched in the cliffs around the waters hold absences in their weathered lines. The mountains' majestic and delicate crevices are poised to harbour women plotting to feed secret longings throbbing in gut and spirit dimensions.

I wonder who will inherit the crown in the underwater kingdom. What creature will take kin's belonging of a doomed woman as a companion until it breaks; its parts dragged around by scavengers or left disintegrating on moss mounds, light bending on the water above becoming its own bright creature.

It is a cool blustery morning; the wind whips my hood from my head, its silken lining grazes my cheek. An amulet in my pocket knocks against the small glass perfume bottle. My white blouse trimmed with lace tightens against my chest. Domingos and his treacherous men are in their boat, further out to sea, as the white waters thrash, pounding against the rocks. The boat undulates unsteadily, a small thing under a sky of white ribbons shifting into the hemlines of kin flashing. I have not spoken to him of these men who stole me from my dreaming place in the crevice of a night. Nor have I asked him if he had a hand in it. It is an unspoken, corrosive thing between us, spreading into the axis in the homestead. There are six men in the boat. Domingos's left arm strains hauling a net, another bounty caught. My ache and anger form again, watching his body from a distance, knowing it afar in the way that I do. I am certain I could single him out from most men in the dark. Perhaps he is afraid of being lost to the sea sometimes or to another hungry entity that has not fully revealed itself.

The bottle clinks in my pocket. I remove it, watching a fennel plant bending in the air as though silently conducting the waters. It glimmers hypnotically in the light, pink veins shoot across it, covered in the dew from a coming morning, its golden leaves tremble. Bulbs of marrow spill off the tip. A cry from the bone fills the air. My body is lighter on this edge. A deafening shriek fills my ears. A cut from a shard of stained glass appears under my tongue. My limbs are weightless. The perfume bottle, a carrier of secrets, is warm to the touch. The plant, a bearer of scents and strange entities, unfurls under my warm breath. I take a bite. Sweet, earthy flavours intermingle with intensity underpinned by a bitter taste that dwindles till only a faint residue is left. It is a sprout of something unwieldy in the mouth. There is the sensation of an unknowable thing bursting through taste into being, into a force longing to consume those around it in loving, small sacrifices, in ways they cannot foresee. I look at the men again. The pink marrow hue from my plant deepens before seeping into the crevices between Domingos and me. They cannot sense the sweetness of doom angling towards their mouths while the catches in their grip twitch in deliverance.

The mountains suddenly seem fragile, even in their glorious power, swimming in my sight like rapturous mounds. A light wind lifts the hem of my skirt, flapping about my legs in reconciliation of beings that cannot be contained. My ache and anger are visible then, a luminous, molten thing gathering then breaking, assembling again before spiralling like a great, untethered instrument, plagued by hearts with tiny ruptures in the wings. I eat half the marrow plant. The boat tips in the water. I turn my back, sure of what will follow, of what becomes on the edge heading towards the centre. Walking away from my hiding spot, I sense every particle of the marrow plant vanishing inside me. Kin's force brews within, all-seeing, all-knowing. It could gift my beating heart to a scene of birth while I wander this land with its shape as a memory, an interloper within. Streams of sunlight are momentarily blinding. I cry out, calling to plant marrow in the veins. Those ribbons in the sky become part of its traffic, heading in the opposite direction. Light on the waters expand, forming bright paths across it, one underneath Domingos's boat of men. The boat tips over again. My ache sweeps between the mountains. The roaring anger inside me deepens. I clutch half a marrow plant with sweaty fingers, watching it regenerate its top half as though it has never been eaten. Domingos and his crew of fishermen are not deep enough in the unknowable parts of the sea to be in real danger, although the waters consume those who underestimate its all-encompassing power. The thudding of his heart beating from the distance is a solemn embrace. He will return to me, wielding the spoils of a stubborn current despite something shattering, patiently awaiting his footsteps in the dark. Saltwater trickles from my right iris down my cheek. A stinging in that eye is a comfort. The pinch at my wrists from my long, white blouse stings. I must get on with the first task of the day: a trip into town to procure a new knife for gutting and soft cuts seeking the solace of contorted bodies angling towards them as sacrifices. A scratching in my throat persists, as though the feathers are writing the secrets of the town in its moist passage. I need cumin, black pepper and a few other necessities from the spice stall run by Rowena and her sister. The sly feathers keep conjuring with restless tips, drawing the silhouettes of burning bodies. I taste ash in my mouth, feel the searing heat of flames on my skin, a terrible guilt fills me as screams of a vanished island rise in my eardrums, growing in weight and density, reaching through me into unsuspecting homesteads waiting to inherit them. My shoulders become stiff despite my determination to prevent this onslaught of sensory invasion from the feathers' tips to dissuade me. The burden of loneliness splinters in my chest. Screams from the vanished island want to be released. The sea's salty coolness fills my mouth, stinging my eyes again. Injuries of octopuses invade my gaze as if waiting to steal my vision. I howl from the depths of myself as the marrow plant trembles in my pocket, recognising my pain. Not even the silken fold containing it can cushion the devastation of an insurmountable loss.

I walk on. The homesteads are murky constructions shrouded in light, anointed by cloudy fragments fading into thin, bluish trails. I take a breath, seeing into these homes, running my fingers over their secret corners, ready to tip the perfume bottle's hidden contents into their cracks. These occupants of Piranu Mountain begin their day with their shadows attempting to migrate to driftwood shrines dotted along the shore like raised carcasses. One woman heats papaya in a pan then eats them slowly, standing in the doorway of the bedroom watching her naked husband argue with himself, convinced his skin are clothes he must take off, reaching for the corroded blade on the floor that slices through fruit, yolk, fennel root, catching his shrunken reflection while his wife licks liquid sweetness from her fingertips. In another I pass, a throbbing starts in my chest. A man on his knees in the front entrance looking up at a dangling string of cloves has a tongue covered in red ladybirds fattened from the mountains' nectar. They suck ravenously, changing his tongue into a twisted, pliant organ. In the third homestead, a woman is frightened of the flashing reflections in her son's eyes. She rinses his irises with cold water to no avail. Her teeth chatter, panic takes odd, fleeting shapes inside her. Her son is confused, his shirt soaked to the skin from having pails of water frantically thrown at him. He attempts to reassure her, even though he feels it too: a slow sense of doom spreading through the town he cannot name. Gethsemane begins to turn on itself, just as Oni and kin intended.

Halfway down Piranu Mountain, the stones roll like tumbleweed. The delightful scent of dandelion patches fills the air. I sense Domingos and his men back in the boat, hauling catches with dangerous bright horizons fracturing inside them. A man pushing a wheelbarrow of large beetroot bulbs, cassava, potatoes and carrots passes by whistling. He nods at me, stopping momentarily to adjust beetroot jostling like blushing purple passengers under a withering gaze.

At the town centre, it is the second of the two weekly market days and the traders are out in force. The main road is lined with tables of sugarcane, cakes, sweet and savoury offerings bathed in streaks of sunlight. There are displays of cooked meats, fowls slick with natural oils and juices turning on a metal rod above a fire; a man minding the fire flicks lint off his orange shirt, stained from the residue of cooking. He hovers over meats seasoned with *cardamom, parsley, mint, gesturing colourfully at passers-by, declaring, 'For your dinner tonight! Try a piece, estimada. The wild goat will melt in your mouth. Why deny yourselves? Take a bite.' A woman further down is making meat pies shaped like parcels, her hands deep in a large bowl of flour, expertly moulding and turning the dough, her head thrown back as the occasional burst of laughter slips from her throat while she converses with customers. Her dark skin is velvety smooth, rich with the history of her African ancestors, her regal features suggesting she is from Sudan or somewhere further north. Her quick hands gather the movements of others, moulding them into a new cartography in daylight.*

Silver coins jangle in my right pocket as I thread my way through. Some people whisper, watching me pass by. 'There goes the healer woman who escaped the guillotine.' Nobody dares accost me, their expressions a mixture of suspicion and curiosity. 'Look at her brazenness,' another fumes. 'No ordinary woman would be so defiant.' A man near the end of the strip plays a drum energetically. Several children circle him, throwing their bodies like rhythm-seized vessels. The scents of fried squid, freshly made batatas, curries and stews fill the air. Tables of colourful materials, silken cloths, handmade jewellery, pantry utensils, knives and decorative items for the homesteads pop up. I pause by the knife stall, watching blades catch fragments of sacrifices threatening to spill them from their tips. I pick up a knife with a wooden handle. Its curved blade sufficiently sharp, perfect for the gutting of corrosive embers, I press my mouth against it in a delicate kiss, attempting to blend in as I move. Despite this, a wire of tension slips into my back, a dangerous stranger amid wary folk.

The Moreaux stall is nestled between a haberdashery stand

and a shoemaker's leather spoils, the tables so close as though to persuade the bright buttons to fall into shoes or spices in sudden disturbances. The sisters are lush, attractive women with full figures, their feline faces harbouring secrets. There is a half-smile here and there from Rhoda, the slimmer of the two, and a squinting of the eyes from Rowena, a measured glint in them while assessing you. Attempting to look past one's clothes and skin to witness what fangled imposters replace a heart. I wonder if Rowena possesses a third eye or could be a challenger of sorts. An uneasy feeling blooms inside me. Rowena's perfume scent of orange blossom teases my nostrils. I dismiss the notion of her as a challenger. It is doubtful, although I enjoy thinking on it briefly. My marrow plant scent bottles clink in the distance. I like my interactions with the sisters, their occasional spikiness, love of gossip and alluring exoticism. They are rare creatures plucked from an Eden into a new season. Unfazed, perhaps even a little impressed by my infamy.

'Come, dear.' Rhoda beckons, 'We have some special things for you today, cherie!' Her right arm flutters over the display of spices in fine gold papers setting an enticing trap. Curly tendrils of hair escape her bun, framing her face softly. She leans forward as she is prone to do in excitement, inviting me closer. 'There is hookah from Marrakesh, brought in via the seas just three mornings ago, right, Rowe?'

'Um hum,' Rowena adds, as if reliving the pleasure of the experience all over again. 'Come see some spice flavours, my dear, perfect for those soups and broths you like to make. And we have white melon seeds, green cayenne peppers for some heat. For you, Zulmira, the mighty healer. That's what we call you in our homestead.' She flashes a smile, fishes out a wooden paddle,

fanning herself dramatically as I make my way over, amused by their flattery. I shield my eyes from the glare of the sun briefly; two boys throw stones at each other. Sunlight streaming fractures, as if the market has been spawned from a feverish hallucination. There is cumin too, nettle spice the sisters made with their own hands, saffron, Ethiopian black seeds, bay leaves, spices from India's havens the Portuguese explorers brought to the town such as cardamom. The golden sheets holding each spice crinkle at the edges in a signature style. Mixtures of scents wafting around are heady aromas. I buy two pinches of cinnamon, several spoonfuls of ground red pepper and a small batch of bay leaves for the wild hare recipe I intend to try the next time Domingos brings me a catch from the fertile forest where the spirits leave their offerings.

Rhoda and Rowena pepper my brief stop at their stall with entertaining anecdotes, wrapping my items in golden sheets with purple ribbons. I slip them in my pouch. The spice parcels want to spill into small gatherings of activities in the market. I wave goodbye to the Moreaux sisters as a drumbeat explodes in my chest. A different beat knocks the breath out of me. The one from my march towards the guillotine. The sisters fuss over their table. Shafts of light intermingling with the beat are an afternoon entanglement. I cannot tell if I manifested this separate beat, yet it feels both in me and apart from me, a loving beast with its own place in the world. A voracious, swelling entity that is slow, staggered then quick then staggered again. That familiar drumbeat rattles through me once more. A feeling of anticipation fills me. The ribbons in the sky reappear, now loose mother tongues bearing their warnings. The clatter of a pot lid falling to the ground rings where a jovial stallholder selling bowls of spicy squid and slender slices of avocado soup serves a new customer. Now the drumbeat is a famished apparition, a reckoning of long-held secrets that are hazardous passengers in the market. I follow the sound all the way down the street before turning right instinctively. At the far end of that road, a crowd gathers in the square just a stone's throw from the market strip. A feeling of sickness fills me. A baying crowd heaves forward, waving their arms in the air, watching the reckoning before them: a man's head placed in a guillotine, hands locked on either side so he cannot escape. The body memory returns to me, painful, crystallised and all-encompassing. My limbs stiffen as if in the vice again. My nervous system is hijacked by the operator. The broken drumbeat gallops towards my dilapidated chest. A siren collapsing rings in my head. The dead tongue slips into my mouth again. The operator, a man dressed in dark attire, stands to the side, fiddling with a small knob. They are on the raised part of the square which doubles as a natural stage. My new blade accepts its first corruption, confessing to the guillotine. The surrounding drooping gumtrees lean into this catastrophic liaison. Boys darting beneath them drop their catapults and instruments of play, their bewildered expressions hanging in the balance. I am lured by the arc of redemption. My body, a sweet, bruised plum turning from a corner. I enter the potent revolution of people wearing devil's teeth, flashing their cruel intentions. The drumbeat dogs my every move. I search the crowd for a drummer but cannot see one. The edges of the square are seams waiting for an unstitching by a careless hand. The man locked in the guillotine has pale skin the colour of curdled milk. His long beard is unkempt, his dark hair shot through with grey. He is shaking, trapped in a hellish contraption, head through a hole, back bent, hands shackled. His copper handcuffs clang against the wood.

'Who is he?' I ask a woman whose green headdress is comically unravelling while she is too enraptured by the display before her to fix it.

'That geologist from Madagascar. He was found wandering through some farms. Now folk feel he is responsible for the bad fortune befalling Gethsemane.'

'Cast him out!' yells a weedy man to my right with a tight, furious expression and hands bunched into fists. Another further back roars, pointing his finger. 'We have no room for those who bring bad blood here.'

'I counted several terrible occurrences since his feet touched our soil,' a haggard woman with a wriggling child in her arms offers. The child's fingers clutch her breast, opening and closing its tiny hands over her nipple like a bud watered by the surrounding chaos. The people of Gethsemane are beginning to turn on outsiders too, just as kin intended. I do not feel my limbs moving, propelled forward, or hear myself say, 'This man deserves a fair hearing.' My tongue throbs, slick with saliva. The dead one shrinks back.

The drumbeats echo around me. Children are the witnesses to a bad occurrence during a ripe afternoon. Forlorn gumtrees bleed into the shadows. I am a stranger in disguise. Filled with internal revelations, hovering above the crowd, arching into their discontent. I begin to murmur an unfamiliar language while the white feather in the guillotine operator's pocket remembering my imprisonment becomes a miniature skeleton. My suffocating small prison holding tumbling above is crooked in the sky. Just as the light-filled guillotine blade drops over the geologist's head with thunderous finality.

Chapter 11

Therese turned the gold lighter sporting a maple leaf emblazoned on its body, a memento from a vaporising night, spinning in her fingers while walking through a snowy Highgate Cemetery. Zulmira had instructed her to go there, whispering urgently between her heartbeats. In the morning light, the cemetery had a crystalline appearance. The dense, winding grounds bearing headstones was elegiac covered in snow. The surrounding trees, temporarily white, housing their wisdom and secret grooves reaching towards the heavens with wild, twisted branches in adulation. The tall black gates contained a sprawling world of death and remembrance. Erected plaques and graves were muted residents calling. Despite the tension from Zulmira's spirit burning inside her, she had dreamed of the prison holding, of being body to body in that space, the hot claustrophobic punishment. The cluster of parts of life spinning before she broke away, running in a white-hot molten path towards this place of the dead. She felt a sense of unease wandering through Highgate, its Gothic allure ever present. Statues bore knowing expressions. Tiny rumblings weaved between the headstones that were fissures making their way out of graves, which saw her trembling figure as new points of entry. It was bitingly cold. Flakes of snow covering the surroundings were melting confetti. Traffic from the road had dwindled to a distant din. The tension in her body from the previous night remained.

It was becoming an addiction, this need to heal sick bodies before the inevitable occurred; a dark, insatiable visitor that had to be fed regularly. She was addicted, and Zulmira, an ancestral architect, expanded her hunger. The latest one from the night before was a man with spina bifida, Vladimir. They'd drunk rhubarb gin and Russian whisky together from short, hollow shot glasses he'd bought in St Petersburg, to break the ice. They'd discussed the wisdom of tarot cards. He taught her a few ancient Russian words, grimaced between confessions. His pained expression was a third figure between them in the plush, maroon-coloured masculine bedroom. A glass side table had an ashtray with a few stunted cigarettes, smoked for comfort, and a stash of *The New Republic* magazines.

Later, she ran her fingers tenderly over his back, that expanse of skin absorbing a series of signatures amid the glow of two chintz lamps. She spoke to his skin using the language from kin, returning to a beginning of sorts, alphabets between tongues. His spine became a string in her grasp, a ripple of dark current, vulnerable, of bone and matter, delicate in her hands. She slipped Ovida's berries into her mouth then the transference of language occurred again. The burst of fruit was a euphoric nectar as her fingers sank into his flesh. This time Zulmira whispered, *Sueli, Sueli, Sueli*. Another name to bloom in her consciousness.

She wound her way through paths, running her finger over the raised leaf etched on the lighter as though it would come to life in cold salvation. She knew there was no solution for shamans like them, destined to straddle parallel worlds and dimensions while riddled with longings they could spend lifetimes deferring to in however many guises needed to be inhabited. The snow fell more heavily, dusting the few visitors at different spots in a steady anointing. A bald, slender man with a sad expression brushed passed her gingerly before scanning and approaching headstones, somewhat unsure of where the grave he was seeking was positioned. A gaunt, auburn-haired woman dressed in a pink sixties rockabilly dress with a black shawl thrown over her shoulders and a black Philip Treacy hat straining upward in an architectural incantation cried gently into a matching handkerchief. Further off to the left, another man had his head bowed, mumbling utterances only the weathered slabs of stone were privy to, his hands folding then unfolding in intimate prayer. Their pain and loss was palpable. Passed as instruments in an orchestral ensemble of death and mourning. Therese closed her eyes, savouring it. Her heartbeats pressed against the corners of that pain where small cracks threatened to spill into her unreliable vision. She could always find those cracks in the darkness, dipping her fingers into them while recovering from the night adventures excavated again in the day. She had learned to not panic when she was hallowed and in need of realigning again, balancing the traces of wonder and euphoria which flew, leaving her fingertips like flickering landmarks inside the bodies of sick people. The sound of a man taking his last breaths multiplied in her eardrums. Gliding things covered in tears. She walked to a black marble sphinx-like headstone, calling her to the skeletal reckoning it marked in burial soil. The wording etched on the headstone in gold lettering faded except 'In memory of . . .' Jeronimo Dorsey, the first victim. Therese murmured his name to herself, fishing out two white orchids from a bag and laying them against the headstone. A plane crossed the sky, loudly announcing its presence. She looked up at the white trail behind it, moving through the clouds as its own form of traffic, picturing the memories of the dead reconfiguring within it, carried to other destinations in flight. And the desires of those buried bursting through them, infiltrating the mouths of new-borns, their shadows dissipating into outlines of other countries. She ran her finger over the worn wordings, her breath shrouding snowflakes in pleasant dialogue, her hands tracking what had been taken away. Heavy on her tongue was a stark absence that would always make its way to her. She knew this grief too well. She'd talked to its flammable contents on painful nights, gathered its corrugated edges, pressing it to her chest in solace, allowing her tears to fall into it as it became an unidentifiable mass in the dark. A shot of pain ran through her chest. She felt like a moving wreckage. Loss was unavoidable in any life, a gaping wound whose circumference couldn't be measured accurately by any instrument, a chasm one could fill with distractions only to find it depleted again the next day. It was a costly price to encounter a loss you knew would always come in different forms yet still be a stranger to its impact. Correctly presuming its hold would lodge inside you like a small bullet still firing itself unexpectedly, sparking a desolate hole within. She fell to her knees, taking deep breaths to steady her wavering body, volatile in the soft fall of weather. Her teeth chattered over Jeronimo's faded, golden name. The familiar pull of Zulmira's hand bloomed, shadowing her movements.

She left Highgate, her body woozy in some temporal state, her legs unsteady in the snow. Her head was full of pale trails from headless origami women that knew the group's secrets. Her throat filled with an inevitable dread, as if insects had stolen the language from her tongue, blindly crawling towards glimmers of light. A kinetic force surrounded her, crackles of energy shrouding her movements. The lighter bobbed in her shirt pocket in collision with the precarious state of her limbs. She needed more peyote to open the channels of flight. They were running low. She'd have to speak to Azacca and Finn about it and their task to finish the new utopia they were building on the other plane for Oni, their bodies as incubators, as hybrid changelings in the warped paradise. A new world which allowed them to see with every part of themselves; where wild-eyed water bulls spilled horizons from their stomachs and processions of butterflies became fingerprints on missions of their own. Once the group had witnessed what was possible, they couldn't stop their need to keep seeing and building, to have the essence of hidden possibilities revealed to them only deepened. Even in this world. Each of them, alert to the wonders and tragedies brushing against their hands. Leaning into it as if to pass through archways into gauzy resurrections. This was Oni's will. The lighter nearly dropped, almost felled by its owner's temperament. In that moment, she knew her Russian companion from the night before was gone. He'd given her the lighter as a parting gift. And just like the others, sacrificed, the signature of a gutting in his neck now a keyhole. His splayed body on the silken black bedsheet, his shadow in the delicate space between worlds.

She had a report to write on the fate of Madagascar's rainforests in the face of climate threats, distracting herself by lingering on ideas. Inside the train carriage, she pictured white orchids grazing against the sphinx gravestone in a caress. As the train rumbled on, she held one paper origami woman that had been slipped under her door after a tender tryst. When she arrived home, she found Finn and Azacca in the living room: the TV volume on low during an episode of *Poirot*, Finn pacing with the remote in his hand and Azacca sitting at the edge of one of the blue sofas, an anxious expression on his face. The TV contained lost conversations in the static. Therese slipped off her coat, dropping it on one arm of the sofa in a distracted manner. She placed her house keys on the rectangular glass table, sensing a tension in the room. The figures in the surrealist paintings on their walls loomed large.

'He's still gone,' Finn said, his gaze lingering on Therese. 'It's been over a month now.'

'What should we do?' Azacca asked, his voice cracked and burdened by the things he couldn't say. Therese sank her body into the sofa, grateful for its silent comfort. Finn's mouth made a sharp 'O'; his half-smile was slightly pained.

'Did you two have an argument?' he asked, turning the thought over before them. 'He was only here because of you.'

'Don't make this her fault,' Azacca offered, weariness creeping into his tone and expression. They had all kept functioning, of course, but they were shaken by Emilien's abrupt departure, wondering which past life had lured him to its wilds, scouring their carefully chosen sites of flight for clues.

'I'm not saying it's her fault but we both know the main reason he tolerated either of us is because of her,' Finn remarked, rubbing his head tiredly.

'He stayed here longer than most places, by all accounts.' Azacca steadied the copper vase to his left he'd accidentally knocked with his leg. 'I don't feel right. I'm hollow inside, Oni still hasn't returned my heart; maybe she took something from him as punishment.'

'Perhaps, no. We didn't fall out. Besides, he knows we need him to finish building for Oni,' Therese said, looking up at both of them, carefully maintaining an open expression. 'I think he'll come back at some point.'

Finn turned to face her again, his body alert, his knuckles whitened. 'When were you going to tell us you've been sneaking off to fix strangers at night?' His confusion was evident, he paced a bit more before finally sitting down, leaving the remote on the table.

'That's my power, I don't need permission to cultivate it,' she said, eyes flashing, trying to ignore the humming in her brain. A headache on its way along with Finn asking questions wasn't what she envisaged on arriving home. 'I'm not poking around in whatever you guys get up to with your abilities.'

Azacca watched her carefully, taking a slow deep breath

that suggested he was struggling to be patient. 'That's dangerous, Therese; anything could happen to you. You're being selfish.'

'Exactly,' Finn added, somewhat surprised that he and Azacca agreed on something. There was a ticking in his right cheek, a trapped bolt of electricity absconding from his brain.

'How did you find out?' she asked, careful not to sound defensive although she couldn't help the resentment in her tone, a subtle warning to them both.

'We're all more attuned to each other since we've been travelling to the other planes. And there's something in Ovida's berries that triggers hidden memories. I saw your hands deep in someone's stomach flash through my head.'

Azacca stopped fiddling with the vase, his interest piqued. 'Are you saying she has stronger abilities than us?'

'Different capabilities; it's an after-effect from the other world. She doesn't know how to control the urge. I can tell, that's the other thing, the hunger ... It's increased for all of us.' Finn's voice was low. 'Maybe it got too much for Emilien.'

'I'm giving people comfort. Human beings need that, especially when they're in a lot of pain,' Therese said. 'Just because my version of comfort isn't out of a bottle doesn't mean you can undermine it. We all have our coping mechanisms.'

Finn looked stung then, his face flushed, his eyes turning a darker emerald green. He shared a loaded look with Azacca. The cuckoo clock above the fireplace momentarily stopped, the bird head chiming in a gap in time. She heard Finn's wounds stretching, the hollowness in Azacca's chest increased from the tips of white feathers running amok. She heard Ovida throbbing in the glass tank, the name *Sueli* growing in stature, thoughts of Ovida entered her brain, murmurings that couldn't be interpreted in the moment. She felt the absence of Emilien. The ache from missing him spread through her.

Later, she played the recording of women giving birth, leaning forward on the bed, moving closer to the sounds, listening carefully while her face contorted. She heard Emilien's voice attempting to communicate with her like its own separate frequency, an entity seeking multiple routes to touch euphoria. They didn't call the police. The law didn't apply here. It wouldn't catch a man who could evade them through universes, reconfiguring himself as and when necessary. He'd just be a missing immigrant to them, slipped through society's cracks, deemed unworthy of sustained efforts to find him. It was clear that Finn and Azacca had previously engaged in conversations without her. Not that it angered her, but it cemented the idea that she couldn't fully trust either of them any more, or herself for that matter. They were all behaving erratically.

Finn knocked on her door bearing a cup of turmeric tea in a chipped white mug before throwing her a parting look of curiosity then holing up in his room, his wounds stretching inside him mimicking the murmurs she'd tried to interpret earlier. She heard Azacca rummaging in the kitchen, the whoosh of the fridge door opening, helping himself to some curry goat he'd made the previous day before heading off to a small gig at a bar in New Cross Gate. Outside, an ambulance pulled up a couple of doors down their street, the siren whirring and piercing through the evening. Therese slipped down to the basement. Ovida floated at the top of the tank in greeting. A few berries had ruptured on one side of her ribcage. The light criss-crossing flickered over her in an unstoppable, alchemic salutation. She sensed Ovida was forlorn. Her loneliness and grief seemed ephemeral in that glass cage, magnificent and grotesque in its blooming of fruit, nectar, waterfalls and moss were miniature configurations that left you breathless. She fished out a small tape recorder from her pocket, lay on the sofa playing the recording of women giving birth again, listening carefully. She sat up. The sounds lengthened, deepened, filling her chest, a vast force seducing her internal rhythms. Emilien's voice rang through even more clearly, but it was darker, pained. He was saying *Sueli* to Ovida, as if it was her true name before it became a garble of static and the light from Ovida's tank filled the walls in a rapturous symphony.

Twelve

After the geologist's beheading, the town is set alight with gossip for several days. Folk become more frightened by this act of brutality seeping through their movements in the aftermath, as though their homesteads salvaged the remnants of his death, tiny embers burning in the quiet hours. Rowena Moreaux makes a short visit from Guverro Mountain, bearing a gift that is a surprise: a painting of me drawn with sure hands using coloured ochre from Topu Mountain's crevices. It is fashioned like a soft white cylinder with a blue ribbon tied over it, Rowena's favourite decorative flourish. There is a sunflower peeking through the ribbon's centre like an accent. I do not take outsiders to my room so offer her a cup of seaweed beer made fresh the day before in the sitting area. Domingos set off early that morning, a man carrying a burden in his heart. Sueli plays with some children near by, while Marguerite shuts herself away in their bedchamber, unable to receive guests, her sickly tremors trapped in the air that morning. Light streams through the windows, making the sitting area warm and cocoon like. The endless blue stretch of sky, speckled white, wraps its infinite parameters around our homes in soft exhalations. My marrow plants' leaves unfurl in their hiding spot, listening, subtly growing from the chatter between women. The homestead's dark treasures wait in the wings to greet Rowena, witnesses turning in the margins. Rowena and I watch each other over the rims of our cups, half smiling in anticipation. 'You must accept this as a token of our appreciation,' she says breathlessly, sliding the painting towards me, her hands fluttering impatiently, her smile now hesitant, assessing, the flash of white teeth. I am struck by the hint of shyness in her expression, her perfume oil with notes of hibiscus filling my nostrils. The scent is robust and alluring. I inhale it quietly, pushing back the flash of us underwater wrestling with the undertow and each other, that nagging feeling rising again. If she were a man, I would think this a seduction. I make sure these inner thoughts aren't reflected in my expression. I take my time opening this latest gift; I like to be the architect of surprises not the unprepared recipient. I am stunned by the painting's likeness of me, the long neck, the proud forehead, the sheen of my dark skin, the planes and angles of an arresting face which draws the eye yet appears unknowable, mysterious. She captures this quality accurately, casting me in a throne-like iron chair, my frame in a midnight-blue gown with lace detailing on the sleeves, my eyes looking past the gaze of the painter's point of view. A half-moon hovers to the right like a mercurial puppeteer, four sets of hands from the future. The hands reach through gaps in the throne, waiting to catch something from me. My hair is braided and pinned up, styled into a labyrinthine crown. The hands orbiting through the throne are a reminder of sisterhood; buoyant, open, willing to catch a fall, or perhaps greedy, grasping, showing broken bonds that mimic my own betrayal in the dark. We sip more beer. It is warm, foamy and rich.

'You must miss folk from home,' Rowena says, her eyes homing in on me in that disconcerting, knowing way that she has. 'Domingos and his family are a beguiling lot, wounded. Forgive my frankness, but I am not certain he gets much comfort, the wife being quite poorly for many seasons.' The green beaded bracelet on her left wrist jangles. Veins there cross over each other like urgent murmurs listening to the surface of skin.

'We get by,' I say, careful to not sound defensive. 'I have my fond memories; I think on when I may see my people again, although this feels like home for now. A place for my body to come to itself in a different way, to gain more wisdom. Gethsemane is wildly beautiful, bewitching even, accosting one's being like a lover.' A heat fills my face, a tentacled creature bobs in my throat, primed to expose itself to my guest.

'It is you that is bewitching, a woman who outwits her own beheading then has the gumption to stay in the very town that tried to kill her.' Rowena laughs, head thrown back as her bawdy rumble fills the room. 'You certainly have a way about you.' Her eyes twinkle. The creases in her voluminous orange skirt feel like whispers. Bits of golden grass are caught in its hemline. I run a finger over the half-moon in the painting. 'You have been generous, thank you. I am taken aback by its likeness to me. I will find a good spot for it in my room that will not cause offence.'

Rowena takes a satisfactory sip, licking foam away from her top lip, hands gesturing afterwards like a reckless conspirator. 'Paintings have a power, my dear, that can bleed through the page. Your stature, the way you move, demands to be captured, though I am certain this is merely one side of you.' The wisdom in her tone implies she wants to say more yet holds back.

My eyes flicker over her collarbone, the mass there beckoning me with its secrets.

The painting's edges tremble as if reverberating from unseen instructions.

Pink mist engulfs us, sucking my limbs into the image. It is daylight there now. I am in the murky, heady folds of meadows and valleys chasing a skull spilling marrow down the valley's spines, its angles undulating like glimmering hypnotised pockets. It is blazingly hot. The sun temporarily vanishes. The azure sky is unrepentant, churning the bloodied white costumes of absent women's bodies. A splintered light fills the plane, shrouding its collapsible corners, steadily becoming brighter, while my body is on the move, hurtling towards the soft skull whose movements are incantations on rapturous land. The iron chair ascends to a great height then tumbles into a molten liquid gulf the pale colour of the nectar seeping from Gethsemane's mountains. It changes to a shimmering crevice anointed by kin's fingers bearing reflections. The arms reaching through the throne become a one-eyed python looming over proceedings with magisterial presence then transforms into arms again, breaching through peculiar pink lava like formations pulsing, crawling into valleys trembling from the trace of a paint-splattered finger. My image in the iron throne goes wandering, temporarily making room for other adventurous spirits borrowing foreign bodies. My reflection gathers the soft skull in a motherly fashion, presses it to her stomach, releasing it again as the marrow spills in rootless celebration. The bloodied white costumes in the sky unravel, collapsing into lines in the molten gulf, hunting for the parts of women that are incantations. The earthy scent of warm soil lingers in the air. A howl emanates from a drooping maple tree, rushing through my veins like a course of medicine disintegrating. I know those screams of birth and memory breaching through bone. The skull lands in the lava that is also a river. It forgets its name. Hollow, skeletal features stretch into a blinding fold of fractured light. I reach for it, chest heaving from this dalliance in the kaleidoscopic plane. The formations from the ground assemble into one entity: curious, encroaching, moving towards me imposingly. The skull sinks below the surface of the lava river just after pleading with me to recognise it in Sueli's voice. The painting trembles. I take a deep breath, pulling myself out of it.

Rowena finishes her beer, unaware of the pink mist in her mouth gathering like a series of cloudy aftershocks. The soft skull's iridescent lines elude us for now, Sueli's skull wailing with Baby's voice in the distance. The plane's valleys shimmer wondrously, shadows waiting for permission to be released, its corners fragmenting then colliding with the edges of Gethsemane. Rowena moves excitedly, eyes rounding, chest heaving, wisps of hair bouncing as she speaks of the beheading. 'I tell you the moment you left our stall, I sensed something change in the air. There was a strong feeling of unease in my stomach – unpleasant, you know? It was equally as uncomfortable as the time I got the hives, feeling a persistent sensation spreading along my left arm. It is its own form of doom, that inkling of a terrible thing about to happen. Do you sleep well, Zulmira?' She places the cup between us, tapping it as an indication for me to fill it. Lifting the jug beside me, I top up both our cups. I know how to soothe women who come fishing for things in disguise.

'Oh mostly, although there are some nights when the

restlessness happens, I remember being imprisoned, how I was not myself there, or I think too much on the future as we are all prone to do at times.'

She reaches across, placing her hand on my arm reassuringly. *'I cannot imagine what your mind endured in that holding, being alone with those guards. During unbearably hot nights, it is hard to let one's mind be still. I struggle myself. You must come up to the homestead to see us sometime. My sister has taken quite a shining to you. She says, "Rowe, she is not like anyone we have ever known!" I tell her we'll try to get to know you!'* She chuckles, a mischievous glint in her eyes. My eyes are drawn to it again, the small bulbous mass on the left side above her collarbone peeking out like a beetle trapped in the skin. *'Oh that,'* she says, catching my gaze wandering. *'It has lived in me for several seasons. I have longed to cut it out, just grab a blade to remove it. I often wonder what lies underneath.'*

'You should not dwell on it,' I offer, aware of a throbbing in my temple. *'It has caused you no harm so far.'* The sound of Marguerite's movements in the other room are delicate forays into the unknown void underpinned by deceptively simple acts: searching for her lost crown swallowed by the sea, reaching for the bowl of warm water by the bed, conversing with the pockets of her husband's trousers lined with pink mist. The soft skull hovers on the plane, now talking with Sueli's voice.

Rowena presses her hand against the mass to flatten it. Her face is suddenly hollow, ashen behind the laughter. *'Sometimes, it grows in the dark,'* she whispers urgently, *'and I need comfort. We all do,'* she says, her gaze meeting mine defiantly. The silence between us is heavy and uncomfortable.

*

Afterwards, I watch Rowena's departure from the front doorway, a green bottle of beer in her tight grip, her fingers clutching its slender neck for dear life, as if she might squeeze it into a shattering, her curvaceous figure reducing before disappearing at the end of the path. I think on the beguiling gap between her front teeth. The way broken shadows invade the whites of her eyes when she ceases rushing to fill silences. Her haunted expressions delicate, hand-drawn companions hovering behind her back. The mass above her collarbone blooms between us, fed by the husk scouring the rooftops of Gethsemane, octopus injuries shaped like bright urchins harbouring parts of an undertow, the dangerous tips of three feathers drawing the shape of the mass in her skin, resurrecting it when it dares to shrink.

My ability to pretend before others when necessary is a gift, to push down feelings of guilt if it does not serve me. It could cause chaos, sustenance for kin if I allow it to take hold. Of course, I knew Rowena had to cross the mountains to visit me, her curiosity would get the better of her. And the mass had revealed its susceptibility to instructions already. I clear the cups away, stopping momentarily to watch Marguerite's feet pad across the gap underneath their bedroom doorway. She sobs after Rowena's visit, shaking in the doorway, unable to say the words trapped in her mouth.

I reach for morning chores to occupy myself, my brain buzzing feverishly. I sweep the floors, gather clothes for washing, the metallic bucket knocking against my knees in protest at the tensions in the homestead. A gentle breeze caresses my skin. Vines in the garden clamber up the back fence. Sueli finds a headless paper woman peeking between growing vegetables left by kin. She plays with these disembodied paper women under a murky sky, feeling a kind of affinity with them. Two blurry buzzards hold a stirring exchange on top of the fence, pale breasts rising. I think of Rowena seeking my counsel. Splinters of pain shoot through me. Small flames licking my hidden portals. I head to the ladder where the new knife beckons like a mercenary invocation. Its sharp blade glints. Above it, a hare I skinned and drained using this very instrument dangles from a silver hook attached to the ceiling, turning slowly, recently spun.

When Domingos comes home late that night, he rushes out back to wash himself but not before I catch the scent, full and filling my nostrils with their revelation: the seductive smell of hibiscus, one of Rowena's scents, spreading between us like a dangerous smog. I think of her brazenness, her visits to the homestead, Marguerite's declining health. And the day she tried to kill me underwater. I sink my fingers into the skinned hare's cuts to stop the shrieking in my temples.

Several days later, Sueli and three other children chase each other along the winding path in a game of tag, touching a shoulder in motion, a back in flight, an arm curving. They laugh in abandon, dark traces of soil on their clothes from wriggling their slight bodies through hiding places or climbing trees. Their laughter rings through the air. I am struck by the joy of children, the ease with which they move, how they regard the world with such innocence. Pure and unspoiled, if only one could bottle that innocence, keep the sweetness unsullied, but the world does not allow that. I recall a memory from my time as a child, darting between a procession of kin confessing to Oni while the sky rattled relentlessly. And me moving through the gaps between their bodies towards something that time obscures from me now. I can still see my small form fit to burst, a catapult dangling from my left hand grazing broken routes for different destinies. Each with its own life and outcomes beckoning a little girl with several mothers dancing under thunder.

Part of Sueli's long braid unravels, giving her a wild, mischievous appearance. The little bandit children are two sisters, cherub faced and talkative, along with one scrawny boy whose deceptively slender figure belies a powerful physical strength. Sueli is clearly the chief mischief-maker, doling out instructions. Her fetching green dress is torn at the bottom. She hikes up the skirt to dance, the others mimic her in amusing displays that are frivolous interpretations, the path coddling them, the stones crunching underneath their eager feet. I carry a bucket of clothes to wash at a nearby river, passing them along the way, informing Sueli of my imminent return. The children form a ring, spinning, chanting a rhyme raucously. 'Mrs DaSilva has the shivers, one silver, three silvers, five silvers, more silvers, throw her in the river.'

The pail of clothes rocks against me, blushing heather sprigs sprout from the path's edges. The day is luminous, the air thick with expectation. The vines in my vision long to take root in the skyline. The children's chanting rises.

Upon my return my hands are raw from scrubbing materials against beating rocks before dipping them in frothy waters. Damp clothes in the gently swaying bucket in my grip dribble from a thin crack into hot stones burnished from sunlight. Gaps in surrounding trees whisper while light streams through skeletal branches. I pause to gather my breath, arms heavy from my earlier task, head buzzing as if a tiny fissure of lightning ripples through it like a trap. I realise through this static that I cannot see the children. The path swells. Red spots in the corner of my *vision become runny yolks. The clay heart beneath the homestead splinters. The marrow plants are shrieking, bending, tiny bulbs of pink marrow seeping from their stems, their unruly rhythms infiltrating the painting of my image causing a shift in the land there. The bone rattling in its hiding place keeps its own time, threatening to uproot secret corners of the homestead in an act of obliteration. A feeling rushes through me that is part excitement, part terror. I run along the path, unfurling towards a hallowed destination. My grip slips on the bucket's handle. The volume of my skirt is too cloying for my legs. My heartbeat increases to an unrecognisably fast pace. My dry mouth is a far-flung instrument on the edge. There is a knowing, a sense of anticipation in my fingertips. A headiness fills my body. Women's silhouettes in the sky thin into departures. I run until my legs ache.*

At the homestead, I find Sueli standing over Marguerite in her parents' bed-chamber doorway clutching the new blade I bought as though it is an anchor. Marguerite is sprawled on the ground in a pool of her blood spilling into an unknown unfettered country, threatening to consume us. Her sacrificial wounds wait to breach her pale nightdress. Her final expression is one of fear, surprise. She is gone forever.

The homestead shudders. I do not ask questions. I take the bloodied knife from Sueli's hand. Her eyes are blank although she is calm. She is unapologetic, a small fierce force in her own right. There is shock, yet an innocence is still in her. The tension between us ripples. She blinks, opens her mouthful of bloodied stained glass, lifting the corners in a half-smile that mimics my own. The mirror Rowena gave me is shattered in my room, a womb emerged through it, beating limply amid broken glass.

*

When Domingos arrives, the roar he emits is a fangled thing collapsing. His expression crumbles. He does not look at Sueli for fear of what he may do to her. He is on his knees, sinking in the blood. Guttural sounds spill from his mouth. Edging towards Marguerite, he seems to harbour hope to salvage what cannot be undone. He strokes her placid face, closes her eyes with unsteady fingers, takes her in his arms, rocking back and forth, muttering, 'What have you done?' He stares into the distance blankly. His dropped sack is left by the entrance filled with the day's catches ready to slither into the bloody pool before them. He does not move for several hours.

Later, I comfort him. It is time. Our bodies in mutual need and hunger. He cannot sleep in the room they shared. I take him gently by the hand into my cavern. The first kiss between us is surprisingly tender. Then his mouth is sweet, full, voracious. His breath grazes the pulsing in my neck. He carries me with sure arms, mumbling things I cannot make sense of, but the urgency of his touch is enough. Our limbs entwine in heady abandon. His fingers thrum against my pert nipples. Naked, we are engulfed in a symphony in my bed. The shadows of stems flicker on the walls, the painting in one corner containing its sacrifices. The newly arrived womb takes shelter under my bed. The rush of desire consumes us. He mutters to the bud-shaped birthmark in my inner left thigh, a confession to a point of solace. His mouth travels further up to my vagina; licking, sucking, caressing and worshipping with a fervour that causes my back to arch, my body to contort. Echoes of pleasure and shock intermingle. A rush through my body softens my limbs. When he enters me, I claim the girth and power of him moving inside. He thrusts rhythmically before hitting the very core of me. I bite his shoulder, digging my teeth in just as our releases happen, one after the other. He collapses on me, rests his head at my breasts. His rapid heartbeat settles, his pain temporarily subsided from our amorous pleasures. I am emboldened by my strength as a woman, lover and new mother, by the forces that bend to my hand. A man at his most vulnerable is malleable after the sweet tryst of loins that drive us. Marguerite lays in their bed, cold, a white sheet draped over her still body. Her terrified expression lingers in the room as a limbless replacement. A trap reeking of washed blood and her favourite scent: lavender. Her body floats, hovering over the ramshackle garden, angling above herbs, irrepressible vines, watering the suffering clay heart with her wounds. I must remove any lingering threat. I take Domingos again as the taunting scent of hibiscus fills my nostrils. Afterwards, I press a kiss behind his ear. Remembering the children's rhyme, I whisper, 'Mrs DaSilva's last tremors ... One silver, three silvers, five silvers, throw her in the river.'

Chapter 12

Azacca and Finn noticed Therese mourned Emilien's absence not by the crying or a melancholy cloaking of her body that one would expect, but in a variety of other ways. She played his favourite Cesaria Evora album, *Sao Vicente Di Longe*, dancing in a loose midnight-blue slip as though possessed by something, a glass of rhubarb and rosehip gin in her hand, moving with abandon in the hallways. She raised her arms to the circular patterns in the ceiling, spilling Moorish alcoholic vices on herself in accidental baptisms, her skin glowing, eyes gleaming, her mouth consuming Ovida's fruit intermittently, chanting an unfamiliar language. A palpable electricity emitted from her body in those few weeks after he went missing. They couldn't determine whether this was a reasonable way to mourn someone, immediately celebrating them rather than recognisable grief or breaking down. Perhaps it was simply her survival mechanism kicking in. After all, they weren't like other people. When she unstitched the pockets of her matador costume, a golden-threaded temptation absorbing angles of memories as she held it lovingly, claiming she saw this unravelling of pockets in one of Emilien's drawings, they knew it was futile to try to intervene. Some days she stood in the kitchen, staring into a void as if she was in her own separate orbit muttering, 'Zulmira, show me your hand, the force of your will, tell me where to find him.' The fridge humming gently; the extractor fan warm, spinning its white blades to an invisible reconfiguration; the cluster of headless origami women she'd arranged lining the windowsill like a small, numbed army.

The anonymous gifts had been from Emilien. In response to this realisation, Therese pulled threads from the matador costume's silken pockets as though expecting to find more revelations dangling at the end of them, saying breathy meditations over small pieces of unravelled silk. She found his sketchbook of caricatures, sat in the living room flicking through the pages, watching for the weather to change in them, her fingers running over scenes he'd conjured. Some she recognised; others were new. She noticed one towards the end she hadn't see before: an image of Ovida spilling new fruit from her bones, the ribcage detail intricate and veins crossing it thick with possible mutations. Ovida was poised over sprawling, rich green land, bulbs of dew dropping to form a reflection, a mirror beneath her. Reflected in the mirror was a young girl, Ovida in her full form. Therese's mouth filled with the name *Sueli*. Ovida and Sueli were the same entity.

She felt heady with this discovery. There was a crackle of lightning in the sky, at the edge of the land stood a little girl holding a dagger or a stick as though she was born to know it, a trick image within an image. The girl was rushing towards Ovida in recognition and relief. Therese stroked the image, the sound of traffic blaring outside on the precipice of rousing it to life. She looked again, she was certain that the girl's expression changed, and the mirror of water underneath Ovida had become a series of unravelled golden threads. Emilien had been sketching images of Sueli to pre-empt her arrival. He had been drawing Sueli – or Ovida, as she was known to them – all along, unaware that she would arrive half formed, blooming with the intricacies and mysteries of Gethsemane.

The Hotel Eso sprang from a street tucked behind a square in Bishopsgate, a kitsch architectural offering that was bright and warmly decorated with sixties references. Therese walked through the revolving doors curiously, her hands stuffed in her pockets, taking in the surroundings as if a capsule had delivered her to these doors. Instead, it had been a tedious ride on the train to get there, standing in a packed carriage with bodies wrangling for stability, uncomfortably pressed up against other passengers while the train stuttered then crawled due to delays, winding slowly through airy tunnels, the figures of advertising posters with static invading their mouths. She had arrived somewhat beleaguered after receiving an email request for help. Tissue regeneration, the message had said, but not which part. Just the address, plus instructions to come alone, which she always did anyway. It was unlike a lot of her requests in its brevity. There was no sense of personality, no indication of how long he had left, no saccharine persuasion or overly familiar context given replete with a melancholy tone. It was brief and signed E^2, which made her think of degrees, unfinished mathematical equations that became theories of relativity. She was surprised at the choice of this retro location – with its labyrinthine feel, it could have been straight out of a David Lynch film, the building situated at the juncture of earth and another ether. The bright orange lobby unfolded into different communal areas. The reddish asymmetrical patterns on the walls were a trick in their own right, immersing passing figures before translating them into irregular angles. At the far-right corner of the lobby was a fountain of pink champagne by a wall-to-wall tank of silvery nuclei steadily pulsing within the glass in slow cycles of movement, as if reporting to a hole in the moon. She couldn't decide if the champagne fountain was gaudy or genius. The revolving doors spun behind her. She was struck by a painting above the tank of a magnificent-looking Black woman on an iron chair with voracious hands reaching from underneath like malevolent roots. Recognition flooded her body. It was Zulmira. Therese whispered her name in reverence. Zulmira's attire was unassuming but there was nothing common about her, with her proud, striking carriage and unflinching gaze. It was powerful, seductive and knowing. Perhaps she was in disguise. Whoever had captured her had done so with respectful strokes, reflecting her true spirit, with the heavens moodily swirling above her head as a series of blue matter. Therese had an intense feeling of fear looking at that image. It made her throat dry, her tongue heavy and the tension ricocheting through her turned her body into a snapped string. There was no indication of who the artist was, no signature to plant a seed. She looked to her left, at the desk, the staff dressed in crisp white shirts and pink waistcoats wore strained smiles as if they themselves were permanent bright fixtures under Zulmira's unswerving gaze.

*

The lift took her to the fifth floor in a flash. The doors slowly squeezed open, used to spitting out bewildered figures with mangled dreams in tow. The blazing, stripy carpeted corridor was at an angle, a slipstream that could fold in on itself. Lights in the pale, mauve ceiling flickered, hinting that the scene could change at any point. The air was thicker up there too, dense with crystalline glass like particles floating. She blinked, thinking her eyes were deceiving her. Whatever was in the pink champagne was beginning to seep into her bloodstream. It was not that she felt unstable, more that she could see hidden things unwinding from her inner landscapes. Like Zulmira in the lobby painting holding the same fruit from Ovida's ribcage, the purple berries edible modes of travel in her hand, threatening to spill from the painting. Therese blinked the image away. Fresh beads of sweat appeared on her forehead and palms. The sweet taste of champagne left an alcoholic echo in her mouth. A ripple from the passageway tried to force entry into the valley between breast and bone. The shadows underneath doorways shifted. Footsteps behind doors on either side of the green flower-patterned walls drew near then faded. She steadied herself, feeling her way along the wall towards room 504, fishing out a copper key just as the blade of light in the gap under the door morphed into an impromptu hologram.

The room was like a scene from a sixties issue of *Wallpaper* magazine. An incandescent red loveseat stood in one corner, a double bed with a purple velvet headboard rested against a wall with a retro gold and green leaf pattern. The clash of colours felt heavy, kaleidoscopic. Large windows overlooked a balcony and the square below. She drew a breath, the alcohol now liquid imprints on her tongue. A man who seemed familiar sat in a big wicker chair facing the window. He turned the gold lighter with the leaf emblazoned on it she had recently lost like a puzzle in his fingers. Recognition filled her limbs, down to her bones. A man who looked like Emilien from the back leaned forward, a coiled spring in the chair listening to her movements. She knew that lean, rangy frame, so like a swimmer's, that she had enjoyed, lovingly, secretly. Her hands trembled. A niggling doubt burrowed in her chest. She couldn't stop the mixed feelings of hope, shock and confusion coursing through her like wildfire. He spoke her name. The man had Emilien's voice and mannerisms, but she was sure it wasn't him.

When he turned to face her, it was difficult not to shrink back stunned. His face had been ripped off, perhaps during flight between dimensions. It was now a perilous dark hole, the equivalent of looking down an endless abyss.

'Querida, I need you to help me grow the tissue back,' he said. It was impossible to tell what his expression was, although the request revealed things. Same voice, same tonal inflections. And yet her instinct told her something wasn't quite right, the uncertainty remained. She felt faint, unmoored. The room swam; the encroaching throbbing in the hallway got closer, the hologram of light intertwined with a shadow. She looked down at him again, as if from a great height, her body pressing against the static, unable to resist its lure; she felt herself catapulting into the abyss.

Thirteen

Rowena stops coming to visit. Domingos does not mention her; it is a barbed thing between us. He mourns Marguerite despite sleeping in my bed. His desire for me and loss of his wife are two sides of a gleaming edge spinning in the balance. The clay heart beneath the homestead shatters after this death. A keeper of time and secrets, its fragments scatter beyond the underworld, seeping into the air we breathe and consume as lifeblood. There is a fitting, small funeral, a return to dust in a plot of land within a burial site on the outer edges of Noma Mountain. A number of people attend while a seemingly inconsolable Domingos is racked with quiet sobs. We bid farewell to her long-suffering body. Afterwards, little by little, I try to remove visible signs of her, a delicate act one cannot rush. I store her clothes, which still possess the scent of lavender, in sacks in the small back room. I throw away the gifts she gave Domingos: a colourful handmade necklace woven with pained fingers; curly locks of her hair she placed in one of his trouser pockets for him to smell, touch and hold dear when he longed for her out on the waters, unsure of what the day's catches would bring, uncertain of what will await him without her. The cold womb Oni sent is still under my bed, covered in ice, a barrier acting as a temporary protective layer. I drag it out to thaw in the garden, running my finger over its cool ridges, and a feeling of recognition hits me. A womb absent of a body is a strange contraption – part trap, part seer. It appears to be in a mourning of its own. I watch it thaw for a little while, trying to decipher what it will consume in the quiet hours.

Domingos's melancholy continues over the coming weeks, although he is still passionate at nights, losing himself temporarily in the physical declarations of our bodies. In the mornings, the depth of his sadness is undeniable. His eyes have a distance in them that cannot be persuaded away. He does not linger. He used to stop on occasion, asking what we would like him to bring for us. Now, he presses a brief kiss to my cheek, pats my back reassuringly, then leaves without further fuss, his shoulders sagging despondently. For a large man, his deflated aura is even more apparent. As if somebody has pricked him with the knife tip his daughter used to kill his wife. These days, he cannot bear to look at Sueli. The resentment between them is a current rippling through our homestead. She is still childlike and cannot recall exactly how she did what she did. Except before it happened, she sees a woman surrounded by a glow in the mirror, her wild curls framing her beautiful face. The woman speaks the language Sueli has been muttering for several seasons and whispers to her about a new paradise with kin waiting on the other side. Oni appears to her, whispering about offerings that needed to be made. When she looks in the mirror again, she sees parts of herself fading, then she notices half of her body hovering in the glass, her chest bobbing as if commanded by a separate crackling sky, bruised marrow berries spilling from the centre of her chest in the mirror. She reaches for it; it flickers like a temptation.

Other children do not come to play with Sueli any more, having been warned by their mothers of the tragic incident that befell Domingos's household. She still amuses herself on the stone-speckled path leading to our homestead, talking to a conjuring of an invisible child companion, who she shares her worries with. She runs along the winding path as though there is a great force propelling her forward, doing handstands, her legs held tightly in a position of upside-down movement before inevitably falling. She takes a stick, drawing those circular patterns from her room wall in the garden. Standing near the womb obscured by an overgrown vegetable patch, poking it curiously with her stick while the white shapes in the azure sky become fading passengers. The womb temporarily becomes a heart, an organ from a future kin Oni claimed, pumping hollow heartbeats slowly within the patch of vegetation.

'Will you be my mama now? Somebody took away my other mother,' she says, standing in the kitchen doorway after playing earlier. Her voice is barely audible, shaky, the catapult in her left hand dangles, an architect waiting for ruinous things to pass through it. I am gutting and salting garoupa fish when she catches me off guard. There is a fear in her expression. My hands are bloodied from slippery insides, the smell of fish in the air is strong. Shimmering scales cover my blue blouse like silver decorations. The few copper pots on the floor at my feet carry the dangerous silences of simmering liquids before they boil over.

'I am your mother now. You do not have to worry.' I offer this with as much reassurance as I can muster. I am still mulling over *other tasks I need to finish. 'Why are you whispering?' I ask, wiping stubborn scales from my chest. Sueli stares at the instrument in my right hand, a bloodied destination, a port for one to receive internal wounds. She is transfixed as I use the knife she killed her mother with to gut other creatures. She moves closer to me, the catapult trembling.*

'Because they can hear me.'

Sueli – like most girls – seeks her father's love, approval and interest. This need deepens in the absence of her first mother, but Domingos rejects her daily. He cannot help himself. When she rushes to greet him at the doorway upon his return, he sidesteps her trembling, confused forlorn figure, initially buzzing at his legs in excitement at seeing him, crying out, 'Papa! What do you have for us from the sea?' Her eyes wide in anticipation, her arms reaching up for some solace, a sign that he still recognises her. Only for him to regard her as a stranger, pull away, the dripping from his sacks a small formation of a stream now between them. At meals, he looks through her as though she is not there. Pulled instead into gazing at a murky horizon that does not have the answers he seeks. On occasion, I catch an expression of unfiltered fear in his face as he watches her dart through the rooms, in one instance her invisible friend at her side as she gripped a stick she painted tightly. The restlessness in her body a thousand traps waiting to strike. This fear of his own daughter's capabilities, a tricky darkness within her, continues to manifest in the homestead's treacherous corners. Some nights, he takes to pacing at the front of our home 'to lift a fog in my brain', he says, or perhaps to reflect on the aftermath of a devastating, protracted loss. I try not to think of what it costs. Kin as architects set certain things in motion. I do not punish myself over already knowing the blade's image in my mind's eye before heading off for the market that fateful day or sensing its gleam moving towards me, its offering of injuries unfurling from the tip like rare moths. The memory of kin's ribbons in the sky that day as disciples is lodged within me. I wash Sueli's hair, grease her scalp then braid her mane. I give her chalk to draw new faces on the invisible friend. I have taken to this role of mother in a way I did not expect. I wear it like a fresh costume, running my fingers through the rips in its lining, throwing my arms around it like a bright sphere in disguise.

Sueli finds Marguerite's dress in the stash I have hidden. A floaty, blue number, cinched at the waist with a trimmed white collar. The sort she would have worn for a special occasion, its billowy skirt skimming her legs, adjusting to her movements, moulding itself to her clammy skin. She gathers it from banishment on a humidly hot day. The sky is vast and unknowable, the mountains like apparitions in the distance; perched surrounding homesteads are desolate caverns waiting to be felled by the dangers lurking within families. I catch her inhaling her mother's lavender scent off the dress, gaining breath from it then burying her face into the material. She stuffs tangerine peelings, mango pits, drooping flower bulbs into the pockets, as though new things she cannot name will emerge from its cacophony, pressing themselves against distortions forming in her heart. Memories of Marguerite unfurl amid the rustling material. She spins the dress around the homestead, watching it flutter in the heat. Its arms as bird wings waiting to be singed. She takes it to the garden, where her invisible friend, lengthy vines and exuberant chorus of flowers, vegetables and herbs offer comfort, growing chaotically beside each other. The soil where my hands have planted and forged paths for creatures in the undergrowth temporarily sated. She passes the warm withering heart now a womb again, collapsed in its position near a vegetable patch, offering silent disintegrations. She slips the dress on. It hangs off her small frame comically. She is amused by the engulfment, laughing girlishly, feeling close to her mother again. I try to ignore the splinter of jealousy that arises in me. Domingos finds her in the dress. The shock followed by the fury in his face is potent. A look of madness appears in his eyes. He grabs her by the arms, shaking her violently, taking her breath away.

'What is wrong with you child?' he bellows, studying her frightened expression. 'What has possessed you? Never wear this again.' The veins in his neck strain as if they may pop. He slaps her twice, the force of it sending her stumbling backwards. I rush between them, pulling her away from him before he throttles her.

'Leave her be, she is only trying to remember her,' I admonish him as she leans against me, tears running down her cheeks, his body folding beside mine, his shoulders sagging, the sound of slaps still echoing around a crumbling family.

It is a bright, warm day when I head off to pick berries in the forest. The air is thick with the promise of a late-afternoon breeze. Birds congregate above in clusters. The trees shudder small spells of wisdom. A brook to my left ripples watery lullabies transporting twigs, lilies, the occasional luminous frog surfacing, noisily announcing its presence. I am humming, gathering handfuls of blueberries from a large brush, when I hear a rustling behind me. Most days, it is safe to go berry picking as a woman in the afternoons, but one can never be too alert to potential threats. I turn around, acutely aware of the tightness of the blade strapped to my ankle, a kindred spirit waiting to seduce its next cut. It is Rowena, whom I have not seen for some time, wary, my expression appropriately benign. She is dishevelled, slick with sweat. Her protruding stomach looms between us, a cocoon in the forest waiting to unspool its contents. The fear in her expression is palpable. She is shaking in confusion.

'The children are gone! The children of the town have disappeared. We do not know where they are and yet this morning, I awoke like this.' She gestures at her stomach frantically, her uncombed hair a contrast to her usually immaculate mane. I think of the unclaimed womb languishing in our garden.

'Are there more like you?' I ask, her panic now the size of a frog's head in my throat. The brook glimmering beside us offers no comfort, only reminding me that this woman, my so-called friend, has tried to kill me over Domingos.

'Yes, there are dazed women pregnant with god knows what spilling from every corner, milling about the town in confusion. I tell you, he never released inside me, so how is it possible? I need to get this unwieldy thing out of me, whatever it is. Please? It is sucking the very life from me. It grows in force and wants to consume me.' She is trembling, reduced to a banshee before me. The mass above her collarbone swells with her admission of guilt. Now the gaps between the trees' branches are stained with blood. The chirping frogs sink towards liquid endings, their shimmering green, silver-flecked skin seeping into my eyeline. My mind lingers again on the womb as a soothsayer, orchestrator and disciple. Rowena harbours waiting wounds. Kin and Oni have placed this temptation before me. My skin turns cold, my mouth becomes drunk in anticipation. My hand reaches for the blade.

The sky's cloudy symphony fills my head. Wound as fountain is all I can see. The hunger is a cave inside me again. I cannot resist it. I must gut her for kin, for Oni. The bloody symphony takes a hold of us in the forest. We are sucked into its white-hot embrace. Dark shapes in the sky reassemble into an ending.

Later that afternoon, the cool breeze does not soothe Gethsemane's panic. Instead, all the fishermen in the town turn blind except Domingos. The pink mist that began in Rowena's mouth spreads like poisonous smog, sending animals scattering out of their pens, making the sweet nectar burst from the mountains spilling down their spines as a travelling ambrosia. Rowena, now depleted, lies in a nook of the forest, the memory of an unannounced birth emerging from her stomach. I set off on my journey back in a trance-like state. The berries jostling in the basket are spattered with blood. Shouting in the distance grows in depth and vastness, reverberating around me along with the shuddering mountains, their pockets of nectar rupturing in alchemic explosions. A robust smell lingers in my nostrils, the scent of hibiscus mixed with blood. I feel unable to control my urges. The might of kin is all around. A sense of doom fills the air. I am still voracious. I could consume whole rivers and my inclinations would not be dampened, the guttings that those around me cannot see. It is the marrow plants that alert me when I reach the path to our homestead, bright, warped and dappled by the duplicitous light on this day of reckonings. A goshawk above shrieks so loudly I think my eardrums might shatter.

 I find my marrow plants strewn all over the floors of our home, half consumed. The feeling of doom spreads through me. I drop the basket of berries. They spill on the floor, scattering in various directions like dice fruit. Domingos sits in the corner of the front room silently rocking back and forth, a look of terror frozen on his face, the fear immeasurable. In my room, more stems are strewn on the floor. The window flaps open like a restless tongue. My bone is out of its hiding place in the wall, lying amid the rumpled white sheet on my bed, twitching, spitting marrow like a porous entity. The stems on the floor keep shrieking. Sueli has ushered her new existence into being after Oni's instructions. Having eaten some of my marrow plants and separated into a death and rebirth all at once. The blade at my ankle glimmers. Now there is no disparity between the blood on the floor and the knife's tip becoming an axis again in my hands. Rowena's final gift, the painting of me on the wall, flaps, its corners lifting. It ripples, pulling me towards it. My vision flickers momentarily. A white feather vibrates at the edge of the painting. Inside it, the background shifts to an unencumbered future, secret visions rise to the fore. Beyond my mirror image on the high iron chair in this hidden world is Sueli's ribcage blooming; shedding fruit, scouring the planes' tremors for new worlds to catapult into. And the four figures from the mirror, future kin, have crossed over into the painting ready to become other entities. Sueli rushes towards them, chasing a new kind of oblivion. She has engineered her own rebirth by eating from my marrow plants. I am bereft of motherhood to fill the absences in me. I offer no words of comfort to Domingos as I pass him, the bone in my grasp again, out in the open, jutting proudly, its shadowy messengers abandoning the rooftops of Gethsemane while the chaos continues. Bone dares him to speak. He cannot. He is reaching for the whispering berries spinning on the edge. I walk outside. The garden shudders, the sky is blinding, the homesteads in the surrounding mountains as playthings for Oni's untouchable force to destroy. I look up. The might of kin's incantation in the sky fills me, surrounds me, holds me. I recognise the sounds of their skirts swooshing, moving as frayed wings. Kin are making off with their bounty, Sueli's head, carrying it towards the horizon like a beautifully distorted macabre sun. And in the painting's undulating grounds, four future kin watch Sueli's blooming ribcage hurtling towards them in euphoric transcendence.

Chapter 13

Therese made it outside the hotel, short of breath, legs buckling and heart racing. She'd stumbled from that room feeling her way through the now dark passage, hands grabbing at the walls before falling into the sputtering lift in relief, away from the purgatory that had almost consumed her. She moved through the haze of the warm, kaleidoscopic lobby, the perpetually hellish enthusiastic faces of hotel staff, the clue from the painting of Zulmira of doublings. Nuclei now starfish took refuge in her brain, their tentacles doubling as an antenna for an incoming danger, a terrifying realisation coursed through her as the revolving door exit spun, delivering her back to the outside world. The man she'd met was a mirror image. A duplicate. A killer travelling through dimensions who'd be impossible to track. There was no precedent for what to do. He'd been killing the men she had been trying to heal, absorbing aspects of them in order to process their memories, imbibe their souls as sustenance. This was done to stop himself from turning into a dark cavity that was spreading, beginning with his face. She found a bench in the nearby square which she gratefully took advantage of, sitting to stop her shaking body, turning the thoughts over in her head like the angles of a magician's trick. He always let her begin on those men only to finish. He'd been in sync with her all along, ever since she noticed the differences between him and the real Emilien, her Emilien. Those strange gifts he'd left around the house to accost her during vulnerable moments, his hoarding of Ovida's fruit, the cruel sketches of her obliteration which appeared to come from a slightly different hand. There was also the rifling through the internet history on her laptop, a darker mindset and the static in the recordings of women howling, birthing that she'd recognised in his voice. It was unmistakable. Those waves crackling in his voice, a chorus of dark passengers changing their movements. She settled back against the bench, closing her eyes, listening to the sounds of traffic and passers-by as a comfort. An imposter had been living among them. And of course, when the cavity in him started to show itself, an imprint of darkness spreading, he made himself scarce while resenting her ability to heal others. The last time they visited the other plane, this break must have occurred with Emilien. His dark double, which had been lying in wait throughout his life, manifested. Splittings, multiples of an entity, were visible and possible on the other plane.

Therese, Azacca, Emilien and Finn were incubators for that dimension, the second plane. Shamans who inherited gifts from carriers in their ancestry; abilities to transform, travel, recreate and to reach beyond the boundaries of what the eye could see. Oni had instructed them to build a new utopia with one immeasurable undercurrent. What would the world look like if no one could recognise it? What could be exaggerated or taken away? Utopia, a second Holy Grail tunnelling through time, needed to be devoid of the perilous infrastructures and destructions of men. Devoid of war, hunger, famine, of man's desire to annihilate. This utopia was a drunken paradise in which to inhabit multiple selves, to sit by brooks doubling as watery chasms. A place where lost memories nourish fertile landscapes; somewhere to run into your infant self imbedded in a dappled valley, watching parts of a future orbiting above the horizon like winged blueprints. All four of them high on the euphoria of peyote, Therese's favourite source of hedonism which she hunts for instinctively whenever they reach this destination of change and triumph. They didn't know what they carried in the blood arriving, the soil rich with new beginnings, an Eden multiplying in vastness and detail by their own hands. There, the trees harbour new languages so a person can learn what it's like to walk in another's cultural richness. The cherry blossom branches contain empathy sap to suckle on for those depleted by the desensitisations of that earth world. Therese knew this from her own shortcomings and the group's struggles. The cost of incessant hunger, of internal wounds separating. Paradise and paradigms couldn't be envisioned, shifted, without parts of the two worlds bleeding into one another on occasion. These mutations were apparent on that plane, limping towards crevices of light in surrender. On the second plane, a fountain translating gaps in religious texts into brainwaves stood flanked by skeletons waiting for new skin.

*

Therese found Finn in the kitchen when she returned. There was a thick tension in the air. His eyes were bloodshot, an indication he'd been drinking more heavily recently. His beard had grown, giving his rakish looks more intensity. Azacca stood leaning against the doorway, half-in half-out of the white frame. His brow furrowed. There was a partially eaten pear in his right hand, poised like a form of sweet ammunition. He'd revealed to her that he was sure he'd never get his heart back. He was certain he could hear it pumping slowly, mutating into another entity in Gethsemane. It happened while strumming his guitar at gigs, his fingers awkwardly pausing against the strings, the lost rhythms of his instrument moving between the bodies in the crowd like a slipstream. The audience watching his expressions, which were collapsing matchstick houses. The pain from Finn's internal wounds was now so acute sometimes he'd black out in bed after drinking to self-soothe. Therese's hunger was insatiable, the need to fill it causing headaches and tremors. At times, she'd get comfort from sitting in Emilien's big wicker chair, but now even that was tarnished because of its duplicate in the purgatory. She could no longer sit there listening to the clock ticking, shepherding time in its own destination when it felt like time was running out. They were all suffering. She waited for a sign from Zulmira.

She put the kettle on, then ducked her head under the tap, a blast of cold water on her face. 'We're struggling because he's not here,' she said, wiping liquid from her cheeks. 'We're all connected. We have to go back to the plane,' she urged, watching them flicker before her like malfunctioning animations.

'So an imposter's been living among us?' Azacca remarked, his mouth flattening into a grim line. 'I knew there was something off about him, something different, but I couldn't identify what that was, why he kept disappearing. I chalked it up to personal issues, that maybe the two of you had fallen out.'

'We knew you were seeing each other. Why did you hide it?' Finn asked, rubbing his beard, watching her closely. 'How do we get to the other version to stop them? You're sure it's not him?' The loud whistle of the kettle a referee between them.

'He was always a little off, Therese,' Azacca added, taking a bite from the pear, still fidgety.

'Because it's not him!' she roared, unable to contain her ire. At that point, the sound of a shattering below disrupted their conversation. They rushed to the basement.

Ovida was gone, the tank smashed, its aquatic lighting flickering, a static hissing in their ears. The mist curled towards their mouths. They walked through broken glass, fruit, ruptured visions. They felt the fire in their veins spreading. Zulmira's voice, having instructed Ovida, echoed in the void, rising like a siren in Therese's eardrums, calling Ovida by her true name again: *Sueli*.

By the time they reached the woods late that night, the mixture of peyote and Ovida's berries had settled into their bodies, a potent hallucinogenic mix that caused their limbs to feel weightless, heady rushes to the brain, their skin warm. They found softened ground made holy by their touch near stacks of wood next to a dilapidated lodge, the door flapping open to release shadows that harboured sharp objects as currencies in the dark. Therese, Azacca and Finn chanted. It rose and grew, becoming its own force ricocheting between the trees, the paths, the curious statues now with tiny trails of moss decorating their cold forms. The group danced for Oni in hazy, disjointed formations, threw their arms up in celebration, in honour of the all-seeing shamanic deity that sustained them who could also strip them, excavate their internal landscapes, reduce them to ordinary beings. They became wild in their rapturous undoings. The nuclei in their brains splintering, linings under their tongues breaking, white-hot unmoored trails beckoning, curbing infants with mouths made of constellations reaching towards them with hungry fists. Throbbing shapes that were embers within them waiting to be released. The amalgamation of cloud gods morphed into one all-consuming tent. It bent and bobbed with the souls picked up as offerings through time. The static in their ears increased, broke, changed, shrouding a ritualistic spectacle among wise trees. By the time the blue light passed through their bodies, their mouths were open in symphony. It was pure, hedonistic flight. They catapulted through kaleidoscopic chasms, long throats of starlight, touched the ceilings of universes which altered their fingerprints, reconfigured languages inside their cells. Bright specks crossed their irises. Then in a shattered, elongated void, the breath was knocked out of them. Earth was reduced to a burnished line. They burst through the chasm into the other hidden world as though there was mercury in their blood.

*

Utopia was bright, drunk, ripe. Blinding in its strange beauty, which rendered fortunate witnesses breathless. The lands rippled; the waters glimmered with half-formed apparitions. The light-dappled valleys undulated, permutations in poetic movements, indelible against a backdrop of a vast azure sky. Creatures lingered, circling and crossing the valleys' spines into small gatherings below. Two suns orbited, a distance between them, one possessing a liquid dexterity that trickled into the trees. Among it an oak tree growing right hands, which doubled as signs to an area where batches of peyote had multiplied, the hands pointing straight ahead where a path of white stones flanking a fountain of tears beckoned. Therese felt Finn and Azacca on either side of her. Their ties as nature's umbilical cords marked by the hands of ancestors. They sensed their carriers' spirits passing through the valleys, talking between trails which intersected into a consciousness only this world possessed. And how lucky were they to have this, how fitting that Oni had shown them the way, giving them a great responsibility that had come to fruition through their abilities. Above them, crows with tortoise heads flapped their wings in a tempered welcome. Below, at one end to the left, goats with human feet frolicked in a stream. The top halves of the water bulls had mutated again, transformed by the songs from their carriers' spirits moving through the land. Some had become fusions of animals and plants, tails springing from wild walking brushes. Others had silver scales falling from them and filmy fisheyes starring in different directions. Others still had heads that were a darkened abyss from splittings marred by their own defections, like Emilien's double, the imposter. The goshawk that had followed Finn's ancestry along the cracks of time passed through their stomachs before resuming its task as a host, its left side a combination of different scenes that slipped in through the ages, flicking their shedding into the sweetness in the air before the scattered residue of an abyss continued to encroach, expanding its foot soldiers. Finn waded into a lake that turned to glass, temporarily capturing his wounds then reflecting them back to him. Azacca's floating heart, now fully released, was pounding on top of one valley, gathering the wings of butterflies as a powdery, purple horizon. He moved restlessly below to ensure his hands were busy with new strings, fresh instruments that would shift before keeping boundless hallucinations company. They were disparate while Therese went searching although she still sensed them. She knew both Finn and Azacca were waning in their respective refuges. A wave of panic then anticipation hit her, like reaching a pinnacle. She could sense Emilien was near by. Following her instincts, she scoured every brimming nook, every overflowing cranny. Finally, on the east side of the plane, she passed through two hovering chambers replete with ruminating veins glinting like circuits of electricity.

She found him in a giant pale egg-shaped concave named mecca. Ovida was leaning against him. She rushed to them, sucked into a vortex of three. His legs were gone, absorbed into a voracious force lying dormant elsewhere in this utopia for now. A well of emotion exchanged silently between them. Now Ovida grew more than berries and mist-shrouded waterfalls from her torso. Glistening stems poked through her ribcage, shrieking. Her Emilien, the real one, was waning but there was relief in his face to see her despite the abyss spreading around his middle, a rot rapidly taking over. The origin of their demise. The sky swirled. The white shell crackled. The heat intensified. A change was afoot. Drunken creatures blurred into a powdery, winged horizon. Therese felt a swell of circadian rhythms fill her chest. The call of carriers and memory rose in her eardrums before exploding into something beyond a spiritual transgression, beyond the very core of being, human essence. Sheets of colour fell from her eyes as thick, velvet curtains of multicoloured realms. She tasted everything and nothing; the curve of unknown pips, the bounds with new life rushing from them, wounds becoming octopuses in mirrors. Therese, Emilien and Sueli, Ovida's real name, felt a thousand stems pressed against their nerve endings in a glistening embrace. They became unmoored, a vortex of three spinning. A renegade light shrouded and filled them so thoroughly, it seared their limbs together indefinitely. They carried the cosmology of human and non-human entities, nature's will to build new worlds refreshed by their carriers' spirits. Then they were as one, conjoined, intertwined. A garish, mercurial spectacle, a three-part Frankenstein beauty. Mutation on the brink hurtling towards infinity, to that second sun, a yolk in the sky obliterating what was, ushering in what was to come.

Fourteen

Bone speaks, marrow seeps, kin wail in triumphant releases. The memory of a life lived on an island destined to become ash prevails. Many moons ago, a young couple fall in love arguing over two coconuts and its bereft tree that marks a strip of dirt road heading east away from the island's centre. The island is lush with vegetation, a thriving, colourful community, natural springs and two dense forests that tremble at night with hidden alchemies and messengers placing secrets in the eyes of creatures who burrow them in the soil like rare seeds. On occasion, when the rainfall is heavy, the forests and their chorus of bright-eyed creatures glimmer in iridescent dew. And the island folk say that if you pass through either of the forests after such heavy rainfall at opposite ends of the island, something unforeseen awaits you on the other side of your journey. There is no way to tell whether it will be good or bad, if fortune will smile at you or turn her back. Only the foolhardy, reckless or brave wind through them in such an instance under the looming gazes of tall trees. The forest of spirits and the forest of memory occasionally consort; when they do, the air changes, patches of colour splatter onto the leaves. The hummingbirds flutter from pillar to post in sporadic, dizzying flights, the forests spitting out travellers as if they are marred dawns ushered from perilous exits.

It is on such a day the young man makes his way through the forest of spirits, bits of his skin stained orange from the porous leaves as if initiated into a hidden ritual. His tall, sinewy frame wandering without fear, his mouth craving a sweet liquid while whistling. He hungers for the juice of coconuts, specifically the coconuts from a particular tree in a specific spot. He does not know why but it is sweeter than most he has tasted, the texture succulent, its shell easy to crack. As if designed for eager hands to mine its contents. But someone else has had the same thought, beating him to it. A young Black woman with a head full of thick, frizzy hair subdued into large plaits. She is long limbed, surprisingly agile, wielding the cutlass in her hand like a sword, with an elegance that implies she could be a horticulturalist. There is a sling-like contraption fashioned from cloth around her breasts which she places the coconuts in, but she drops two. It causes her to look down, noticing the stranger below holding the fruits of her labour as if he could just stroll up and take them.

'Give me my coconuts!'

'Come and get them from me.'

'I have been shading under this tree before climbing to get them.'

'Well, I have walked a long way with them in mind. What do you have to offer in exchange?'

'Nothing, I picked them, therefore they belong to me.'

She is aware of how trivial this exchange is, how petty, yet she cannot help herself. Sweat from her brow falls into her eyes. Her throat is parched and an ache she is becoming familiar with spreads through her. She is irritable contending with the breadth of this ache, the way it seems to accost her unexpectedly. Sometimes, she is a little dizzy from its intensity, trying to steady herself for several moments, orbiting with silhouettes in a reverie. She makes her way down the tree in swift, efficient movements, careful not to allow her small bounty to spill from its cloth holding. She grips the cutlass tightly; sweat from her fingers makes it a slippery instrument to hold. The mercy of a cool breeze arrives, tempering their bodies somewhat and the instinct to escalate what could become a protracted squabble over a resolvable issue.

'Look here,' he says, taking an authoritative stance, his tone more conciliatory, the expression on his face softened, a glint in his eyes which highlights his handsome, rugged appearance, 'you keep the ones you have, and we share these two?' he offers. She does not think it an important factor then but his ability to shift from one mood to another in the space of moments is a subtle indication of what lies ahead. She is certain, taking in his strong imposing figure, his comfort in his physicality, the gift to quickly reassure a person when they view him as a threat. She can see that this is a man who knows how to make others feel seen, valuable. She thinks it an interesting quality. There is an intense aura about his person, an alluring pull that tugs her towards him as if a thick rope bobs between them, inching near their fingers, and the only way forward is to the centre towards each other. Her irritation fades somewhat. His presence is a distraction from the ache that comes in waves. She agrees to share and pass a little time with him under a cooling, pliant palm tree a short walk away, with the sounds of thrashing white waters lapping at the shore and an invisible bind forming between them. And so an unexpected breaking of bread but with coconuts becomes more.

*

The young pair wed in a burnished, precarious shanty house on the shore, where their joy dodges a bloody tide. The man gazes at her with his smile lingering after they say their vows, as though registering every detail of her face. The woman, a striking beauty, is certain his keenness means he will want to live up to those vows, despite a persistent sensation in her stomach as if a procession of fireflies are losing their wings travelling through her intestines. The man appears enchanted by her.

Those first few seasons, they live in relative tranquillity except for the occasional argument, though this is no surprise since they are both strong-willed characters. Gifted using his hands, he is able to see things built from different raw materials on the island. He sets up trade as a local carpenter, making items that sometimes means he toils in their small outhouse into the early hours surrounded by evidence of both his successes and his failures, furnishings and objects colliding into each other in contained chaos, while she makes crab soup, mutton broth, banana bread. He whispers sweet promises for the future while he is inside her as the pleasures of their bodies intertwined consumes them. She is sure he will keep his promises. Sometimes, on long, slow afternoons, she weaves baskets from broad banana leaves, selling them to other women. She is also contending with her own gifts: an ability to see with certain parts of her body and the utterings of women in her peripheral vision who feel like relatives. She senses their movements in her blood, their burrowing of memories and flight in her, but she does not share this with him. After all, a woman must have secrets for herself in a union. He is popular on the island, possessing a gregarious, outwardly generous nature others are drawn to. He sits on the council offering direction on how the various communities can sustain each other, carries chopped firewood and sugarcane sticks to the old ladies of the island who bend his ear about the various monotonies of their lives. He takes food to the vagabonds on the outskirts, often peppering his visits with humorous stories to lift them.

More seasons pass.

The reckless moon injures itself. Harvests fail. A gumtree in the forest of spirits traps an apparition. A lace dress in the forest of memory moves through the lake in search of a reflection. The handful of umbilical cords teeming with memory, achings and bloodied departures is found in the shanty house on the shore. Something shifts. Storms start to brew in the young man.

He begins to neglect his wife. Hs moods are darker. He starts to drink more, blaming her for his unhappiness. It is a sudden blow that she cannot do anything right in his eyes, tumbling from the doomed pedestal he placed her on. His criticisms flow freely: her soups do not have enough spice or are missing ingredients he cannot name; her cocoa yam porridge gives him gas; her boisterous opinions are unseemly and make his head throb. And can she not see how other women know when to keep quiet, for the love of the gods? Her touch turns him cold. The sweet mischief of lovers leaves their bed. Some days, she thinks her vulva may seal itself shut as she aches from a hunger and loneliness tearing through her. The man uses his tools to build furniture with glazed eyes, to chip away at her until she is a husk floating through the rooms of their modest home in shock and confusion at these intimate assaults. He is unaware that his wife is no ordinary woman whose power continues to form within her despite her suffering. It is impossible to identify what makes this man change towards her. Perhaps his dark side was always there, carefully hidden under a mask, a quick smile, the instinct to bend things to his will, but brought to the fore by a series of incidents that no matter what order they arrived would always end in the same result.

He disappears for days, coming home smelling of other women, paramours he gathers behind her back, mocking her with his refusal to hide it. She starts to drink plantain juice, dancing under the moonlight, cementing her channel to the women's voices that draw closer, speaking a language he does not recognise. The unfettered joy she displays despite his cruelties makes him want to break her spirit all the more. Soon, he is standing before her in their bed, watching her toss and turn with a blank expression. Something rotten takes root.

His first mistake is strangling her to death thinking she will die.

His second is burying her body in a shallow grave in the forest of spirits where the porous entities, spies of kin, keep a slither of breath in her body.

His third mistake is fleeing the scene yet leaving his decayed, marauding shadow behind.

Kin start a raging fire in his carpentry outhouse, set it on his heels. Folk are unable to stave the fire. It roars on, claiming all asunder in its wake, consuming the island.

The man escapes through the tremulous forest of memory onto a boat big enough for two, although the right side of his face is burned, scarred for ever. He sets off on the boat over choppy waters, perilous tides. Kin send three white feathers to follow him.

He starts a new life in another place. Here he is a fisherman. He takes on a new name. Domingos.

After Domingos leaves me for dead in a different life, I give birth to myself again with a new face under the watchful gaze of kin. I *break the circle then set off on the twisted, stony path towards the man I have loved before. Domingos's fractured selves, his treacherous duplicity, his ability to remake himself into a good man before the eyes of others while battling his secret demons, make him both lover and enemy, source of solace and pain, a crumbling terrain to stand on while the wilderness inside me demands to be heard. Once kin stake their claim on Sueli as sacrifice, vehicle and penance, they tell the winds she belongs to them, long before knowing her mother's puckered nipple made sour to her wailing mouth. Oni's debts should always be paid. I must give thanks to Oni and my kind, kin.*

My kind stores breath for me.

My kind keeps bone for me.

My kind sheds the elements for me.

I shall honour them, reckon with their fruit in the blood, press my lips against Sueli's ribcage beating in the bounds.

I must always carve my name in the bone.

Now the homestead is filled with Sueli's absences and echoes. The loss of her laughter, often arriving in a room before she does, her wily body and quick hands conjuring something playful and disruptive, is felt in this trap. Her equally childlike and knowing expressions are webs I still run my fingers through. Her absence is profound, changing the fabric of life in the homestead. Her invisible friend lingers in the garden, searching for memories of her amid bruised peach skin, vines clambering, nettle arguing with seeds sprouting into sunflower, orchid and rose. Plant life calligraphy is necessary. Plants and vegetation keeping me company, to call relatives when my body needs their internal rhythms. And the decomposing womb quietly shrieking its last existence under changeable skies, a relic between star and fire.

It is a punishingly hot afternoon when the twisted, parched path beckons again. The bramble breaks, the garden splinters. Fence gates marking homes crack open in indication, scattered white stones double as misshapen seers. Children's voices trapped on the burning island become an ash language. The barren, dazed homesteads are collapsed, excavated traps wielding the shadows of an obliterated shanty house as a molten core. New fruits raise their heads in the blood. Animals flood the roads in confusion at their freedom, as if ceremonial clarions ring loudly in their ears with the force of a thousand echoes. A purple mist spills from their mouths that will soon engulf the town. Domingos shuts himself off in the dark as his days bleed into one, his face hollow, his mouth grim, his eyes pained and body a wreckage.

He sits in the room he shared with Marguerite, moored by the undertows of actions he dare not name. There is a flicker of shock, of possible recognition, when I bring him a bowl of peppery plantain broth humming a song from long ago that quietly breaks him, sending him over the edge. But I have no words of comfort for the reckoning that awaits on the other side. Instead, I kiss his neck in a soft exchange, a last betrayal between lovers. I take few belongings since I came with nothing, only bone and marrow plants slipped into my white dress's pockets, humming like wasps in the void. The three white feathers remain weightless disciples. One scales Noma Mountain unmoved by its murmurings. Another commands the children on the burning island to cross into their mothers' memories through the unclaimed relic womb in our garden doubling as a bridge. One travels across the rippling landscapes of my painting. I am drawn again to the painting's corners. The feather changes the world there with its stirring tip, turning it as though it is a revolving door, a wheel spun by the breathless point of a feather. Inside the painting, Sueli's ribcage hurtles through the green land blooming red berries, chrysanthemums, orange blossom, teeth. My mouth is flooded with sweet nectar spilling from the mountains. There is the passing of a lace dress unravelling in the heavens. Oni's blue tent of souls collapsing in the margins is a form of traffic. Baby, my real child, calls to me, hovering between distant clouds before falling into the hands of multiple mothers known to her as kin. I rush out into the slippery, light-filled afternoon. Walk through the bright, thunderous carcass of Gethsemane as the tragedies of this mountain town become lines in my palms, a tale I may whisper to a new-born self before it gains its first mother tongue.

Only bone as anchor, only marrow as sustenance, I head towards the pernicious, disparate embrace of kin, changed again.

Acknowledgements

Curandera was forged through the fire, it's a book I fought to manifest into existence during tricky periods. Working on this novel gave me light and courage. I hope it encourages others to follow their own paths. I must thank my supporters whose belief and faith in me means everything. Dad, I know you're somewhere watching over us, you were an unforgettable force of nature. I'll miss you always. Thank you for being my biggest champion. Mum, you're my heroine, I love you beyond measure, thank you for your irrepressible spirit. Amen, Ota, Iredia: my glorious ones, my world is so much better because you guys are in it. Thank you to my grandmothers as well as my aunties for invigorating me during difficult times. Thanks to Gogo for the vibes and magical walks.

A big thank you to my terrific agent Jessica Bullock. I appreciate your support and encouragement. Many thanks to wonderful publisher Sharmaine Lovegrove for your passion and energy, to my editor, the brilliant Hannah Chukwu, for eagle eyes and advocacy. Thanks to Millie Seaward and the Dialogue team for their efforts. Apologies to anyone I've left out. Much thanks to fiercely gifted fellow women art makers Bernardine Evaristo, Gaylene Gould, Yvvette Edwards, Leone Ross and Hannah Hutchings-Georgiou for sisterhood and communion.

Bringing a book from manuscript to what you are reading is a team effort.

Dialogue Books would like to thank everyone who helped to publish *Curandera* in the UK.

Editorial
Hannah Chukwu
Adriano Noble
Eleanor Gaffney

Contracts
Megan Phillips
Bryony Hall
Amy Patrick
Anne Goddard

Sales
Caitriona Row
Dominic Smith
Frances Doyle
Hannah Methuen
Lucy Hine
Toluwalope Ayo-Ajala

Design
Duncan Spilling

Production
Narges Nojoumi

Publicity
Henrietta Richardson

Marketing
Emily Moran

Operations
Kellie Barnfield
Millie Gibson
Sameera Patel
Sanjeev Braich

Finance
Andrew Smith
Ellie Barry

Copy-Editor
Alison Tulett

Proofreader
Karyn Burnham